Winter Journeys: a novel of music and memory

Audrey Driscoll

Published by Audrey Driscoll, 2025.

WINTER JOURNEYS: A NOVEL OF MUSIC AND MEMORY

First edition. July 7, 2025.

ISBN: 978-1999424077

Written by Audrey Driscoll.

"These songs please me more than all the rest, and in time they will please you as well."

Franz Schubert, speaking of his song cycle *Winterreise*

PRELUDE

OCTOBER 2007

He stands on the corner by the red brick church, oblivious to passersby—an old man, seemingly, thin and grizzled, with the marks of a hard life on his face and body. He is dressed in the accreted layers of poverty—multiple shirts and sweaters, topped with a stained and abraded coat. A blue knitted cap covers most of his hair, except for a protruding grey fringe. His feet are encased in work boots, cracked and sole-split. They shift restlessly on the pavement as he executes a perpetual, jittery dance in time to whatever incoherent tune he plays on the harmonica nearly hidden in his hands.

Three weeks after the autumnal equinox, a crystalline blue sky arches over the city, the product of a zone of high pressure that has persisted over the western edge of North America beyond the season commonly known as summer. Wafted on a fresh breeze, gulls sail and call above the streets. The water of the little harbour mirrors the sky's endless blue.

Ilona Miller waits for the traffic signal to change so she can make a quick visit to the bank before she's due back in her cubicle. Her thoughts dart like hyperactive hamsters between the spreadsheet awaiting her and the bills she needs to pay.

She hovers on the edge of the curb, ready to step out. The man is still there. Or he's there again, because surely she's seen him before. He seems to have staked out this corner as his personal territory, but he isn't asking for handouts. There's no hat or other receptacle awaiting donations, no gaping guitar case or felt-marker-on-cardboard sign saying "Homeless Please Help." There's only the man himself, big hands working the harmonica, big feet shuffling in a private dance.

No one else seems to see him, but Ilona has observed that most people bop along in a state of happy oblivion. The lunchtime crowds surge and part effortlessly around them—him and Ilona, who has paused without knowing why. She watches him intently from a distance of ten feet. Two things about him strike her as peculiar. One—she cannot hear the tune he plays so deliberately on his instrument. It occurs to her that it might be broken, or not a harmonica at all, merely a salvaged piece of junk the right size and shape. Two—there's something familiar about him.

A deep-toned bell tolls, rousing Ilona from her thoughts. She's missed the "walk" light and has to wait through another cycle. Now she'll be late getting back to the office, not a good move with everyone under pressure to finish the report. Especially not good when you're the junior member of the staff, a newbie, in the eyes of some an intruder.

Banking done, Ilona hurries back to the office, calculating a quick estimate of expenses for the coming week. What's left in her chequing account should be just enough until next payday, if she's careful and nothing unexpected comes up.

"Katherine was looking for you," says Trish, the eagle-eyed receptionist, not bothering to lower her voice. "I told her you were due back by one, but hey, what's twelve minutes?" She shrugs and smirks as Ilona hurries to her cubicle. A note from the section coordinator rests on her keyboard. *I need those figures by 4 p.m. today. Please!* Ilona mouses her sleeping screen into wakefulness and turns on the printer. "Don't you start bleeping at me," she mutters to it, "or I'll give you something to bleep about."

Outside, two crows confer in one of the locust trees that line the street, already showing golden leaves amid the green. Behind them is the pure, depthless blue of the sky, but Ilona ignores it all, busy wrangling numbers, gathering and assembling them, earning her keep.

Three and a half hours later, the office empties with exhortations of "Have a nice weekend!" and "See you Monday!" Ilona turns her back on downtown and harbour and begins her homeward trudge up the hill. She reminds herself how lucky she is to have this job—civilized hours and a half-decent salary. So it isn't perfect—what is? At least she's supporting herself, making a fresh start after the muffled years. And she does like the actual work—tabulating figures, putting them into coherent displays, making them useful.

But what if it happens again? *Never mind that. Just remember—first one foot, and then the other. Right, left, right, left, nothing to it.*

Nothing, until—clunk—you trip and fall on your face.

The job ensures a place to live, a home. It's just a basement suite, but as long as she can pay the rent, it's hers. She turns into her street and pauses in front of her door. The marigolds and verbenas she planted in May glow a greeting as she rummages in her bag for the key. There's another bill in the mailbox, but at least it won't be due until after payday. It could be worse, she thinks, remembering the man by the church.

She stops in the act of putting the key in the lock. *He did look familiar, didn't he?*

Something about that man with the harmonica—the way he moved, the tilt of his head and the slope of his shoulders—trickles out of the depths of her mind and links up with long-dormant memories. An hour later, when she is cooking supper, a name swims into her consciousness from the shadowed past. She and Davy Dawson were the only ones from their high school's graduating class to go to university.

Davy Dawson. Ilona hasn't thought of him in years, or of university, but she lets the memories come while she eats supper, does the dishes and watches the evening news. It's fall—time to leave home for college dorms and rented apartments, for long hallways, lecture theatres, crowded cafeterias, and campuses entering the dishevelment, dampness, and disorder of autumn on its way to winter.

Fall on campus is magical and fleeting, maybe because you're always so conscious of time passing. High school years seem endless, but in university it's no time at all from the start of the year to midterms, even less to Christmas exams. Every week there are assignments due; every day you're putting something off or frantically trying to get something done.

And outside, the whole world is changing. The summer says a lingering goodbye as the light drains away earlier each day. Campus walkways are carpeted in golden leaves that make the air around them glow. Any day the rains will start, weeks of grey skies, water dripping everywhere, windows steaming up and broken umbrellas abandoned in garbage cans.

By the end of October, wind pulls the remaining leaves from the trees, revealing their structure in a new austerity. The gaudy colours fade to brown and ochre. Contingents of yellow-clad grounds staff rake up the leaves, revealing the dark earth and wet pavements. They herd the flying leaves with roaring leaf-blowers, suck them into trucks with giant vacuum hoses and haul them away.

As the year turns toward solstice, rain and clouds occasionally give way to clear days and frosty nights. On such afternoons, walking from residence to the library, you see the bare trees silhouetted against a sky of cold orange, remote and brilliant. You shiver with awe at the beauty, yet are glad and relieved to reach the shelter of the fluorescent-lit building with its fixed boundaries and bustle of human activity.

Then there's the slide toward Christmas exams and the sudden release of two weeks off. When you come back, it's a new year and a whole new world.

Yes, Ilona, but what happened then?

1

You didn't know me when I came,
You didn't know me when I left.

NOVEMBER 2007

That was the last good day, Ilona thinks. Last month when I went to the bank and saw that homeless guy who reminded me of Davy. Everything changed after that. If I'd given him money, would that have taken off the curse?

After that day, things got jittery. Everyone in the office knew something was up. Supervisors were called to sudden meetings and came back looking grim. Everyone did their work, but there was a feeling of pointlessness about it. Some people knew things but weren't talking. Others talked but knew nothing, were just speculating and trading rumours. No one talked to Ilona, except to say "Good morning" and "See you tomorrow."

Then comes the day when everyone knows. The department is being downsized and jobs are being cut. The announcement comes by e-mail on Halloween—definitely a trick, not a treat.

The next morning, Ilona pulls up her current spreadsheet, ignoring the buzz of talk on the other side of the divider. She has work to do and wants to do it, even if the others don't. Let them gossip. If she had a choice about which of them would be laid off, it would be Trish—she of the braying voice and wealth of random opinions.

Ilona looks up to see Katherine, the section coordinator, standing by her desk. "Excuse me, Ilona. Would you please come into my office?"

There's something about the tone of her voice, something about the respectful way she escorts Ilona toward her glass-partitioned office, that makes Ilona's stomach feel heavy and sick, even before she sees the balding pate of the department head behind the glass.

Ilona's co-workers call him "Mr. Talbot," even when they're gossiping about him, commenting snidely on his choice of ties or the way his comb-over comes unstuck by mid-morning. Katherine is the only one who calls him "Larry" on his occasional visits to the office.

Ilona sits. Katherine gives her a weak, sympathetic smile and leaves, closing the door.

"Ah, Ms.—" Talbot looks at a piece of paper on the desk. "Ms. Miller. I'm afraid I have to tell you that your position has been eliminated. I want to make it perfectly clear that this wasn't my decision. I was given very strong direction from my superiors." He raises his eyes toward the ceiling as though appealing to a higher power.

Ilona clears her throat. "So I'm being fired?"

Talbot blinks and produces a smile. "Oh no, you're not being fired. One position had to be cut from this department, fortunately only one. Other departments weren't so lucky. We made the selection based on seniority, you understand, and you were the most recent hire. This is in no way a reflection on your performance, Ms. Miller. You'll be given a good reference, don't worry. Unfortunately, the policy in this case is immediate termination." His eyes flick ceilingward again. "You will be paid for the full day today as well as the severance package. Three months' salary, and of course you'll have access to advice on finding new employment and moving forward."

He asks if she has questions, and when she doesn't, he tells her the whole thing over again, not forgetting the bit about "moving forward."

Talbot stands and holds out a hand. Ilona stands too, but her legs feel as though they don't belong to her any more, and she's afraid she might fall over. Talbot's hand is soft and spongy, like part of one of those inflatable Santas people put in their yards at Christmas.

"Thanks for working with us and good luck." Talbot utters, and hustles off.

Katherine reappears, carrying a cloth bag emblazoned with the logo of the public broadcaster. *Nice bag!* Ilona thinks. She always listens to the early morning radio program while getting ready for work.

"I thought you could use this for your personal things," Katherine says. "I don't know if Larry mentioned it, but your final cheque will be mailed to you. I'm really sorry about this." But she doesn't look Ilona in the eye, just hands her the bag and turns away.

Less than an hour later, Ilona is half way up the hill to home (carrying the bag, which contains her coffee cup, a sweater, a calendar, some photographs, a hairbrush, and an extra pair of shoes), when the reason for the "immediate termination" policy hits her. They don't want to have doomed people in the office any longer than absolutely necessary. It's like the meat business—everyone likes the sizzling steak, but no one wants to see the animal being killed. That part is best done out of sight.

They were all there to say goodbye and wish her luck, with the right expressions on their faces. *But I'll bet they're feeling relieved right now. And I'm unemployed. Jobless. Laid off. Downsized.*

The words echo through her head in time with her footfalls on the pavement until they lose their meanings. A few minutes later, she looks up and realizes she doesn't know where she is or what she is doing. She's supposed to be at work, isn't she? She'd better get back; it's so late!

No—not any more. It doesn't matter any more. It's all over. You blew it. Again.

Cars go by like they always do. A bus wheezes to a halt and people get off. A woman loaded down with grocery bags nearly bumps into Ilona. When she sidesteps to avoid her, a man hurrying from behind steps on her foot.

Ilona freezes. *Oh shit! What am I doing here? Home—I need to get home!*

Home, where the heart is, right? Well, Heart, you're going to have to move soon. Better get used to being out on the street.

Home. Up the hill. One foot forward and then the other, step, step, step. That's right, keep going. Past the shops, past the banks. Up the hill. One, two, one, two, like you do every day. *Except now everything's wrong. The light's too bright. The day's been zapped. I've been chopped, I've been cut, I've been axed, I've been sacked. Won't be back.*

A group of girls giggles by, pony tails and purses swinging. A woman with a cane, a man muttering into a cell phone, frowning.

Everyone has somewhere to go, things to do. Not me. I'm out, don't count, got the boot, didn't suit...

Three years she worked there. She thought she was doing well. But when they had to pick someone to cut, it was her. Why?

Because it shows, that's why. No matter how hard you try to hide it, no matter how much time goes by, no matter where you go, it still shows. People always know.

"No reflection on your performance." What a crock.

Here is the familiar street. Here is the house where she lives (but for how much longer?). Today the flowers look ratty, with their tired leaves and slug-nibbled blooms. Even the sky is dull and flat. There's a crumpled tissue on her doorstep, probably dropped by whoever stuffed the wodge of flyers into the mailbox.

Didn't last long, did it, your try at a new life? That's because there's no such thing as a new life. It's just the same old life and you're the same old failure. They didn't have to look very hard to find someone to get rid of, did they? You were right there, the obvious choice.

I'll do some work in the garden tomorrow. That might help. Maybe I'll plant some pansies for winter, tulips for spring...

Who're you trying to kid? You won't be here in spring! You won't be able to pay the rent after February or so.

But I can find another job. I managed to get this one, didn't I?

Barely. You got it only because you glossed over the previous seventeen years and called seasonal farm labour "resource management." And okay, there were those computer courses you took. But who do you think will hire you now? No one wants a middle-aged failure whose only skills are typing and data entry. Everyone's downsizing, haven't you heard? I can't see you in retail, somehow. "How may I help you, Ma'am?" "Have a nice day, Sir." Not likely; we're not dealing with a well-rounded, marketable individual, are we?

Ilona dumps the bag on the couch and shuffles through the flyers. "Well, I have to do something! Don't I?" *Do something. Have to. Or else. But what? Stuff on sale. Selling. I have to sell myself. Promote my assets.*

Your assets. Ass sets. No, it sits. Sit on your asset. Haha!

Okay, there's no hope. All gone. It's over. Over. There's nothing. No thing. Oh, what a cute jacket, and it's on sale. I should get one for winter.

And why, pray tell, do you need a new jacket? To impress the crows when you feed them in the park?

Feed crows? Why would I do that?

That's what crazy old women do.

• • • •

1987

My parents wanted me to go to university. My father thought it was a great thing to have a kid in college. It meant he had brought me up right and achieved more than, say, Joe Thorsen, who owned the farm down the road from ours. His two daughters both stayed around home and got married to local guys, and his son went to Alberta to work in the oil patch. But Carl Miller's daughter, *she* went to the university to get a degree. It didn't matter what kind—a degree was a degree, as far as Dad was concerned.

My mother decided it would be a B.Ed. "Four years and you come out with something that will get you a good job," she said. "Those English and history B.A.'s are just a waste of time. Look at that girl working in the drugstore—the one who thinks she's so great because of her degree in English. But the only thing she can do with it is work for Larry McKee, selling sunglasses and makeup."

It didn't do any good for me to remind her that the girl was working in Mr. McKee's drugstore only until she saved up for a trip to Europe, or maybe grad school. I'd overheard her talking about both of these possibilities with her friends when I'd been hanging around in the drugstore reading magazines.

And it certainly didn't do any good when I said I didn't think I'd be very good as a teacher, and maybe I'd like to be a writer.

"What do you mean, a writer? Someone who writes for newspapers and magazines? Or movie scripts, maybe?"

"No, Mom. A *writer* writer. You know, novels and stories. Like Margaret Atwood."

"Oh, Ilona! That kind of writer—what an idea!" Mom said. "You have to be practical. Qualify as a teacher and you won't regret it, no matter what else happens. Then you can write as a hobby, if you still want to. At least you won't end up like me—a part-time accountant and glorified janitor." And she gave me that look, smiling but worried, that she got when she was wondering how I would turn out, like a cake that wasn't rising properly in the oven.

"Uncle Jim isn't a janitor. 'Building maintenance specialist,' that's what he calls himself." What was Mom's problem? She did all kinds of jobs—accountant for the local farmers' co-op, cashier in the co-op store, and of course helping Dad on our farm. The odd times she filled in at my uncle's building maintenance company didn't make her a janitor.

My first couple of years in the College of Education, I reasoned that I could always switch to Arts if I couldn't stand it. But I knew how hard my parents worked to pay the bills, so they got to call the shots, which Mom certainly did. By fourth year, I was just about through the teacher factory. My courses had titles like Educational Outcome Management, Concept Development, and Program Synthesis. The big buzz at the beginning of fourth year was practicum placements and the eventual job hunt.

My fellow students were mostly clean-cut, idealistic young women and a sprinkling of men. There were the drearily practical ones with detailed Life Plans: work for 4.5 years, get married, work for a further 3.5 years and have babies—2.5, probably. Once the kids are in school, back to work. Their entire lives were mapped out, unrolling before them like a hallway runner—jobs, babies, houses in the 'burbs, mini-vans, PAC meetings, soccer coaching. Eventually, the retirement condo or townhouse near a golf course, cruises to Alaska or the Caribbean, the short illness, death and cremation. Nice and neat.

I wanted something different. I didn't hate my courses. A few of them were actually interesting. I was friends (or at least friendly) with some of my classmates. But when I was honest with myself, I had to admit I wasn't looking forward to teaching. I wasn't enthused by the prospect of nurturing young minds. I guess I'd been waiting all along for something to happen before it came to that.

In three years of university I hadn't really experienced what I had always thought of as "college life"—radical, intellectual coffee-house culture, all-night debates about life and politics, wallowing in the throes of artistic or literary creation with a group of like-minded bohemians. The closest we got to that in Ed. was arguments about whether the special needs child did better in an integrated or separate situation, or whether educational video games did more harm than good. I suppose I hoped that proximity to the campus intelligentsia would draw me away from my mother's program for me, but so far it hadn't happened, and it was almost too late.

In fourth year, it turned out that I had space for three free elective credits. Here was my last chance to experience something outside of Education. I paged through the course catalogue, scanning the descriptions. I knew it when I saw it: Arts 375—A Survey of German Romanticism. It sounded artsy, intriguing and not too difficult. "Knowledge of German not required." That was good. My Dad's grandfather had changed his name from Mueller to Miller because of World War I. He forbade his kids to speak German and always said the family was one hundred per cent Canadian.

The classes were on Wednesdays and Fridays, 2:30 to 4:30. Perfect. On Fridays, there might be a chance of something extracurricular.

The instructor was a woman named Mona Lang. She was young to be a prof, and in fact it turned out she was a grad student, working on a PhD. in German Literature. She was clearly an intellectual, artsy type. I could tell from her asymmetrical haircut, her elaborately smocked dress in peacock blue silk, and the Gitanes cigarettes she smoked outside the building during the break. A few students joined her, puffing on their own smokes and talking about trips they had taken, plays they had seen, books they had read—or were going to, some day. I was intimidated, but hung around the fringe of the group, hoping for osmosis.

There were fifteen people in the class. They didn't look like Ed. students, but the gender breakdown wasn't much better—ten women, five men. Most of them were a bit older than me; a couple were quite old, forty or fifty. I wondered if they were career students or rich stay-at-home wives trying to alleviate boredom by taking university courses. Sophistication hung over the group like a subtle perfume, emanating from their clothes, their accents and the things they talked about.

Everyone except me wore nuanced colours—ochre and puce and celadon. Shoes and boots had oddly-shaped heels and buckles in unexpected places. Two of the men sported earrings, and the women wore jewelry that looked as if it had been dug up from burial mounds in Central Asia or hand-forged by loincloth-wearing men in remote mountain villages. Leather pants, suede vests and wrap skirts with fringe were not uncommon, as were vintage velvet jackets and hats from parts unknown.

And there I was, in my wrinkle-resistant chinos and pink sweater. Judging solely by appearances, I was in the wrong place. I took a seat at the back of the room and tried to remain inconspicuous

In that first class, Mona Lang gave us an outline of the course and a long list of suggested readings. There was no set textbook; instead, we were encouraged to start with the reading list and explore the resources of the university library. "Once you become aware of Romanticism, you find it in all sorts of unexpected places," Lang told us. "It has manifested in nearly all the arts, but also in more mundane places, like advertising. And it didn't stop in nineteenth-century Europe; even today, there are Romantics among us."

People looked at each other. A few laughed.

"It's true!" Lang said, laughing herself. "All of you probably know someone who never thinks twice before indulging their impulses, even the wildest ones. Romantics don't plan and consider possible outcomes before turning thoughts or feelings into actions. Maybe some of you are Romantics yourselves. Maybe that's why you decided to take this course."

She stood there, smiling at us, daring us to laugh again.

The course outline was about what you would expect: What is Romanticism? Why Germany? Romanticism in Literature, in Art, in Music. Romanticism in Politics and Society. The Romantic Tradition. The classes would consist of lectures, followed by discussion. There would be no exams (a murmur of appreciation here), only two short papers the first term and one major project in the second. People would be expected to present that one to the class. The paper and presentation would be worth 70 per cent of the mark.

Leaving the classroom, I found myself following two of the women from the class across a wide lawn between the Arts Building and the main road. The blond was tall and willowy, her hair gathered into a loose knot skewered with something that looked like a jeweled chopstick. The other was petite and dark-haired, with serious-looking horn-rimmed glasses. I nearly decided to catch up to them and introduce myself, but they began singing something that sounded like it came from a Gilbert and Sullivan operetta. Their voices rose and mingled in the cooling air of late afternoon. Intimidated, I hung back and listened until they were out of sight.

2

Why should they care about my grief?

2007

Invisible waves of air interact with the tides ruled by magnetism and the enormous journey of the earth through space to produce the weather for each place and each day. These forces operate without reference to humanity, and humanity is largely oblivious to them.

In November, the temperature of both air and water falls. The jet stream repositions itself, slipping southward so it is aimed directly at the northwest coast of North America. The giant ripples of air that move over the Pacific Ocean deepen into eddies of low pressure. Caught in the easterly flow, they move onto the land, watering the untended forests, filling the beds of rivers for the death-journey of the salmon, perturbing the human inhabitants with wind and rain.

On Monday, Ilona takes Larry Talbot's advice and phones the Human Resources Department. A chirpy-voiced woman sets up an appointment with an advisor for the following day.

The advisor, whose name is Nicole Burke, is young, plump and earnest. She quickly assumes an appropriately sympathetic expression when Ilona describes her situation.

"Oh, I know—it's so hard for all of us! Our client base has tripled since the cutbacks began. We've had to bring in extra staff, even." She breaks off, realizing that this may not be the best news for someone just laid off.

"I can help you develop some skills to manage this transition," she says, returning to the script.

Once launched, she goes on at some length about how to turn challenging situations into opportunities.

"...so you need to list your strengths and present them to potential employers in a way that matches their needs..."

There are diplomas on the wall behind Nicole's desk—a B.A. degree from the same university Ilona attended, and below it a Certificate of Public Administration. Apparently these testimonials are sufficient qualification for her to tell Ilona how to manage her life.

The appointment is from 10 a.m. to 10:30. Thirty minutes to learn how to pick up the shards and glue them together. Presto—a new life! Another one.

"You know," Ilona says, interrupting, "I did all that stuff. Three years ago, when I moved here and got my job, the one that just disappeared. I listed my strengths and put a resume together. I did that. And so what? When it came to the crunch, they thought it was perfectly fine to show me the door. And now you tell me it's an opportunity to grow. I'm having trouble with that."

Nicole's cheeks are several shades pinker than when the session began. Oh, oh, you've made her mad, Ilona thinks. You're making a great start on the self-reinvention process!

"I'm sorry you feel that way," the advisor says. "Anger is one of the stages of processing a challenging situation, but you don't want to get stuck in that place. It stops you from moving forward."

"But I didn't want to move forward," Ilona says. "I liked it just fine where I was." *That's right—stick out your tongue, cross your eyes, be a bad girl.*

It's clear to her that Nicole is out of her depth. Her face is even redder, and her eyes dart from computer screen to window to her own fingers; she looks anywhere but at Ilona, who sits and gazes at her. (Ilona has done this before, but now she is doing it differently.)

Nicole clears her throat. "Ah, Ms. Miller," she says. "I'm not sure I can help you with your present attitude. Before we can talk about the things you can do to change your situation, you have to embrace the idea of change."

"Well, change has embraced me, hasn't it? I don't think it really matters whether I return the favour."

"Oh, but it does!" Nicole turns, if possible, a shade pinker. "It makes an enormous difference. Resisting change uses up valuable energy that would be better put to making positive moves—"

"If life hands you a lemon, make lemonade," says Ilona. "I've heard that one before."

"Exactly!" Nicole smiles and looks relieved, but Ilona can see that she isn't sure where the conversation is going, or who is in charge.

"Ms. Burke," she says, standing up, "as you can see, I'm a few years older than you. I've experienced things you can only imagine. Perhaps you've read about them in books. I don't think there's any advice you can give me that I haven't been exposed to already. So I'll just thank you for your time, and, as they say, move forward."

Ilona doesn't look back as she leaves Nicole's office, but she makes a bet with herself that if she did, there would be sweet relief on the plump face. The crazy lady's finally gone. Thank God!

Outside, the sun is veiled in high clouds and the wind has picked up, heralding rain. The ornamental cherries planted for their masses of pink flowers in spring are now in full autumn colour—rose-suffused golds and oranges more gaudy and complex than the innocent springtime bunting. The fallen leaves that have accumulated under each tree lift and stir in the breeze.

Ilona walks up the hill to her home in a whirl of leaves. It's just as well that the rain is holding off, because it's too windy for an umbrella. Behind her is the building that houses the H.R. Department. Sane and safe behind the swaying trees, poor Nicole is probably taking a break, telling a co-worker about "this really weird lady I had to deal with. I thought she was about to pitch a fit right there in my office. I can see why they picked her to get rid of, but you have to wonder how she got hired in the first place."

C'est la vie, kiddo.

Emerging from under the trees, a shambling figure moves slowly, a knapsack on his back, a bulging plastic garbage bag in one hand. Somewhere on his person is a harmonica. His blue knitted hat bobs with each step. Up the hill, up the hill, up the hill he goes, just like Ilona. She's going home, but where is he going? Somewhere, everywhere, nowhere.

• • • •

1987

For the first few weeks, I maintained my low profile in the German Romanticism class and observed my fellow students from the back of the room. As usual, a definite group of stars emerged—Joyce and Helen, a pair of eternal students who seemed to be working their way through the Arts curriculum. Gudrun, nicknamed Goody, the willowy blond I had noticed the first day, who never let us forget that she had read Goethe in the original. Harold Neville, a master of sarcasm who provoked arguments for the sheer joy of it. Maria, an older lady who didn't say much, but when she did, displayed a profound knowledge we all respected. I couldn't figure out if she was showing off or not. Libby, Goody's sidekick, was a self-proclaimed feminist intellectual and critic. And Mike. Mike wasn't one of the in group; in fact, I noticed him because he was definitely an out, a geology major who needed three Arts credits and didn't give a damn about German Romanticism. He didn't last long.

It took more than one class to answer the question "What is Romanticism?" For a while it seemed we were studying German history, beginning with the Holy Roman Empire, which morphed over the centuries into something that was "neither Roman nor holy," ruled by the Hapsburgs. This lasted until the First World War put an end to old-fashioned empires.

Through Mona Lang's lectures, and the books I tracked down in the Main Library (so much bigger and more complicated than the one at the College of Education), I learned of the statesman Count Metternich, with his spies and secret police, the extravagance of the Congress of Vienna, and the resulting combination of frivolity and repression. Some features of Romanticism sounded curiously familiar—the rise of the middle class, with its bourgeois values, but which meant more people were literate. An emphasis on the individual rather than society, on emotion rather than reason, conventional religion rejected in favour of nature worship or mysticism. All this led to a whole generation of lyric poets writing in German, with recurring themes of lonely wanderers, shepherds and shepherdesses, wild nature and the enchanted world.

Far from being bored, I found it all new and interesting. The good study habits I had cultivated for three years served me well and I soaked up the facts eagerly. I didn't put myself forward in class discussions, however; all those artsy people were too intimidating. Without a body of relevant reading to draw upon, I couldn't drop names and quotations to embellish my opinions. On the other hand, I did hit a few vintage clothing stores and equipped myself with some long skirts (velvet and tweed), lace-trimmed shirts and satin vests. Patterned stockings and shoes with floppy bows complemented them quite well; I thought I looked quite the Romantic, in fact.

About this time, I bumped into Davy Dawson on the way back to my residence room one Friday afternoon. (The invitations to post-class socialization sessions had not, as yet, materialized). Davy was in the College of Engineering, so our paths hardly ever crossed, and when they did, it was usually a hello-goodbye thing. This time, for some reason, we ended up going for coffee in the Student Union Building.

There we sat, opposite one another, next to a pillar in the cavernous SUB cafeteria, coffee cups steaming between us. I thought

Davy looked older, as in more mature. He had lost a bit of weight, and his round face had more definition. His curly hair was a little longer, but I was pretty sure it wasn't a fashion statement. He wore the familiar glasses, though, and pushed them up his nose when they slipped, just as I remembered from high school.

"So, you been back to the Valley?" I asked. That was how most of our conversations started.

"No. Too busy. Christmas. You?" Davy was a man of few words.

"Yes, I went back for Thanksgiving." I shrugged, reluctant to provide details.

"How was it?"

"The usual." Mom talking too much, Dad not enough. Same old stuff. "How're your classes going?"

"All right. What about you?"

"Great. I'm taking something different this year, an elective. German Romanticism."

"Is it romantic?"

I guessed this was a Davy joke, and did a small laugh. "Not really. We sit around and read old German poems, in translation. Then we talk about the social forces that led to them being written. We're going to start on music next week."

"Okaay. I guess someone has to do that stuff." He was looking at me as though I had sprouted a third eye. "You really like that?"

"It's different from Ed. So how did your midterms go?" I figured that would divert him, and I was right.

3

How have I not noticed
That I have been weeping?

2007

Ilona sits at her computer, trying to work up some enthusiasm for writing a resume and beginning her job search. The pattern is by now too familiar. Begin work on resume. Decide it's too hard to write an all-purpose one; better to tailor it to a specific job. Look at job postings on the Internet, until the relentless sidebar ads, with their bouncing, flashing colours and images of happy, successful people sporting big, white smiles begin to wear on her. So does the language of the job hunt—creative, enthusiastic, passionate, change agent, progressive, leadership material, proactive, and—always and especially—dynamic. Whatever that means.

She doesn't feel any of the desirable qualities in herself, can't even fake them on paper. The wastebasket is full of rejects. "I believe I will bring to your business a degree of excellence and enthusiasm which will be an asset and bring about positive change." Or, "I am enthusiastic about working in an environment of constant change. I believe I can display the requisite degree of nimbleness and proactive leadership you are seeking."

Shit.

She gets up and goes to the kitchen to make tea. Since she lost her job, her kitchen—her whole apartment, in fact—has never been cleaner. She spent three days in a furious cleaning spree, attacking grime and dust bunnies as though they were to blame for everything. Then a reaction set in and she barely moved from the sofa, sat mindlessly watching old movies and cooking shows.

Now she is trying to come to grips with her situation. Never mind what she said to Nicole Burke, she knows that after several months of no income, the none-too-generous severance package will be gone and she will be not only jobless but homeless.

See what happens when you continue to make poor choices?

There's the voice again. Sometimes it's her mother's voice from decades ago, before Ilona learned to tune it out. Sometimes it's Dr. Polansky's—precise, bloodless, relentless. She shakes her head. There's no way she's going to listen to Polansky again, even in imagination. That would be a really poor choice.

But as usual, her mind doesn't obey its own advice and goes off on a little excursion down memory lane, all the way back to Dr. Polansky's office, with its shiny, pale green paint making the little bumps in the plaster stand out like goose pimples. His diplomas hang on the wall behind him, proclaiming in scrollwork-surrounded Latin his qualifications to ask her personal questions and give her unwanted advice. There is the window through which she has stared so much (in preference to the view of the doctor's pouchy little face and his mud-coloured eyes behind their thick glasses).

There's that tree. Something's been eating holes in the leaves. There's a bird. A crow. Hi, Mr. Crow. Wish I was out there with you on that branch, instead of in here with Dr. Polansky. But the branch would break and down would fall baby, crackup and all. "Ha ha ha ha ha..."

"No hysterics, please, Ms. Miller!"

"Pardon me, Dr. Polansky. I'm having trouble concentrating. That crow out there distracted me."

Oh boy, what a flashback that was! Get a grip, 'Lona!

She takes her mug of tea and goes over to the window that looks out on the narrow side yard that is her private garden. She hasn't bothered to pull out the dead marigolds and other annuals, so it's a pretty bleak scene, especially on this cold, grey day. It's hard to believe how proud she'd been of this little patch of ground, how she thought of it as an oasis from the outside world, kept safe from scrutiny by cedarwood lattice panels. She used to relax out here on weekend mornings with a cup of coffee, summer evenings with a glass of wine...

It's stupid to cry about something like this, stupid.

But she does. As though getting fired (laid off, not fired) has broken some sort of internal dam, she's turned into a regular weeper. Almost anything sets her off these days—a tune on the radio, the sight of happy people having fun, even those goddamn dead marigolds out there.

There's something lying by the bench. Ilona wipes her eyes with a tissue and leans closer to the window to see it better, but still can't make it out. She puts down her mug and goes out to investigate.

It's an apple core. Quite fresh too, only slightly brown. Ilona can see the marks made by the teeth of the person who ate the apple, most likely while sitting on her bench, just a few feet from her rooms. But the bench is so private, invisible behind its lattice screen, except from inside her apartment. Someone probably tossed the core over the fence and it landed near the bench. That has to be it.

But no. As Ilona turns away, holding the apple core gingerly by its stem, intending to put it in the garbage, she sees something else—a cigarette butt, one of those brown ones, so it hadn't caught her eye against the brick pavement the way a white one would have. There's no way it was tossed in, because she can plainly see the smear of ash where it was stubbed out. She drops the apple core and hurries back inside, closes and locks the door and pulls the curtains.

That night, the atmospheric pressure builds and the flow of air over the region changes from the prevailing westerly direction to northeasterly. Cold air breaks out of the interior and spreads over the coast. By morning, there is a thick layer of frost on roofs, grass, roads and sidewalks. Early risers slip and curse, complaining to one another that winter has come early.

••••

1987

It wasn't that I disliked Davy Dawson. *Au contraire*, as my fellow Romantics would say. But when I wasn't with him I didn't think about him much. No one would ever call him "hot." He was just an ordinary guy—about six feet tall, slightly chunky, with curly brown hair and hazel eyes. His face wasn't bad; it had two eyes, a nose and a mouth in the expected places, but that was about all you could say.

But he was an old friend, the only friend from home I had on campus. We came from the same small town and had gone to the same high school. That common link to the past made our friendship too special to dismiss.

Maybe because I was thinking about him, I wasn't surprised when he phoned me a day or two later. I had just gotten back from spending a few hours with some of the Romantics. We had started adjourning the Friday afternoon class to the Paradox Club, a dark little watering hole frequented by students with pretensions to the campus intelligentsia (as opposed to the much larger and rowdier Pendulum, where everyone else went).

By this time, I had achieved a certain comfort level with my fellow Romantics. Every show needs an audience, a perfect role for me. I was quiet and inconspicuous, certainly no threat to anyone. I would sit nursing a glass of wine and watch the others score points off each other, occasionally throwing out a question or venturing an opinion. Sometimes I added fuel to the fire by reminding them of a statement someone had made that directly contradicted their latest pronouncement. I loved this; I felt I had actually found a shortcut into their rarified milieu.

And of course, there was Harold. Harold Neville, the unquestioned King of the Class. He was thin but not tall, with a bony, expressive face and a mop of straight, blondish hair which he was always flinging out of his eyes. He wore a vintage overcoat and a long, fringed scarf. Between the hair and the scarf, his hands were always busy, adjusting and repositioning. He carried an old-fashioned canvas book-bag, in defiance of the ubiquitous nylon backpacks, and wore Doc Martens before anyone else did (or maybe they weren't really Doc Martens, but only reminded me of them later, in retrospect). Harold was eloquent, opinionated, sarcastic, brilliant. Or so I thought—but then, I was wildly infatuated, with his style, his hair, his wicked smile, the whole package.

Harold reminded me of boys in high school I thought of as dangerous but interesting. Most girls thought they were weird. Some were class clowns, "brains" or "geeks." A few were inseparable from their rear-end-jacked-up cars, with an aura about them of lonesome heroes who fought criminals in their spare time (but more likely were criminals themselves). In my circle, you didn't admit to being attracted to guys like these, you just admired them guiltily from a distance. However interesting, they were odd, and in high school, oddness was an often fatal disease.

In university, things were different. Harold was, in a circumscribed way, a celebrity. So was Libby, she of the fringed wrap skirts, suede vests and silver jewelry. In our Friday get-togethers at the Paradox Club, she, Goody and Harold would thrash over topics introduced in class. Would Mozart have been the first of the Romantic composers if he'd lived long enough? Harold said no, Goody said yes, of course. Libby didn't care; music wasn't her thing. Was Romanticism a cause or merely a product of the political situation in Europe? Harold, no; Goody, yes, definitely; Libby, maybe, but... Were the Romantics a bunch of shallow, selfish dilettantes, mentally ill individuals or true artists? On this one, everyone agreed that they were all of the above, depending.

Someone inevitably brought up that ultra-Romantic character, Goethe's Werther. His passion for Charlotte was patently irrational, Libby declared, because she seemed such an ordinary sort of girl, hardly the type to provoke suicide. At this point the discussion split into two—one group went on to debate Goethe's poem versus the opera by Massenet, while another pursued the psychological angle.

Eventually, we would drift away from the strictly academic. Was Mona Lang a lesbian? (Goody said yes, Libby, no; Harold didn't care).

I listened to them argue, watched Harold (the way he held his cigarette, the way he sipped his drink) and thought how lucky I was to be sitting at the same table. Sometimes, when we met on campus or in the library, he actually greeted me by name.

That Friday in the second half of October, I had just gotten back to my room when Davy phoned. It was too late for residence supper and I was wondering whether I had anything in my emergency food stash.

"Hi, Ilona. Davy here." He sounded cheerful and nervous at the same time. "You're still in. Must be my lucky minute."

"Hi, Davy. What do you mean, I'm still in? I just got in, and I don't have any plans." As soon as I said this, I knew I'd made a mistake.

"Really? That's great, because... ah, because I wonder if you'd like to go out. With me, I mean. We could go to a movie or something. Have you had dinner?"

"Ah, no." I was still trying to process this. Davy's asking me out?

"Great! I mean—I haven't either, so we could do that first, then go to a movie."

My first thought was: Why couldn't it be Harold? He always drifted away after our Paradox Club sessions, usually with Libby, but often with a big, lumbering guy everyone called Aardvark even though his name was Leonard. He was reputed to be both a black magician and a genius, for reasons not evident to me.

My second thought? Well, why not? It won't be a real date. This is *Davy*, for God's sake, and going out with him is better than staying in and eating Squeez-a-Snak on crackers.

We went to a campus pizza joint, and then to the Student Union theatre, which was showing *A Room With a View*. I was surprised that this should be Davy's choice, and even more surprised when he said, as we were leaving the theatre, "Thanks for coming out with me tonight, Ilona. I really wanted to see this movie with you."

"With me? Why?" I stopped right in the middle of the aisle, causing several people to bump into me.

Davy took my arm and steered me clear of the crowd. "Just because," he said. "It kind of reminded me of you, that's all. Because it was romantic, maybe."

A Room With a View reminded him of me? Did he think I was a rebel against the established order, like Lucy Honeychurch? I wasn't sure I wanted to know why, but it certainly made Davy seem more complicated. I wasn't sure how I felt about that, either.

At the door to my residence building, he said goodnight, in a formal, old-fashioned way. I thought he was going to say something else, but he didn't. And for a second, I thought he was going to kiss me, but he didn't do that either.

4

Shall I, then, take
No memento from here?

2007

The interview is over. It has not gone well. When they stand up and shake hands, Ilona can see it in the interviewer's eyes: *No, not this one*. She's too old, not dynamic enough. And there's something funny about her.

"You'll hear from us by the end of the week," the interviewer intones.

"Thank you. I'm looking forward to it," Ilona says brightly, flashing a big, fake smile. *Just cut the crap and tell me the truth right now.* On the other hand, does she really want to be a receptionist at Grumble, Fumble, and Boggs, or whatever their name is?

No, except there's this little matter of the rent.

Out on the street, she hits her going-places stride. Money money money money. That's what it's all about. Find yourself. Be yourself. Sell yourself.

"Hey Ilona! How's it going?"

A voice. *Who? Oh shit!*

"Oh, hi Trish!" What a coincidence—the mouthy receptionist from her old office. Once, she had earned more than this woman. Once. "I'm just fine."

"Doing some shopping? I guess it's nice to have all that free time."

You always were stupid. "No, actually I've just been to a job interview."

"Oh, great! That's great. I just know you'll get the job, too. What kind of job is it?"

"Just 'general office duties,' you know." Ilona doesn't want to admit that the job isn't much different from Trish's. Especially since she's almost certain she will not be offered it. "How's everyone at the office?" *Better head her off before she asks for details.*

"Oh, fine. Yes, everyone's okay. Busy, busy, busy. Reports, meetings, courses, the usual routine. Well, you know."

She knows. It doesn't sound like anyone misses her much. "Well, I have to get going. It was nice seeing you, Trish. Say hi to everyone for me." *If they remember who I am, that is.*

"Okay. Bye, Ilona. Drop in sometime, will you. We can do lunch, have a drink, whatever."

Sure, you really sound like you mean it, too. "Bye, Trish."

I wonder which of them has my spot. Her cubicle hadn't been that much different from the others', except that if you leaned sideways there was a scrap of a view through a window thirty feet away. At least you could see if it was cloudy or clear outside, dark or light. And for some reason it was exempt from the HVAC-induced wind chill that materialized every afternoon.

Charlotte's probably grabbed it. She was always whining about being cold. Or maybe Jean the Queen Bee. Yes, most likely Jean. Her gallery of grandchild photos and finger-painted "art" would have supplanted Ilona's Gustav Klimt calendar and the picture of her Dad next to Bambi, his prize-winning Jersey cow. Good old Dad. He was such a simple guy—so happy with his farm and his cows. Too bad his daughter let him down. Just as well he doesn't know about her latest screw-up.

Up the hill. Clump, clump, clump. Know yourself, be yourself, present yourself, sell yourself. *Well, they're not buying. This product has passed its best-before date.*

The world feels dangerous again, like the day they kicked her out. The light is harsh and everything has sharp edges that sting and scrape. Cars go by faster, the drivers accelerating with evil intent. People passing by wear false faces; under the human masks are the mirrored eyes and everted mouth-parts of insects, or nothing at all—smooth blanks, like in a Japanese ghost story she read once. A couple of boys leer like gargoyles. She can feel their thoughts. "Look at that stupid old woman. Look at that washed-up old bag," their rubbery, grinning faces seem to say. A young woman taps by in high-heeled boots and a short coat, cell phone pressed to her ear. "...Darcy's party tomorrow night. We're all gonna be..."

Ilona can't remember the last time she was at a party. The office Christmas bash last year, that was it. She made herself go, because you have to leave your comfort zone, go out and meet people. It's not healthy, sitting around at home alone all the time.

But then, parties aren't your strong suit, are they? That's where things went really bad that other time, didn't they? At a party.

Ilona doesn't want to think about the Good Old Days, and even less about the Bad Old Days. That doesn't leave much. It already seems like a long time since she climbed up this same hill, tired after work, with groceries in a plastic bag swinging by her side, anticipating food and rest and eventually sleep. Then another day much like this one had been, and another. The weekends spent cleaning her apartment, doing laundry and grooming her tiny garden. Then reading and relaxing. That was good enough.

Now everything is different.

There isn't much food left in her kitchen, but she finds a loaf of bread in the freezer and makes herself a couple of sandwiches—one cheese, the other peanut butter and jelly, followed by the last, slightly wrinkled apple. She turns on the television, mostly for the illusion of company it provides, but the people are too happy, too perky, too sexy, and she turns it off. She ought to beaver up a couple more job applications, but the idea makes her feel sick. She flips through some of the magazines that have piled up on the coffee table, but their relentless messages—look, look, look, want, want, want, buy, buy, buy—disgust her too, and she throws them down.

She prowls her living room, looking for diversions. There's that old box, out in the storage area. Maybe it's time to look through that.

She hasn't looked at the things in that box since before... well, *before*, and she isn't about to now. Not now, when she's feeling kicked down. No.

No? Okay, but you can't put it off forever.

Before going to bed, Ilona peers between two slats of the venetian blind at her "patio." There is no one out there now. She had forced herself to clean up all traces of the apple core and cigarette butt. A couple of nights ago, though, she'd heard footsteps, quiet but distinct, and a faint cough. She lay paralyzed in the dark for what seemed like hours before finally drifting to sleep. The next day there was something on the brick pavement—a granola bar wrapper, Nature Valley brand.

The wind must have blown it in. Sure, except stuff never blows into her part of the yard. The walk is sheltered between the house wall and the fence, and anyway, there wasn't any wind that night.

In mid-November, after a series of equinoctial storms, another ridge of high pressure forms, centred over the interior land mass. Cold air falls down the pressure slope, deflecting storm systems and spreading over the coast. Northeasterly winds sneak below the relatively warm layer of marine air. Frost and chilly fog in the morning give way to cold, brilliant days. After sunset, a white moon rides the dark blue sky, making the cold seem colder.

The night deepens, sharp stars pierce the blackness overhead. A shrivel of low cloud gathers over the cooling ocean.

Ilona wakes, listens intently. Are those footsteps she hears? Is that someone playing a harmonica, far away?

• • • •

1987

In late November, we started on Romanticism in Music.

"For many, music is the most direct way to experience the Romantic spirit," Mona Lang said, introducing the topic. "Consider, for example, the difference between a Bach chorale, or even a Mozart symphony, and a symphony or concerto by Brahms, or a Wagner opera."

This didn't help me much. I had never given much thought to music. It was ubiquitous but not compelling. It was just there, on the radio, on TV, in shopping malls. My parents were not musical people. Sometimes my mother hummed or sang along with the radio while washing dishes or ironing, and I dutifully jerked and bobbed to the beat at school dances (the few I went to), but it didn't excite me. Some of my friends were fans of bands or singers, collected their recordings, drooled over their posters and occasionally went to their concerts. I did none of these things, and wondered what all the excitement was about.

Classical music was even less present in my life. A few of the kids I knew took piano lessons or were in the school band. A couple of times I ran across concert broadcasts on TV, even watched them for a while if there was nothing else on, just because they seemed so weird. There was the conductor, silver-haired, waving his arms. There were all these serious people dressed in black, sawing away on violins or puffing out their cheeks blowing into horns or other cylindrical instruments. There was a grand, impressive sound, but I wasn't sure what to make of it.

I came into class to see Lang setting up a portable cassette player and some speakers. A couple of the guys instantly gravitated over to help her untangle the cables and plug everything in.

"Today we will look at—and listen to—one of the quintessential Romantic composers, Franz Schubert," Lang began, "but first I want to tell you about your major assignment for this course."

Several people groaned. The spectre of Christmas exams was already looming.

Lang held up her hand. "First, the good news—it's not due until the end of February." Cheers erupted. "But," she continued, "I want a major paper from each one of you, as well as an oral presentation. That's what we'll do in class during March—everyone will deliver their presentations, and we'll discuss them afterward. This is a multi-faceted course, and I expect a multi-faceted project from each of you. I would encourage the use of multimedia as much as possible. Demonstrate your thesis with sound and vision.

"Pick an area of German cultural life in the 19th century—painting, poetry, music—and show how it was influenced by social, economic or political forces. I want you to be specific—to zero in on a particular artist, writer or composer and cite evidence of these influences in their life and work.

"Or you can do the reverse—examine the influence of the arts on political and social trends. The main thing is that you identify the trends we have discussed here in class and cite their manifestation in specific lives or works. Are there any questions?"

There were plenty—some naïve, others just plain dumb; a few, fortunately, were exactly the ones I would have asked, were I not intimidated by Frau Lang (as Harold called her).

The questions and answers dragged on for so long I was beginning to think we wouldn't have time for Schubert that day. I had heard of him, in a vague way, lumped in with "those German classical music guys," Mozart and Beethoven. That was all, though. I wasn't sure exactly where he fitted in musical chronology, and the only work of his I could name with any degree of confidence was the Unfinished Symphony. Because of that, I had it in my mind that the composer was unreliable or pathetic. The poor guy couldn't even get his symphony done before he died.

Mona Lang said that one of Schubert's claims to fame was his songs—more than six hundred. I had never heard of them, had never heard the word "*Lieder*."

"Franz Peter Schubert," Lang continued, "was born in 1797 in Vienna. A schoolmaster's son, he was educated in a school attached to the chapel of the imperial court, to which it supplied choristers. Young Schubert got a pretty good musical education, and although his father wanted his son to follow him into teaching, it soon became evident that Franz wasn't inclined that way. He was a musician and composer first and last, and that's how he made his living, meagre though it was at times.

"The main thing you should know about Schubert," she continued, leaning forward for emphasis, "is that he wasn't some stodgy old music-master. He was a *bon vivant*, with a large circle of friends who lived for the present. Planning ahead wasn't something he did; when he needed money, he could always crank out a few songs or other pieces and sell them. Schubert was a grasshopper, not an ant. If you want to make an analogy to our own times, think of singer-songwriters like Gordon Lightfoot, Stan Rogers, or Leonard Cohen, except that Schubert never wrote his own lyrics. He was always looking for other people's poetry to set to music, everyone from pillars of German literature like Schiller and Goethe, to the amateur efforts of his poetic friends. Even Shakespeare, in translation of course. Some accuse him of being indiscriminate in his choice of texts, but that's not true; the poems he chose to work with may not always have been great literature, but they were great material for creating music.

"Before we go much further, I want you to hear a few of the songs," Lang said, turning to the cassette player. "Don't worry about the meaning of the words, but do listen to them, the sound of the words and the piano accompaniments."

She pressed the play button. There was a brief silence, a few notes on a piano, and a voice...

If you could hold a voice in your hands, touch it with your fingers, how would it feel? What colour would it be? How much would it weigh? What value would it have? Can a voice be like water, like glass, like silk, cool and smooth and perfect?

Yes, oh yes, it was all those things.

His voice was at once soft and clear, flowing and solid, settling into my being as a glass globe nestles into the palm of your hand, but supple as a skein of silk. It wasn't colourless, but certainly transparent. Limpid, like the water that ripples through so many of Schubert's songs.

What did he sing, that first time? The memory has been nearly obliterated by everything that came after, but there was "*Die Forelle*," I'm sure of that, and "*Der Zwerg*" and "*Auf dem Wasser zu Singen*," which was so beautiful my knees went weak. When Lang turned off the player and started speaking again, I felt like I had been rudely yanked out of a lovely dream.

"Well, that's a first taste of Schubert," Lang said. "Cheerful, beautiful, and grotesque; and remember that the sinister is never far away, even when the song seems happy and carefree. That's a feature of Romanticism, as I hope you realize by now. Well, next time we'll get right into Schubert's masterpiece, *Winterreise*, which is neither happy nor cheerful, but absolutely Romantic. And start thinking about those projects for next term."

I had never before gone up to talk to Mona Lang after a class. Others did it all the time in the most casual way, as though they were pals. I always told myself they were just sucking up, and if they had to do that, maybe they weren't all that bright. But today I had a question I couldn't ignore, and no one else had asked it.

"Excuse me," I said, sidling up as she was unplugging the cassette player, "could you tell me more about that recording? Who was that singer?"

She looked at me seriously through her glasses, as though she was doing a sincerity check. Then she smiled. "Pretty good, isn't he? At least, I think so. He's a tenor, Julian Northridge. He's British, not German, but he seems to have a knack for Schubert, doesn't he?"

"I guess so," I muttered. "I haven't listened to that kind of music much, but I liked it."

"That's good," said Lang. "I'm glad. I have one suggestion—get a copy of the texts, with translations, and follow along while you listen. That really makes the songs come alive, especially in a good performance, like Northridge's. His diction is perfect, which makes it easy. Or there's Fischer-Dieskau, if you prefer the classic baritone treatment."

I was out of my depth. "I don't really know what I prefer," I said, feeling silly again.

"Well, then you have an adventure ahead of you." Lang picked up her briefcase and the cassette player. "Go to the record library. Listen to different performers. Everyone brings something different to the songs."

Some people from the class were standing around outside the building. "Isn't that great—no Christmas exam?" Goody said. "But a big project in the middle of next term kind of sucks. It's too easy to put it off forever, and it counts for so much of the mark for the whole course."

"Do you have any idea what you'd like to write about?" I asked.

"Hey, give me a break—she just assigned it. I have no idea. I'll have to look at my notes and hope I get inspired. Later." She laughed. "See what I mean?"

Harold leaned toward her. "I'm already inspired. The sorrows of poor young Werther and all the spin-offs, right up to our time. Like Ian Curtis."

"Who's he?" I asked, taking a chance.

"Was," said Harold. "He's dead. He was in that British punk band, Joy Division."

"They weren't punk, Harold," said Libby. "Post-punk. There's a difference."

"Post-punk, neo-punk, whatever. Curtis was the lead vocalist and wrote a lot of their stuff, too. Anyway, he killed himself five or six years ago, and there were a bunch of fan suicides after. That's very weird, don't you think? Why would they do that? Just like those Werther copy-cats. The dark side of Romanticism is still with us. I bet I can dig up all sorts of stuff about that."

"I think Werther's been done to death already, Harold," Libby declared.

"Well, yes—he did himself in. That's the whole point. What love can do. Unrequited love, that is." I thought Harold suddenly looked sad. Maybe there was something personal behind his choice of topic.

"Did you—" I began, but Libby spoke up, and her assertive "I am Woman" voice drowned me out.

"I think I'll do something on women in the Romantic age—women as objects and subjects. How they created works and inspired works by men. Compare and contrast, you know." She turned to me. "What about you, Ilona? Any ideas?"

"Not really. I think I'll wait 'til I've heard more from Schubert." *And from Julian Northbridge.*

When I got back to my room, I found another message to phone Davy Dawson. I crumpled it up and threw it away.

5

"Come to me, friend,
Here you will find rest."

2007

The ridge of high pressure moves inland and breaks down. The flow of upper air switches to westerly, opening the door to a parade of weather systems from the mid-Pacific. They suck warm air from near the equator and use it to fuel their eastward journey. The air pressure falls and temperature rises. A solid raft of stratocumulus cloud arrives, blocking the sun as the days shorten. It hangs over the city like a wet, grey quilt, and it rains. Weather-wise residents of the coast talk about a "pineapple express." "At least you don't have to shovel it," they say, cheerfully hoisting umbrellas.

Now that the last leaves have fallen and turned into pulped brown heaps on the boulevards, the landscape darkens. The world becomes grey and brown, punctuated by tired greens—dull, sullen, acidic. On rainy evenings, the wet blackness of pavements glitters a kaleidoscope of reflections.

Ilona sits. A mug with an inch of cold tea sits beside her, along with a wad of crumpled tissues. She studies the shoal of fluff balls and dust which has gathered along the edge of the carpet and the baseboard. An enormous task, she thinks, to clean all that up. Maybe later.

Every evening, she tells herself to get up early next day, clean the apartment, do a laundry, restart the job search. Or at least go outside, walk around, get some fresh air, rejoin the world. She thinks of sunlight streaming through clean windows, a mild, blue sky with fluffy white clouds. Hot, soapy water, the vacuum cleaner sucking up fluff balls, the virtuous feeling of order restored.

But then she sits up late, watching stupid programs on TV, falling into bed at some nameless hour. Next thing she knows, it's nearly noon—too late again. Reality is the sink full of unwashed dishes, gritty, sticky floors, the overflowing laundry basket, the rumpled bed.

Maybe later.

Ilona is dangerous now. She doesn't go out because she can't be sure how she will react to any situation. If someone looks at her the wrong way (and maybe there is no right way any more), she may shriek curses at them, or burst into tears. It's safest to stay inside, sitting in her own mess. At least things can't get worse.

But she can't get away from her stupid, weepy self. Anything can set her off—a gush of music during a tender scene in a movie on TV, a picture in a magazine of a couple sharing an umbrella, the photograph of her Dad on the wall. Thinking about the morning she lost her job, on the other hand, or the interviews she's had since (all uniformly unsuccessful), makes her feel sick and dirty.

Eyes staring, mouths moving, puckered holes emitting hateful words. "Skills, challenges, solutions, goals, change-readiness." *Shut up! Enough! I've had enough!*

Tears smell like ammonia. You put bleach in the white loads and ammonia in the coloured ones. Ilona's mother didn't use ammonia, so she'd never smelled it at home. It smells like tears. Isn't that funny? Whether you're crazy or redundant, it's the same.

Larry Talbot told her that day—she's redundant. (Actually, he said your job was redundant, not you. *Never mind, it's the same thing*). The world doesn't need another middle-aged low-achieving woman. They've been telling her that for years; it's time she accepted it. She's not a wife or a mother and will never be a grandmother. So what's the point?

You're too old to be useful or interesting, and of course there's that little problem of mental instability. Who needs you? No one.

Another bout of tears, like a shower of rain. Eventually, it lessens and clears. Ilona reaches for one more tissue from the box beside her on the sofa. She wipes her eyes, blows her nose and sinks back against the cushions in an exhausted peace.

Through the window, she can see a tree. She doesn't know what kind of tree it is. A maple, maybe. She has never paid much attention to it, beyond noticing that it leafs out in spring, casts shade all summer, turns yellow in fall and drops its leaves. She can tell when a day is windy by the swaying of its branches. Ilona and the tree have been like neighbours who nod to one another in passing, content never to speak.

Now she looks at the tree and really sees it for the first time. The tree is naked, an intricate black shape against the somber background of clouds. The solid bulk of its trunk divides into several main branches, embracing a wide swath of the darkening air. Swiftly, they attenuate and multiply, forking repeatedly, thick branches to thin, thin branches to twigs and more twigs, until the outer perimeter is reached, swaying gently in the rising wind.

This is my shape, the tree says to Ilona. This is what I am, this particular interlacing of my thousand limbs. I stand here, showing myself to you on this ground which is mine, because I have grown into it a corresponding mass of roots, delving the earth. So there.

Ilona stares and stares, effortlessly giving her entire attention to the tree. There is nothing else for her. She can almost see the ridges and bumps on the trunk, the mosses and lichens that use it as their substrate, the thick bed of discarded dark brown leaves beneath it. On such a bed, a weary traveller could find rest and peace. The tree wouldn't care. She could burrow into the leaves like a small animal, a squirrel or a mouse. No one would see her. She and the leaves would decompose together.

Decomposition—the reverse of composition?

It would be easy. There would be no need for the ultimate, wrenching decision, no trigger to pull, no endless fall, no puking up the handful of pills and the slug of bile. Only a gentle yielding of the self, giving in to the universal urge to rest and sleep. Once you stop shivering, they say, you're nearly there. Yes—first a long, long walk through the cold night, to an indifferent wood, a grove of trees, a bed of moss and leaves. Then sleep and silence, forever.

A gust of wind brings Ilona from her thoughts. The tree's branches are swaying now, back and forth, as though it's trying to get her attention, beginning a crazy dance or cursing her wordlessly. She gets up from the couch, nearly stumbles on numb feet, goes to the window and pulls the curtains closed.

• • • •

1987

Winterreise means "winter journey." That was all I knew. I imagined something bracing, an adventure ending in a welcome, a coach making its way through a snowy landscape with mountains in the background, through quaint villages, past rustic farmhouses. There would be difficulties, of course—bad weather, early darkness, a broken wheel, even robbers. But all would be resolved and finally there would be an arrival at a well-known place, to be greeted by well-loved people, perhaps one who was especially dear. Then warmth and merry-making and conviviality, like an old-fashioned Christmas card.

Of course I was dead wrong. Schubert's *Winterreise* is a cycle of twenty-four songs based on poems by his exact contemporary, the teacher, librarian, and poet Wilhelm Müller. They trace the aimless journey of a man from the home of the woman who has jilted him, through countryside, towns, and villages, to madness.

Mona Lang already had the cassette player set up when we arrived for the next class. "We'll start by listening to the first few songs of the *Winterreise* cycle. Grab a copy of the texts so you can follow along. Keep in mind that in *Lieder* the singer does not act, the way an opera singer is expected to. Instead, he or she suggests. As you listen, you form your own ideas of the character expressed by the words and the music. To illustrate this, we'll listen to two different singers." She turned to the cassette player. "First, a baritone."

Again, it began with a piano, deliberate, regularly-spaced notes in what I later learned was Schubert's favourite walking rhythm. Then a rich, warm voice filled the room. *"Fremd bin ich eingezogen..."* The jilted lover has come one last time to his sweetheart's house, to write a farewell on her gate, so she will know that he thinks of her even as he departs.

When the song was over, Lang pressed the stop button. "Quickly, now—first impressions. What kind of guy is this?"

"Sincere," said Joyce.

"A solid, steady guy," said Goody. "I feel sorry for him already. That girl was so selfish!"

"Oh, I don't know, maybe he was a bit of a bore," Libby contributed. "You know—meat and potatoes. Maybe she wanted someone a bit more exciting."

"No—her parents wanted someone with more money," said Harold, lazily. "That comes out in the next song, I seem to recall."

"Maybe, but we're talking about personalities here," said Lang, swapping tapes, pushing buttons. "Let's see what you think of this one."

The same bleak melody on the piano, like a steady rhythm of footsteps plodding doggedly along. Then a voice that was higher, clearer, sharper than the first one. *That* voice. The lurch in my stomach told me it was the singer who had thrilled me before. I listened intently, following the translated text. "I arrived a stranger, a stranger I depart."

The five and a half minutes passed quickly. "Well," said Lang, "what about this guy?"

"Is he really going away?" asked Helen. "If I was that girl, I'd be scared. She should be glad he's taking off."

"He's full of bitterness and irony," said Gudrun, smiling in her superior way. "You can hear it in that bit about how 'love loves to wander'—it's supposed to be a quote, isn't it? Someone said that to him to explain why she changed her mind, but the way he sings it, so quietly and so... nastily—it makes me shiver."

"It's like he's a stalker," Libby said. "He's obsessed with her, can't accept that it's over."

"Give me a break," muttered Harold, and then, more loudly, "The poor guy's been dumped and he's hurting, that's all. And he doesn't stalk her. He writes 'Good night' on her gate and leaves town. Eventually. He runs away, with crows throwing snowballs at him, he says. Then he gradually goes nuts. There's no need to make him out to be some kind of monster."

A debate began. Mona Lang had to intervene a couple of times to maintain order and keep the discussion focussed. In the end, the consensus among the female majority was that the character portrayed by the tenor was one of those fascinating but dangerous guys who were best avoided. "She did the right thing, breaking up with him, in the long run, anyway," Joyce summed up.

The few men in the class, led by Harold, said they couldn't see much difference between the two performers. The main thing for them was that the man had been wronged and was angry about it. Who could blame him?

I sat silent through most of the discussion, but just as it showed signs of ending, I felt compelled to speak up. "Maybe she should have stuck with the baritone," I said. "He sounds like a nice guy, so that makes her a greedy little—" I broke off, realizing that I had almost said the b-word. "But the tenor... he does sound more exciting. I'll bet he was a better dancer."

Laughter. "Why would you think that?" asked Lang, when the giggles were over.

I shrugged. I could feel my face getting hot and knew I was blushing. "That's just the impression I got," I said. "You told us to give our impressions."

"There you are," said Lang, smiling. "Ilona has put her finger on it. The words, the music, the phrasing, the dynamics—they should all result in an impression, a feeling, an emotion. That's Romanticism."

"But the Romantics weren't the first to convey character and emotion in music," said Maria, the quiet, scholarly one. "Look at Mozart's operas. That was forty years before Schubert. And what about Beethoven?"

"Beethoven is the great exception," said Lang. "He reminds us of the fundamental artificiality of these categories. And some believe he is transitional between the Classical enlightenment and the Romantic. As for Mozart, there is a difference between opera or drama and a focussed individual art form such as the song. Mozart has more in common with Shakespeare, perhaps, than with Schubert."

"Ah, but what about Shakespeare's sonnets?" Harold was all ready to take the debate in a new direction, but the class was nearly over.

I happened to leave the room at the same time as he. "How's your Werther paper coming?" I asked.

"It's on hold." He laughed. "I've got so many, and since this one isn't due until next year, it'll have to wait. Besides, I get a real rush from the last-minute effort. The inspiration of desperation and perspiration. How about you?"

"Well, I've decided on a topic, anyway. Just today, in class." I had been trying to think of a way to ask him to come for coffee with me. First, I had to get him away from the others; if he turned me down, at least it wouldn't be in front of an audience. It seemed to be working; we were drifting down the hall together, and soon would turn the corner and go down the steps to the exit. "I'm going to write about *Winterreise*," I said. "I really love it, what I've heard so far. It's so—"

But Harold was looking around like he'd forgotten something.

"Hey Hal, my man!" A leather-clad creature came up to us, jingling buckles and chains and sporting a mohawk, a rare sight at the time.

"Hey, Poco!" Harold lit up in a way I'd never seen before. "See you, Ilona." The next thing I knew, the two of them had vanished into the crowd.

But it was true, what I had told Harold. I was going to write the truth about the man of the *Winterreise* songs—the poet, the hero, the singer. I wanted to know him and to make him real.

6

Tell me, where does your path lead?

2007

Overnight, the rain ends, as the weather system that produced it leaves the scene. Crossing the strait, it gathers fresh moisture and goes on to wreak snowy havoc among the peaks and valleys of the interior. On the coast it is replaced by a building ridge of high pressure.

The temperature falls. In the morning, the sun swims up out of clouds and mist, over roofs and trees sparkling with frost. Stealthy black ice covers north-facing slopes, eliciting curses from early risers without sensible shoes, and causing several minor car accidents among those in a hurry.

An immense flock of starlings settles into the maple near Ilona's window. They hop and flutter among its branches, chirping incessantly.

Ilona does not hear them. She is sleeping. At three in the morning, thinking oblivion preferable to the thoughts replaying themselves like bad movies in her brain, she had taken a purple pill from an ancient stash she keeps on the top shelf of a kitchen cupboard, and is still under its influence.

In the small hours the world operates by different standards. Even the most deluded optimist has trouble seeing the bright side at 3 a.m., and Ilona is not an optimist. Once asleep, she no longer has to listen to anything, internal or external. She has spent too many nights doing that. Small sounds emerge in the dead hours when there is no passing traffic, no wind or rain –slow, deliberate footsteps, a hoarse cough, a snatch of music.

By the time Ilona wakes, the frost has melted and the starlings have left. She pulls on pants and a sweatshirt and goes out to check the mail. There is none, but on the middle picket of the gate that separates the paved walk from the driveway is a glove—a red woollen one. The picket supports it like a fingerless hand, with the result that only the index finger points upward. The thumb and other fingers flop down and inward. It's as though a disembodied someone wants to tell her something. "Now hear this..."

Ilona walks slowly toward the gate, but stops a few feet short of it. She peers at the glove, looks vainly around for an explanation. After a moment, she reaches out, snatches the glove from the gate and turns back to her door.

She pauses, her hand on the knob. On the step is a patch of frost, preserved from melting by the shade cast by the house. In it is the faint impression of a lugged sole.

Hours pass. Ilona is curled in an armchair, wrapped in an afghan, but still cold. She has drawn the curtains, despite the bright day, and the room is dim. She can't stop shivering, and getting up to make tea seems like a major project. The red glove, incongruously cheerful, lies on the coffee table among the plates, cups, and glasses which have accumulated there.

Someone is stalking her. There's no point in denying it any more. The apple core and cigarette butt nearly a month ago, the sounds she has heard, mysterious scrawls on the fence, and now the glove and footprint—they all prove beyond any doubt that someone has been here, right here on her doorstep.

So who is it? Who is making a point of showing her his presence, telling her "I was here." He? How can she be sure it's a he? Maybe it's one of those women from the office, Trish, for example, spying on her so she can tell the others that Ilona is still unemployed, and going downhill fast, poor thing.

Maybe someone lost that glove, and someone else put it on the gate in case the owner came back to look for it. Or if it is someone you know, maybe it means they want to keep an eye on you or help you.

Sure. Like people ever do things like that outside of books and movies. Not to me, anyway. I'm not one of them, never was. Besides, if they really want to know how I'm doing, all any of them has to do is pick up the phone.

Ilona's phone never rings. One day, after she's stopped paying the bills, it will be disconnected, and she probably won't even notice.

The phone! She digs out the phone book from under a pile of magazines and finds the police non-emergency number. She presses the right buttons and waits.

"Police department. How may we help you?" A woman's voice, clear and dispassionate.

"I... don't know. I—I think I'm being—that someone's stalking me. I keep finding footprints and cigarette butts. And an apple core, once. What should I—?"

"One moment. First, I need to know your name and address."

"Ilona Miller." Of course—name, address, serial number. She complies.

"Do you have any reason to suspect that someone might be stalking you? Anyone in particular?"

"Well, no, not exactly."

"No ex-husband or boyfriend, for example?"

"No." *How "ex" does he have to be, to count? Twenty years?* "It's just that I've seen... evidence that someone's been... visiting my place for the past few weeks. Hanging around outside. There was an apple core and a cigarette butt left by my garden bench. And last night someone left a glove on my gate, and there was a footprint by my door. Right by it."

"Has there been any vandalism? Anything stolen?"

"No, not really. A few marks on the fence."

"Graffiti?"

"I suppose so. Scrawls. They don't really say anything." *Not that I can understand, anyway.*

"Sounds like tagging. Ms. Miller, I'm glad you've alerted us to your situation, but aside from advising you to use common-sense personal safety measures, I can't really help you at this point. If there is any personal threat, or if you see an individual trespassing clearly enough to describe him or her, then we could take some action. But aside from noting these incidents so our officers are aware of them, there is little we can do."

"I see. Well, if someone murders me one night, I hope my neighbours will be able to give you a description of the murderer. Maybe then you'll be able to take some action." She hangs up. She isn't even surprised. The police never listen to people like her.

The neighbours... The people who live on the main and second floors of the house. She barely knows them. They're all younger—the couple above her, two girls on the top floor, probably university students. The couple have jobs and a busy social life. The girls usually go away on weekends. Flurries of friends come and go. Sometimes they have parties. That's what earplugs are for.

But they might have seen something. Picking up the glove, Ilona goes around to the front of the house and rings the bell. A wait, and then footsteps. The woman (*I don't even know her name*) stands there, sleek in black yoga pants and a blue top, her blond hair gathered into a pony tail. "Hi," she says, uncertainly, looking Ilona up and down.

"Hi, I'm your neighbour—downstairs, you know." Ilona swipes her hair back, wishing she'd taken the time to pull herself together before doing this. "I'm just wondering—did you happen to see someone around my place the last few days? Last night especially? Someone left this glove on my gate, and there was a footprint..."

She stops, out of breath. The hardwood floor is shiny. Several pairs of shoes, a man's and a woman's, keep company in the coat closet. An umbrella stand holds—surprise!—umbrellas.

The look on the girl's face isn't encouraging. "I've never seen that glove before," she says. "And we haven't been anywhere near your place."

"I didn't mean that." Silly bimbo, Ilona thinks. "I just thought you might have noticed someone hanging around."

"No, I haven't," the girl says. "Do you have any idea when this happened?"

"I told you—last night, and it's been more than once. I've found things in my part of the yard—things that show someone's been there."

"Well, I'm sorry, I don't know anything about it." She starts to close the door.

"Is there a problem?" A man looms up behind the girl. "Anything I can do?" But his eyes are wary.

"She thinks there's been someone around her place," the girl says. "In the basement suite." She stands in the curve of his body as he hovers protectively near her.

"Has someone broken in?" he asks. "Maybe you should call the police."

"No, no one's broken in. Not yet, anyway. I was just wondering if you'd noticed anyone suspicious around."

"No, not really." They sneak looks at each other. "I'm sorry," says the man.

It's quite clear to Ilona that the only suspicious person these two have seen recently is herself. Figures, doesn't it?

"Thanks anyway." She turns and goes down the walk, to her own place, leaving them standing together in the doorway.

Going back inside, she catches a glimpse of herself in the mirror near the door. No wonder Little Miss Sunshine and her man were so inhospitable. Ilona's hair is dirty and wild, and her clothes look like she's been sleeping in them (because she has).

She spends the evening mulling over the possibilities. Who could be stalking her? A total stranger? Why? No—it has to be someone who hates her and wants to make her life more miserable than it already is. The bitches at the office. Former office. Loud-voiced Trish and her pal Jean. They were always talking and sniggering together, probably about her. That glove would be just like them; it was meant to say, "Hi there, Ilona. Screw you!" They probably meant to make the middle finger stick up, but couldn't get it to cooperate.

But what about the rest of the evidence? It suggested a man—the big footprint, surely made by a boot, the cigarette butt, the deep, chesty cough she'd heard more than once in the pre-dawn hours. And had she heard a harmonica, or only dreamt she had? She'd seen the guy only once, downtown, just before things went bad. He looked like Davy Dawson. Could it be him? Why?

Are you sure you want to ask that question, Ilona?

• • • •

1987

I dived right in. I didn't hesitate. It never even occurred to me that this wasn't like me. My usual style was to think everything out carefully and approach anything new with caution.

I went to the classical record store I'd heard Harold mention and asked for recordings of Schubert's *Winterreise*, sung by Julian Northridge or the baritone Dietrich Fischer-Dieskau. Mona Lang had recommended him as an alternative to Northridge, and I'd even gone to the trouble of going to the library and looking him up, to make sure I got the unfamiliar name right.

The fellow I talked to was young and weedy-looking, but obviously knew everything. "Fischer-Dieskau is the guy you want for Schubert all, right," he said. "He's the gold standard. I've never heard of Northridge."

"I want a tenor performance as well," I said, hoping I sounded like I knew something. "Didn't Schubert write a lot of his songs for a tenor voice?"

He looked at me with a spark of interest. "Some people think so, but no one really knows. It seems he was a baritone himself, but the original versions of some of his songs were written for a high voice, then transposed down for other singers." He'd been rummaging in a display of cassette tapes as he spoke. "Well, you're out of luck with Northridge. Unless—wait a bit."

He went over to a glass display case, opened the sliding door and peered in. "Here you are," he said, pulling out a couple of square plastic cases, thinner and taller than cassettes. "*Winterreise* on compact disc—Julian Northridge, brand new, and Fischer-Dieskau, reissued. The latest technology. Do you have a CD player?"

"No, I don't." But I thought maybe Davy did. "Not yet. All right, I'll take them both."

"You'll love the sound quality," the guy said. "It's better than live, believe me."

The discs were quite expensive, but I didn't care. This was meant to be.

That evening I had another date with Davy. Almost without thinking about it, I had slipped into a habit of getting together with him every week or two. It was easier to go out with him than to keep thinking of reasons not to.

This time we went off campus, to a Chinese restaurant, the meal followed by the inevitable movie. It was my choice this time, and I picked an "arty" theatre that specialized in the foreign and the obscure. Davy hated subtitles, so it was just as well they were showing a tenth anniversary revival of *Bobby Deerfield*. I sold Davy on it by telling him it was about a race car driver, but of course it isn't really. He was bored after the first five minutes, and his sighing and fidgeting pretty well killed any enjoyment I might have found in the picture.

Sometimes we went for coffee after, but tonight Davy said he had something special for me in his room, so we decided to go right back to campus. There had been snow in the weather forecast and a few wet blobs were mixed with the rain that began to fall as we waited for the bus. Davy pulled me close to him and hummed a few bars of "White Christmas." It sounded funny to me, as though my musical senses had been retuned. I started to say something about this, but just then the bus came, which was just as well.

The special surprise was a bottle of wine (Ruffino, of course) and two wine glasses—real ones, with stems and all. That was the real surprise, as far as I was concerned; it was so unlike Davy to think of details like those. Then I got it—he'd asked someone for entertaining tips. What it came down to was that I was about to be seduced.

While Davy wrestled with the corkscrew, I pretended to look at the books on his shelves. Next to them sat his stereo, and (just as I thought) a neat black box. "Wow!" I said. "Hey Davy, I didn't know you had a CD player."

He looked up. He had successfully impaled the cork and was about to begin the tricky process of extraction. "Huh? Oh yeah—my folks gave it to me last birthday. I guess they thought it would be a great gift, but I don't have a whole lot of CDs yet."

Davy wasn't big on music; I was surprised he had a stereo at all. A few LPs leaned against one of the speakers—the Beach Boys, the Beatles and—dare I say it?—ABBA.

"So you don't use it a lot?"

"No. Why?" He was pouring the second glass of wine.

"Do you think I could... borrow it for a while? Just until Christmas? I'm going to be writing a paper for my German Romanticism course, about music, and it would be great to have a CD player. They say the sound quality is amazing." I took the glass he offered me and leaned close to him. "How about if we listen to something romantic right now, so you can show me how it works?"

It turned out that Davy's idea of romantic was Barry Manilow, but he was in his element, showing me the shiny disc and telling me how the sound was encoded in tiny pits on the surface of the metal and read by a laser beam. "There's no distortion like you get with analog playback," he said. "That's why the sound is so good."

I gave him my full attention, and, after another glass or two of wine, my complete compliance. The wine wasn't bad and neither was what followed. It just didn't do much for me. There were no fireworks, more like nice, glowing embers.

Davy didn't seem to notice. He was happy as a clam, as pleased as Punch, as contented as a cat with a bowl of cream. Pick your simile. While he slept, I took the opportunity to look over his stereo system to see where the CD player was plugged in and to figure out if it would work in my more modest setup.

I needn't have worried. Davy brought it over the next day and installed it himself. He fussed with cables and jacks, shifted parts around, told me my system was "low-end crap, but it should do." Finally, he straightened up. "Okay, she should be good to go. Got any CDs so we can give it a test? I forgot to bring any."

I had only two, and suddenly I realized I didn't want to play either of them with him there. Davy Dawson and Franz Schubert seemed like an unlikely combination, but I couldn't very well refuse, under the circumstances. I picked up the Fischer-Dieskau recording, sliding the other one under some papers. "Well, there's this," I said. "I have to listen to it for my class."

Davy took it from me, looked at it and frowned. "Winter-rise," he said. "What is this, anyway?"

"It's German—*Winterreise*. What's called a song cycle." *Just get on with it, will you!*

"German songs? Like leather shorts and Oktoberfest? Oom-pah-pah? Wow." He dropped the silver disc into the player and pushed a button.

Silence. The piano, and then Fischer-Dieskau's voice, pouring from the speakers on either side of my desk.

"Sounds good, eh?" said Davy. "No oom-pah, though—kind of gloomy stuff. Do you really have to listen to this? Better you than me. Oh, I brought my headphones too; they're better than those speakers of yours. I suggest you use them. They plug in right here."

"Okay, I'll try it. Thanks, Davy. It's really sweet of you to do this for me." I kissed him on the cheek, but he put his arms around me and started one of those kisses that goes on and on and usually leads to more. After half a minute or so, I extracted myself. "I thought you said you were on your way somewhere. I wouldn't want to make you late."

It was like when you're in a restaurant and the waiter has brought your meal, you're drooling for it, but the person you're with is still waiting, so you have to restrain yourself from digging in.

"Just a study group with some of the guys." He seemed inclined to linger, but I pushed him gently toward the door.

"Thanks again. See you soon."

"I'll be cramming for the next couple days, but I'll see you on the weekend. Bye, 'Lona."

At last. I locked the door and turned to the CD player. The first song was just ending. With a mental apology to Mr. Fischer-Dieskau, I pushed the stop button and took out the disc. I got Julian Northridge out from under the pile of notes and popped him into the player. Then I plugged Davy's headphones into the jack and clamped them over my ears, adjusting them to fit. I was ready.

I pushed "play" and sank onto my bed with a sigh.

The Voice. The one true voice, now singing for me alone. It filled my ears, flowed into my soul like balm on a sore, like water down a thirsty throat.

"Fremd bin ich eingezogen, Fremd zieh' ich wieder aus..."

Bliss. You arrived a stranger, and a stranger you depart, but let me go with you, all the way to the end, whatever it is.

7

With a hard, rigid crust
You have covered yourself.

2007

Now it is December. Cold, dry air filters onto the coast under the influence of a building ridge of high pressure. A breeze, small but relentless, blows from the northeast, bringing a wind chill factor to a place that prides itself on ignorance of such phenomena. Christmas shoppers grumble about the cold while enjoying the brightness of the day. The sky is a pale, enamelled blue, the sun a distant white star, moving farther away each day.

There are no more yellow leaves, except the odd holdout here and there. Dull greys and browns form a subdued backdrop to the coloured lights of Christmas, which increase after every weekend.

Ilona does not decorate. The two past Christmases, she put up lights along the top of the fence that encloses her tiny patio, and hung a wreath on her door. Not this year. She has no idea where the lights might be in the disorder that prevails in her apartment these days, and doesn't care.

Piles of unopened envelopes have joined the unread magazines on her coffee table. Envelopes from the bank, from utility companies, from the unemployment insurance office, are interlayered with ads on stiff, glossy paper, for luxury condominiums and self-indulgent spa vacations. The envelopes give her a headache and the ads make her sneer. She ignores them all, except to use them as an improvised cushion to rest her feet on while she sits on the couch.

It is late morning, long after rush hour. The busy people have gone to their places of business. The aimless folks are stirring—old people trying to fill their days, stay-at-home moms liberated from their school-bound offspring, hooky-playing teenagers, the unemployed and unemployable.

Ilona decides to leave the scene of her crimes, the evidence of failure. She needs to get away. Being outside, walking and breathing the cold, fresh air, might help her to get some perspective on things.

There hasn't been any more evidence of the intruder. Maybe he knows she's on to him; he may even have guessed that she has talked to the police. Every morning she checks for debris around her door, under the garden bench, in odd corners outside, but there's been nothing. If he sees her go out, will that make a difference?

Ilona pulls on two pairs of socks, laces up her hiking boots, shrugs into a coat, stuffs gloves and a woollen cap into her pockets, along with her keys and a few dollars for eventualities. She takes no identification. She's a free agent now; her business is hers alone.

She closes and locks her door, strides down her walk and out the gate, which shuts with a clang. There is no glove on it today, neither greeting nor waving goodbye.

The day is sunny, but it is a veiled sun, remote behind a scrim of high cloud. The sky is a non-colour, neither blue nor grey—light diffused through water vapour or ice crystals. If there was frost it has melted, but the air retains a chill.

The usual route used to be downhill, downtown. Not any more. Today, Ilona strikes out along the crest of the hill, into regions unknown and unexplored. Past the grand mansions of days gone by, now partitioned into rental suites, stratas, or b&bs. Past scenes of demolition, excavation, reconstruction, and renovation, ever more common in a city intent on reshaping itself to the demands of those with dreams of granite and stainless-steel kitchens, hot tubs, and expanses of polished wood floors—and, of course, the money with which to manifest these visions.

Ilona walks. One foot, then the other, right, left, right, left, go, go, go. No hum, no haw, no hesitation, no destination. The concrete of the sidewalks is damp. There is moss growing in the cracks, like green velvet trim. There are pits and blemishes, scars and chips. This is an old neighbourhood. Tall trees line the streets, reaching their topmost twigs toward the sky in extravagant, futile gestures.

Trees. Grass. Dog shit. Crows. Nice houses. No people. Where is everyone? Ilona wonders. Working, shopping, sleeping, fucking, living, dying. And here I am, walking along, walking alone, walking, walking. A loose pebble rolling along. No moss on me.

Two bobbing figures come into sight where the street curves toward the Lieutenant-Governor's mansion—joggers, two young women, clad in nearly-identical form-fitting pants and zippered jackets, pony tails flicking, expensively shod feet rising and falling. They puff out little bursts of steam into the cold air. Their faces are delicately pink.

These days, Ilona hates meeting people on the sidewalk, even total strangers like these two. These days, everyone is a total stranger. She knows she doesn't look right any more. Along with her job, she has lost the thin veneer of normalcy she had worked so hard to construct the past three years. Now that it's gone, the bumps and knobs of her real self stand out, raw and sore for all to see. She knows that nice people see them; nice people look too, they just know how to do it sneakily.

It's too late to cross to the other side of the street, and she's damned if she's going to do them the favour of removing herself. It's too late; they are upon her. "We're going up Thursday," one of them exhales. "They're joining us there for the weekend."

"Sounds like fun," puffs the other. "Have you ever skied at Whistler? We're thinking about..."

The words become a faint twitter and fade away, punctuated by the rhythmic slap-slap of their feet. Ilona doesn't look back at them. She never looks back. That would be too obvious.

• • • •

My heart, do you not recognize
Your image in this brook?
Admit it, for beneath its ice
A seething torrent roars.

• • • •

1987

Davy's CD player and headphones were a Godsend. Every time I used them, I recognized my debt to him. Fortunately, I had the means to pay, and all it cost me was a little time. Even though Davy wasn't exactly Prince Charming, sex with him was a source of a particular kind of energy that meshed neatly with everything else in my life. Davy's course load meant we could get together only once or twice a week, which was just about right.

I had never listened to any music with such attention. Until now, music had been only a background for studying, drinking coffee or shopping for groceries or clothes or books. This was different. It became a ritual, a ceremony.

At first, it was the technology that impressed me—that a voice could be captured and reproduced so perfectly on this shiny disc the size of a large cookie. Davy had explained it all, but to me it was still magic.

I began with Fischer-Dieskau. Following Mona Lang's advice, I read along in the tiny print of the booklet that went with the CD, tracking the texts and translations. I heard both the words and the music. I tried to pay attention to things she had noted in her lectures—how the piano suggested the wind blowing, frozen teardrops falling, the fluttering of the lonely crow, always the footfalls of the protagonist, finally the spectral hurdy-gurdy of the *Leiermann*.

But that was only the appetizer. The real thing came after, when I put away Fischer-Dieskau and summoned Northridge from his silver disc.

The headphones made it a totally private experience. Some people in my residence liked to turn up their stereos to the max, advertising their musical tastes to all. They never played Schubert. I knew that anyone who demonstrated an actual preference for this or any kind of classical music (as opposed to simply enduring it for the sake of course credits) would be branded as weird. So far, I was considered simply quiet and dull, not worth razzing. But it was never a good idea to show an embarrassing enthusiasm for the unpopular, so I kept my door locked when I indulged.

Even with my rudimentary knowledge of German, I was able to follow the texts of the songs. After a few listenings, they became familiar. Contrary to all preconceptions, I began to find the language beautiful. Or maybe it was Northridge's handling of it that made it so. The consonant clusters, harsh and crude in—for instance—Hitler's speeches, here were models of precision. Vowels were soft by contrast and carried the melody. It was interesting to hear the effect of the umlaut on a vowel—the difference between the "u" in *gute* and the "ü" in *glühten*. Certain words and phrases would pop into my head at odd times during the day, such as "*ein lauer Wind,*" or "*Die kalten Winde bliesen,*" or "*Die Liebe liebt das Wandern.*" This last was sung by Northridge so quietly, so insinuatingly, with such irony, that I wished I could fondle the sounds in my hands, take them into my mouth like cherries and taste them.

It's funny how long it took me to apprehend that there was a person, an actual human being who produced those sounds. Maybe because the songs were so new to me and so perfect, I accepted them as I would have the music of an instrument, a flute or violin.

On the last page of the booklet that went with Northridge's CD was a photograph of him, in black and white. One night, when I no longer needed to follow the words on the page, I studied it instead. He looked boyish (how old is he, anyway? I wondered) and very English, with his thin, bony face, high forehead and long, straight nose. There was the slightest downward curve to the corners of his mouth, and a just-perceptible (or perhaps imaginary) trace of apprehension in the light-coloured eyes that gazed seriously at the unknown photographer. His hair (light brown or dark blond) had been cut carefully around the ears, but left long enough at the crown that its luxurious abundance had to be held in place with mousse or something. Otherwise, a shake of his head would bring it down over his forehead.

He must have been wearing a tuxedo for the picture, since a white tie secured an immaculate collar. I imagined him on stage, dressed like that, singing Schubert. How strange, when you thought about it, that this young Englishman of the late twentieth century should get dressed as though for a formal wedding to sing in German about sorrow and loneliness. This was how he made his living.

He sang with such care and precision, each syllable precisely enunciated, given a particular emphasis and expression. He must have worked hard to be able to do this. He had trained his voice, learned how to pronounce the foreign words, studied the texts and the music. I had read somewhere that some singers had their tonsils removed to enlarge the acoustical space in their throats for a more resonant sound. Had Northridge resorted to such measures? Was that professional dedication or something a Romantic might have done? The face in the photograph gave me no answers.

He was a musician whose instrument was his body. Unlike the violinist or pianist, he needed no manufactured object to produce music. This realization gave me a strange thrill, and I closed my eyes, concentrating even harder on what I was hearing.

Mein Herz, in diesem Bache
Erkennst du nun dein Bild?
Ob's unter seiner Rinde
Wohl auch so reissend schwillt?

Now I could actually see him in my mind's eye, shaping these words with his lips. I even heard him breathe at times, a faint inhalation at the beginning of a phrase. And the way he sang "*Mein Herz*" (my heart) made my knees weak.

I owned this part of him, his voice. By buying that shiny disc, I came into possession of this emanation of another human being. I would probably never see this man or talk with him, or know very much about him, but I owned these sounds made by the exhalation of his breath, shaped by art and desire into music and words. There was no relationship between us, but there was this disembodied, intense experience. It was not nothing. It was *real*.

That night, I began writing my paper.

• • • •

<u>The Winter Journey: A Symbiosis of Music and Poetry</u>

The composer Franz Schubert and the poet Wilhelm Müller were nearly the same age when they died, Müller in 1827 and Schubert the following year. They never met, but are joined forever in Schubert's song cycle, <u>Winterreise</u>, which is a musical setting of twenty-four of Müller's poems, published in 1823 and 1824.

Despite being exact contemporaries, the two men were quite different from one another. Müller, the elder by three years, was university-educated in philology and history, a teacher of classics and a librarian at the ducal court of Dessau, in northern Germany. Müller was sophisticated and worldly. He had visited Italy and belonged to a literary circle. His poems were famous in his lifetime, but probably would not have survived into the present day if Franz Schubert had not set many of them to music.

Schubert was always poor, mainly because he did not want to work as a schoolteacher. He wanted to write music instead, but never managed to earn much money that way. He never travelled very far from Vienna, where he was born, and most of his friends were young men who wanted to enjoy life, although a few of them were more prosperous than he.

Schubert had already used twenty of Müller's poems in his first song cycle, Die Schöne Müllerin, in 1823. He was delighted to discover, four years later, the twenty-four poems which became Winterreise.

Much has been written about this song cycle. A particular focus of the literature is the use of irony by poet and composer. Some regard Müller as a sophisticate who was poking fun at the folk poetry of his time, and Schubert as sincere and straightforward. This may indeed be said of the Müllerin cycle, but not of Winterreise, in which irony is clearly evident. This distinction can be heard in interpretations of both works by different singers.

In this paper, I intend to explore the theme of irony in Winterreise, in order to demonstrate that Schubert was not a naive tunesmith, but a mature and skilled artist who deliberately used Müller's texts to achieve a particular musical effect.

• • • •

That was my intention. But it didn't work out that way. The next time I put my fingers to the typewriter keys, the words that came out weren't the ones I intended to write.

• • • •

He knows it's over. There's no reason now to stay in this town, where he might see her, out with her mother, or, even worse, with the new fiancé. He's finished with her. He hits the road. But first, he stops by the bridge. The river, which flowed so merrily all summer, is frozen now, like his heart.

He climbs down the bank, picks up a sharp stone, and walks out onto the ice. He bends down and scratches into the ice a picture of a tombstone. On it, he writes the date he first met her, last May, when the lindens were in bloom and birds sang everywhere. Then the day in November (only a few weeks ago!) when she told him she could no longer see him. He straightens up and throws the rock as hard as he can at the ice in the middle of the stream. It breaks through and vanishes, leaving a hole through which he can see black water flowing swiftly.

He climbs back up the bank. Only when the cold wind strikes his face does he realize that his cheeks are wet with tears.

He crosses the bridge and turns his back on the town where she lives.

8

The crows threw snowballs and hailstones
Onto my hat from every house.

2007

The northern hemisphere darkens and cools with the approach of the winter solstice. A large upper low over central Canada retrogrades and pools cold air over British Columbia. A surface low spins up past the Washington coast and injects moisture into the cold air which has oozed out of the interior. Weather forecasters cautiously predict snow, hedging their bets with "mixed rain and snow at lower elevations." Commuters hope that "it" will hold off until the weekend, or not happen at all. Kids hope it happens, now, tonight, three feet of "it."

Ilona neither hopes nor cares. She is no longer a commuter, and she has boots.

The trick is to be unpredictable, to come and go at different times each day, not to form a pattern. That would make it too easy for the watchers. If she does things right, she will be able to catch them in the act and give the police the facts they insist upon.

Ilona walks. She walks early and late, morning, afternoon, evening, and night. She walks uphill, downhill, eastward and westward, downtown and uptown, and to the nearer suburbs. She looks at the map, picks a time, a direction, a route, and goes.

Not so long ago, she would have been afraid to walk alone at night, especially in places known to be unsavoury. But now it doesn't matter. By removing the coating she needed to play the role of a normal person, she has made herself transparent, perhaps even invisible. In her dark green duffle coat, with a black knitted cap over her hair, wearing black pants or blue jeans, she could be anyone, man or woman, any age between the flaunting teens and the onset of limping decrepitude. Thus attenuated and disguised, she floats past bars and 24/7 convenience stores, pool halls and dubious hotels. She drifts along trim suburban streets whose time-conscious householders put out their identical wheelie-bins of garbage in perfect concert, ready for pickup the next day.

All kinds of sidewalks get to know her boots as December deepens—old concrete ones with gently rounded curbs and a patina of time, or tilted, cracked, weed-sprouting slabs by seedy, rented houses. Fresh, raw cement showing the striations of the finishing tool fronts spiffy new townhouses with potted Christmas trees decorated with tiny white lights. Interlocking bricks support matched bay standards housed in Italianate tubs flanking shiny doors with brass knockers and designer wreaths.

As she walks, Ilona inventories the things she sees on the sidewalks—dog shit, wads of phlegm, cigarette butts (just like the one by her bench), fast food litter, spurned pennies. She doesn't pick up the coins; start doing that and next thing you know, it'll be the french fries, or the butts.

It is late, and a raft of stratocumulus hangs over the city, like stuffing falling out of the sky. A cold north-easterly breeze threatens snow, but it remains an empty threat.

The street undulates from east to west, past tall old houses, corner grocery stores, small coffee shops, used book stores, a laundromat. Ilona's thoughts hang and drag like the clouds—thoughts of times past and things lost. Long-ago Christmases, with snow and sunlight and laughter. Even last year's artificial jollification in the office, chatter among the co-workers about gift-buying, recipes, and the doings of children and grandchildren. Coloured tins of homemade cookies and foil-wrapped boxes of chocolate indulged in at coffee breaks. The cozy comforts of a solitary dinner, even the dubious conviviality at the home of a co-worker—even that, remembered now, has a faint, nostalgic glow.

"Have yourself a merry little Christmas." The silly tune runs through her head, inanely repeating itself in time with her footsteps.

This year is different. Home is no longer a haven. She no longer has co-workers. Now, unlikely as it seems, it's possible she has watchers. She is trying to discover them for herself, out on the streets.

Since the incident of the glove, her call to the police and the conversation with the upstairs neighbours, Ilona has done some investigating. No one else is going to help her, that much is clear. She has been keeping her eyes open and her wits about her.

There is more than one watcher. First, the man who left the footprint, the apple core and the cigarette butt. She has heard his heavy steps and his muffled coughs. She has found what can only be his belongings, stashed in the no-man's land between the fence and the garage—a garbage bag containing clothes and a burlap sack full of beer and pop bottles.

Then there's the black car with tinted windows that drives slowly down her street several times a week. She has never been able to see the people inside. She doesn't know how many there are, or if they are men or women.

The question is—what is the connection between them and the other, the harmonica man, who could also be Davy Dawson?

Maybe it's only Davy Dawson. He was studying something practical at university—engineering, wasn't it? Could be he just dresses up like a bum sometimes, to fool you, suck you in. Other times he drives by in his car to do a quick check.

Or maybe the people in the car are from the unemployment insurance office, making sure you're following the rules—waiting, because you're in the waiting period. You never know.

She snorts laughter into the gathering dusk. No, you sure don't!

Just ahead, up a small hill, is a neighbourhood park—grass, a few trees, benches, a set of swings and monkey bars, a teeter-totter. It's the kind of place where parents bring small children to play, where people walk their dogs, where old folks come to get away from their apartments, where everything is the same, day after day. At night, of course, it's a different story.

As if on cue, a gang of teenagers appears, their heads moving like pistons in an undisciplined but purposeful engine. They enter the playground, arguing in loud, staccato phrases. One jumps onto a swing and propels it with violent lurches of his body. Two others grab the chains, shouting, and try to jostle him off. The first kid curses, laughs, jumps off. The group coalesces and heads for the street on the opposite side of the park.

Ilona pauses behind a large holly bush. Best to wait until they've passed; it won't be long.

The black car comes down the street, sleek and gleaming. It slows and stops. Ilona freezes. It's the one, the very same one she's seen on her own street, several times. Just this morning she watched it glide by, an hour before dawn. So they're really tracking her now. It's more than just sending her forms in the mail and checking to see if she's at home. They want to know exactly what she's doing. Someone must have tipped them off. The upstairs neighbours, probably. Or Trish. Or Davy?

What are you waiting for? Run! Her muscles loosen and she plunges into the park, right through the gang of boys. She bumps one of them with an elbow, ignores the ensuing barrage of hoarse shouts and curses, keeps running. Through the park, through the park! They can't drive their car through the park!

She runs, her panicked breath coming hard, catching in her throat. Ahead, four paths meet at a water fountain. Ilona dodges left, trying to throw them off if they're chasing her on foot. She hears running feet, but can't stop to look back. Maybe it's only those kids, maybe it's *them*. Just keep going!

There's the far edge of the park and another street. It's dark there, but a dozen yards ahead a street light illuminates a tree covered in...

snow! Mystified, she stops under it and looks up. Not snow, but blossoms. The tree, a rather small one, with a lumpy black trunk and a tangle of twiggy branches, is blooming. In December. The flowers are white or pale pink; it's hard to tell in the harsh artificial light.

Slowly, Ilona's breathing returns to normal. No one is following her. The new, strange street is quiet and empty, except for a woman walking a white dog on its far side.

• • • •

1987

In no time, I was immersed. It was like falling down the rabbit hole—a new world whose existence I had never suspected. I didn't stop to think, I just let it happen, night after night.

Because it was so wonderful.

I would start up Davy's CD player, put on his headphones and start typing. By now I knew the words so well, I no longer needed the printed text. I let the music inhabit me, and I wrote.

I had to know what he looked like, the man of the songs. The only detail in the texts was that he had black hair, "*schwarze Haare*" in the fourteenth song. Schubert himself was a short, chubby fellow with wire-rimmed glasses. Pictures of him showed curly hair that was probably brown, a snub nose and a chin dimple. He didn't look like my idea of the Romantic hero. In fact, if he reminded me of anyone, it was Davy.

Wilhelm Müller looked more promising in the single picture I was able to find, but there was something of the schoolmaster about him, which put me off.

The only other face available to me was that of Julian Northridge. Listening to him, I pictured the figure of the protagonist moving through a snowy landscape, alone except for a few crows. I waited until he was close enough for me to see his face—yes, those patrician features, lips made to express irony and bitterness, a fringe of that abundant hair visible under his hat, and now a week's worth of stubble on his chin. He gave me a bleak glance, without a trace of warmth or recognition, and moved on.

Yes, of course that's how he would be.

I turned back to my writing.

• • • •

A great deal has been written about Winterreise. Musicologists, music historians, and students of German literature have analyzed the words, the music, the original poems, and posited their theories. But to the present-day listener, who approaches both words and music naively, without a background in musicology or literature, it is a story, the story of an individual.

This is his story:

In the spring of a certain year, a young man came to a certain town in Germany. He met a young woman, fell in love with her and began to court her. She responded favourably to his overtures, and—most importantly—so did her family. As the summer progressed, her mother even began to hint that marriage was a distinct possibility. The birds sang and the linden trees bloomed and everything was lovely.

In November, the door of her house was shut in his face. The last time he saw her, she turned her eyes away. It wasn't girlish modesty—oh, no! Too late for that. It was guilt, because she had transferred her fancy to another, one with finer clothes, smoother ways and (as her Mutti would have pointed out to her) more money. Yes, love delights in wandering, and it had wandered on. Now it's time for him to go too, but before he does, he will write "Good night" on the gate of her house, to show her that he has not forgotten her.

• • • •

I stopped to ask myself: what's his name? Franz Peter? Wilhelm? Not necessarily. It could have been Karl or Josef or Heinrich or Christian or Dietrich. What did The Girl call him in their intimate moments, when they walked arm in arm across the green meadow, in May? Before she dumped him.

It seemed strange, that I was getting to know him so well but had no name for him.

Why not Julian?

Silly—that's not even German! And this is an academic paper, not a novel. Back to work!

• • • •

At this point, we must consider why Schubert was so attracted to these poems. Surely it was the story they convey that impelled him to set them all to music. Was there something in his own life that predisposed him to explore so deeply the consequences of a broken engagement?

First, let us deal with the contention that it is in Wilhelm Müller's life that we must seek the explanation. The poems are his, but Müller was a successful, happily married man with a circle of prosperous friends. To them, these sorrowful poems were only a literary parlour game.

There is also evidence that the subject of the forsaken lover had engaged Schubert before he discovered Müller's Die Winterreise; in 1826, he composed nine songs to poems by one Ernst Schulze, another short-lived poet (1789-1817), who was obsessed with a woman who didn't want him. Several of these songs seem to foreshadow Winterreise, for example "Im Walde" (D. 834), "Über Wildemann" (D. 884), "Um Mitternacht" (D. 862), and "Tiefes Leid" (D. 876). This indicates that it was not merely the musical possibilities of the Müller poems that attracted the composer, but their theme as well.

Schubert was no Casanova. There are only two women with whom his name is romantically associated—Therese Grob, a widow's daughter, a year younger than he, and the young Countess Caroline Esterhazy, who was socially far beyond his aspirations. Therese was the more likely prospect, but the poverty (and the underlying flightiness) which characterized Schubert's entire adult life probably prevented him from offering her marriage. She eventually married a wealthy baker. One of Schubert's friends related that Schubert expressed regret and hurt over the ending of this love affair, if it can indeed be called that.

Listening to the first song of the Winterreise cycle, one can certainly see a parallel with the composer's situation. It is not beyond the range of the possible that Müller's poems recalled this unhappy experience a decade afterward, and elicited the twenty-four songs.

• • • •

I was lost in Schubert's world, my head full of his music. His lonely protagonist, embodied for me by Northridge's voice, moved through a white landscape on the screen behind my eyes. It was as though I, invisible, was standing and waiting for him at the next crossroad. He came slowly toward me. I could see his battered hat, the knapsack (*Rucksack*) on his shoulders, the walking stick (*Wanderstab*) in his right hand. Soon, he would be close enough for me to see his face and speak to him...

There was a loud but token knock on my door, immediately after which it banged open (Shit! I forgot to lock it!) and two of my floor mates burst in. I must have looked at them like they were aliens come to abduct me. I saw their mouths moving, but whatever they said didn't register at first. I was waiting for *him* on the snowy road outside the Town of Inconstancy, watching him alternately run away from it and stand and look back longingly at its distant towers.

"Hey, Ilona, have you got a curling iron we can borrow?" Tiffany picked up a hank of her own hair and shook it. "Dawn's is bust and I can't go out like this."

"She's got her ears on," Dawn said. She came up behind me and pulled my headphones off. "Wow, are you out of it! What're you listening to, anyway?"

"Hey! Give those back!" The abruptness with which I had been jerked out of my total concentration produced an almost physical pain. I snatched at her hand, but she backed away, laughing, and clamped the headphones over her ears.

"What is it?" asked the other one—Tiffany, I think her name was. "Air on the G-string or something, I'll bet. Ilona's into serious music." She nudged her friend, giggling. "Get it? G-string?"

Dawn made a face. "Weird!" She pulled off the headphones and thrust them at me. "Some guy singing in... Russian or something. Gag me!"

"It's German. German, not Russian," I said.

Tiffany piped up. "Hey, you've got a CD player! Awesome! Can I borrow it some time?"

"I don't think so," I said. "It actually belongs to my boyfriend."

"Okay!" Tiffany said, in that tone that means it's not okay at all. "I just asked." She picked up the CD booklet from my desk. "Winter... ise? What you do to your car in the fall? Who's this guy Northridge?" She showed the picture to Dawn. "Look at that hair."

Dawn looked and grinned. "I bet Ilona thinks he's cuuute."

"Will you two knock it off?" I stood up and snatched the booklet from Tiffany. "Give me a break. I'm working on a paper."

"Sure you are." Dawn was still grinning, showing her teeth and gums in a repulsive way. "When we came in you looked like you were about to have an orgasm or something. Listening to this guy." She threw back her head and held out her arms. "Oh, take me, take me, I'm yours!" she cooed.

"Get out of here!" I yelled. "Get out, get out, get out!" I grabbed a mug from my desk and hurled it at them. It grazed Dawn's shoulder and shattered against the door frame, spraying pottery shards and tea all over the room.

The two of them stared at me, mouths open, eyes shocked, while I stood by my desk, vibrating with the unexpected spasm of rage. The crash seemed to go on and on. If one of us didn't say something, we would stand there frozen forever, listening to it.

"Get out, please," I whispered, and that did it. They were happy to oblige. I closed the door and locked it. Out in the hall, there was a faint hubbub of voices. "What's going on? Is everyone okay over there?" I guessed Dawn and Tiffany told them it was, because no one came to get my point of view.

9

How I shall find a way out
Does not trouble my mind.

2007

The western sky gate stands wide open to the weather systems that breed in the Pacific Ocean. They hitch rides on the jet stream, heading eastward over the continent. One after another, they shuttle through, depositing rain on the west coast and snow farther inland. The pattern doubles and repeats—southeast wind, gathering clouds, southeast gale, rain: ten millimetres, twenty, thirty, fifty. Then the wind drops, the periods of rain fragment into showers, the cloud blanket shreds, the wind becomes westerly, weak or strong depending on the depth of the low-pressure zone exiting the region. The sun comes out, or the moon, pavements dry, umbrellas close. A day or two later, it all begins again.

For Ilona, it's a day to stay home. Her whole body aches after last night—the long walk, the terror of pursuit, running, running, taking a circuitous route home, partly to throw off the watchers, partly because she got lost. The topography of the city, with its several hills and irregular seashore, does not lend itself to a squared grid of streets, oriented by the compass. It's easy to become disoriented, even without people chasing you.

Another weekday, another workday. Houses and apartments stand empty while their occupants earn money, or spend it. For Ilona, of course, it's another non-work day. She keeps her blinds down, doesn't show her face in daylight. She makes a pot of coffee, rinses out a mug, rummages in the kitchen for something edible, finds a package of ancient fig bars—rock-hard, but they'll do.

She makes a nest of blankets on the couch and curls up in it, the mug of coffee clasped in her hands. Home. She is home. They can't drive her out. Not yet. Her rent is paid for this month, for the rest of the year, in fact. Why should she worry? Her time is her own. She should relax and enjoy it.

Except she can't, because that other Ilona, her dark sister, whom she thought she had left behind in the cellar of her mother's house, has broken out and tracked her down. At this very moment, she is on the couch with her, under the blanket, warming her claw-like hands on the very same mug (a blue one with three fat yellow stripes—so cheerful!)

A conversation is inevitable.

"Well, well, old Ilona! Look at you! Down in the mouth again! What happened to all that perkiness?"

"Where did you come from? And what's this 'old' stuff? I'm no older than you."

"You know where I come from. You know damned well. You were there too. But at least you recognize me. I'm impressed. 'Admitting you have a problem is the first step toward solving it.' Remember that?"

"That was a long time ago. Why would I want to remember any of that stuff?"

"Why indeed? But that's what happens when you're cursed with a retentive memory. Hey, want to hear a joke I made up? What's the French word for odd, like an odd number, you know—three or seven?"

"I don't know. What?"

"Impair. Neat, eh? Suits us to a T. We're odd and impaired, all right. But at least I learned stuff there. I studied. Not like you, sitting around in the so-called library, moping and breaking the No Sleeping rule too, I'll bet."

"Stuff it. So where have you been in the meantime, smarty pants?"

"Boy, was it ever a mean time. First you hide out at your Mommy's house for years and years, and then you pretend to be Ms.

Goody Two-Shoes over here. Ms. Office Worker. Bo-ring! Didn't work out so well, though, did it?"

"It worked just fine. For more than two years. Now it's done. And it's all your fault."

"*Moi?* No way, José. You can't pin that one on me. I wasn't there, remember? I just got here."

"They knew about you. They could smell you. It took almost three years, but they figured it out and got rid of me, because they could tell."

"If you smell, they can tell. And if you walk like a duck and quack like a duck, eventually they see your webby feet and act accordingly. *C'est la vie.* Who cares what They think, anyway? Now you don't have to sit in that office every day from 8:30 to 4:30, pretending to keep busy. We'll have time to get acquainted again, have a happy reunion. So, tell me, Ilona, what's on your mind?"

"Besides being out of a job, you mean? That's a pretty big thing."

"Sure, but you'll get over it. What else? There's something else, I know."

"Well, that guy that's been coming around here. Sitting on my bench, smoking. And those people in the black car. Someone put that glove on my gate. I'm thinking maybe it was the guy."

"Cute. His way of saying, 'Hi there, Ilona!' Or maybe, 'Bye-bye, Ilona!' Is he someone you know?"

"Well, that's the funny thing. He wanders around and plays a harmonica. I think he left some stuff behind the garage—a bag of clothes and another one full of bottles and cans. But the really funny thing..."

"Well, what is it? Come on—tell, tell, tell!"

"I think he's Davy. Davy Dawson, you know."

"No way! Davy never played a harmonica. He was an engineer, and they don't."

"That was a long time ago, as you've just reminded me. But I admit I've forgotten a lot of that stuff."

"No kidding! You've forgotten just about everything important. Too busy being Ms. Goody Two-Shoes."

"Like what kind of important?"

"Well... I'll tell you when I remember myself. But at least I know it's important. That's why I'm here, actually—to help you remember."

"I wasn't aware that I needed help. Yours, especially."

"Sure you do. Look at you—moping again, going crazy, thinking about suicide. What a waste! Okay, you're going to die anyway, but why run and meet it?"

"*I'm* a waste—that's why. Look at me—a middle-aged failure! No job, no husband, no kids, no friends. All because of—well, you know."

"That's right, I know, and when we're done, you will too. Let's start with Davy."

"Start what?"

"Remembering, you dope. You started already, when you dredged him up, all by yourself (applause, applause). Now let's work on him some more. Your mission—and you have to accept it, no choice—is to figure out just what happened to Davy Dawson. How did he get from studying to be an engineer twenty years ago to playing a harmonica and collecting trash and pop bottles here?"

Well. That's a question, all right.

Ilona sets down the cup of cold coffee and contemplates the ceiling. A mobile of dusty cobwebs hangs from the ceiling and oscillates slowly, impelled by the constant, inevitable movements of the air. Back and forth, back and forth.

How *did* Davy get here? How did *I* get here? Maybe if I find out about him, I'll find out about me, too.

• • • •

1987

Nothing.

That's what happened after the scene with Dawn and Tiffany. I expected a delegation to arrive at my door and haul me off to a combination of trial and encounter group session. They would try to figure me out and show me The Right Way To Be. But all that happened was the next day the social work major who (inevitably) was our floor monitor approached me rather timidly as I came back from breakfast.

"Is everything okay? I heard there was an... incident last night."

"Of course it's okay," I reassured her. "I blew up at Dawn and Tiffany, I admit it. Stupid, but I've been working on a major paper and I guess I'm kind of stressed out. I broke a mug, but that was the only damage." I put on a smile I hoped was rueful and reassuring. "You know how it is."

"I guess," the social work major said, looking relieved. Then, with a stiffening of authority in her voice. "Next time people bother you, just ask them to leave, and pound your pillow instead."

"Hey, I'll have to remember that!" Another smile (a smile makes everything worthwhile). "Sorry, got to run."

That was it.

But that was the next day. That night, after they left, it took me a long time to unfreeze enough to pick up the mug shards. By the time I was done, it was so late that everyone else was in bed, so I had no encounters, awkward or otherwise, when I went to the bathroom and washed up.

Back in my room, I began gathering up the books and papers spread out over my desk. The headphones lay where Dawn or I had dropped them. The disc was still in the player. (Actually, it just about lived there; I rarely took it out).

I put on the headphones and pushed "Play." I sank into my chair and placed my fingers on the keys.

• • • •

He is a long way from that town now, such a long way he doesn't think he can ever go back. Even if he does, they may not recognize him there, and if they do, they certainly will not welcome him. Her mother, on seeing the unkempt, hairy thing he has become, would probably faint, and her father would call a couple of stout servants to see him off the premises. And she, herself? The possible answers to this question occupy him for another mile.

Every now and then, it occurs to him that he is being impractical, foolish, even mad. He doesn't need to do this, to wander like an outcast through the countryside. He could go home; his family has no reason not to take him back into its collective bosom.

But he won't go; he knows that, without knowing why. This is the road that is laid before him, and he will follow it to its end, whatever that is. These fields, white with snow and mist, these black trees, this frozen mud—in some way they are a memento of her, the only one he will ever have.

• • • •

It was nearly three in the morning before I went to bed.

In a day or two, everything was almost normal. Almost but not quite. I had never been much of a socializer in my residence, had kept my dealings with the others at the level of "Hi, how's it going?" and small talk in the hallways. I kept to myself. That was okay—I filled a niche. I was the Quiet One.

Now I had a new title—the Crazy One. Word would have gotten around about my tantrum. Now when I said, "Hi, how's it going?" I got only the briefest response. "Fine." No small talk, not even the smallest. Sometimes just a nod. No smiles.

Well, that was fine with me. I had other things on my mind. I had never become so involved in any paper or project at I was with my *Winterreise* paper. It was more than a paper for me; it was a person. I wanted to see him, to know him, even though I didn't know exactly who "he" was. An Austrian composer? A German poet? A British tenor? A young man in love, who has been jilted and who is not, as they say, coping well with change.

He never left my mind. The music was always there now, ready to play at the slightest provocation. A door latch clicking shut would launch the sound of frozen teardrops falling. The rhythm of a word or a phrase, even a noise such as footsteps in the hall or the clink of cutlery on a plate, could trigger any one of the twenty-four songs. It would play itself over and over in my head—my own personal recital, except I didn't have any control over it. As though something had pushed a "Play" button inside me, I would hear Northridge's voice and the accompanying piano that so perfectly represented wind, ice, a coach horn, dogs barking, or the spectral hurdy-gurdy of the final song.

I sleepwalked through the last few weeks of classes, slept through some of the classes, in fact, because I was staying up late every night, listening, imagining and writing. My Education classes seemed unimportant and easy to skip, now that the world had changed. This was a new thing for me; I had always been Ms. Dependable, the one others came to for notes when they skipped. Now I was scrounging around for other people's notes. A few of them even asked me if I was all right. "You look sort of funny," one woman said, digging the relevant set of notes from a binder. "Have you been sick, or...?'

"Or," I said, taking the notes. "Thanks. I'll get these back to you next class."

"That would be great, you know, because I really need them to study for the exam. It sucks that it's the first day, doesn't it?"

Exams! I had totally forgotten about them. "It sure does," I said, trying not to show my sudden surge of panic, "but it means we'll get it out of the way early. Okay, I'll get these back to you Thursday."

I hurried to the bulletin board where the exam schedule was posted. Not too bad—two the first week, two the second. And, of course, none for German Romanticism.

I didn't miss any classes the final week, but even though I was physically present, I wasn't paying full attention, even to Mona Lang's lectures. I did stay after the last class to ask her some questions: Had she ever been to Vienna? Yes, once, a few years ago. Had she ever seen Julian Northridge perform? She never had, because he didn't come to North America very often. Like me, she knew him only through recordings. (But not as well, I'll bet.) What did she think *Winterreise* meant to Schubert?

By this point in the course, we were deeply into Brahms. Lang smiled. "You've been quite captivated by Schubert, haven't you, Ilona? Or maybe by Julian Northridge?"

I felt a small spurt of resentment. Was she being patronizing? I didn't have to justify my interests to her. "Both, actually," I said, trying to sound casual. "You were right—really listening and understanding those songs made them come alive for me. In fact, I'm doing my paper on *Winterreise*."

"Are you? That's great. Once you get started, feel free to ask any questions you might have." She finished packing up her notes and put on her coat.

"Oh, I've already started," I said. "I'm quite a way into it, in fact."

"Really? Don't you have exams to study for? The paper isn't due until the end of February, you know."

What business is that of yours, lady? "Well, sure, but I had to make a start on the paper. I was... inspired."

Another smile, somewhat fleeting. "That's good. Well, I wish you luck, both with the paper and your exams. And Merry Christmas too. See you, Ilona."

She hurried off. I stood in the hall, empty now that most classes were over, students and instructors gone. Posters and notices tacked to a nearby bulletin board flapped lazily in an HVAC-induced breeze, as though they were waving goodbye.

10

You too, my heart, so wild and fierce
In battle and in tempest,
In this calm you feel the serpent stir,
Ready to strike and sting!

2007

Three days of clouds and rain give way to one of cold, brilliant sunshine. Then the Eastern Pacific Storm Express makes another delivery. On satellite images it shows as a great comma-shaped arc, its top in the embracing curve of the Aleutian Islands chain, its tail drifting down to Hawaii. Forecasters murmur of 975 millibars, of warm and cold fronts, of significant QPF and flood watches on susceptible rivers, of gale-force winds. In the rain shadow of the Olympic Mountains, there is mainly wind, a relentless flood of five-degree air galumphing over houses and roads, power lines and trees, carrying leaves, twigs, discarded tissues, shopping bags, wrappers from cigarette packages and chocolate bars, hair, grit, and dust.

Once the wind would have kept Ilona at home, but not now. She bundles up and goes out into the thrumming darkness.

Now she is looking for the harmonica man. Maybe he doesn't know that yet. Or maybe he doesn't want to be found. He has become elusive. Ilona hasn't seen any trace of him in more than a week.

She starts with the obvious places—downtown and its fringes, haunts of the night people. She may as well get used to them; soon she may well be one of them. Under cover of her apparent invisibility she can check things out, but she has to forego its protection if she is to ask questions.

Ilona's pockets are stocked with change—loonies, toonies and quarters. She has to buy her way into this world, because she still has a home, a place where she can be alone and private, clean and warm. For now.

Here are a couple of people sitting on the steps of a fountain in a public square. From a distance they are dark, nondescript lumps sheltering from the wind. Ilona can't tell if they are male or female. A point of orange light passes intermittently from one to the other. They are smoking something.

"Excuse me," Ilona begins, then realizes they haven't heard. She speaks louder, "Excuse me, can I ask you something?"

This time, they hear. Two hood-framed faces look up at her. They are much younger than she expected, both girls.

"What's up, Mom?" asks one. "Want a drag?" She holds out the cigarette.

"No thanks. I'm just looking for someone... a man."

"Hey, join the club." Laughter that ends in coughing.

"No—I mean a specific man. He's an older guy, about six feet tall, with grey hair. He plays a harmonica."

The two look at each other with nearly identical mascaraed eyes. "Lots of old guys around," one says. "They all look the same. Old." Giggles ensue.

"I think I have seen a guy with a harmonica," the other offers. "What's his name?"

"It might be Davy. Davy Dawson. But maybe not. I'm not sure. That's why I want to find him, so I can ask him if he's Davy Dawson. That's a guy I knew a long time ago."

The girls nudge each other and giggle again. They're just two kids hanging around downtown, looking for thrills or trouble. "No, I guess we don't know him," one says. "Sorry."

They don't ask for money and Ilona doesn't know whether to offer them some change. Suppressing the impulse to give them enough for bus fare, along with advice to go home, she turns away.

"Bye, Mom! Hope you get lucky." Followed by giggles.

She has no luck. She doesn't see the man with the harmonica, and no one else she asks tells her anything about him. Wearily, she turns homeward. Halfway there, she passes a church. The door of the church hall stands open. Light and the noise of a crowd spill out onto the street. "Christmas Supper," says a sign propped up by the door. "All welcome."

Ilona nearly passes by. This has nothing to do with her, whatever it is. Some sort of charity effort. But he might be there. She stops, and after another hesitation, goes inside.

The long room is bright with the harsh light of fluorescents. It's also hot, from cooking and from the massed body heat of several dozen people who sit at rows of tables covered with red and green paper tablecloths. The meal appears to be nearing its end, judging by the slices of pie, the cups and saucers and crumpled napkins scattered over the stained and wrinkled table coverings.

Ilona scans the faces of the diners. Would she even recognize him?

"Better late than never," says a voice at her side. She turns and sees a smiling, mostly bald guy standing there. "There's some turkey left, and maybe even stuffing," he says. "You're lucky. Last year we were picked clean by this time."

"Uh, I'm not exactly here for the dinner," Ilona says. "Not really." She can smell coffee and roasted turkey, and is suddenly hungry. How long has it been since she had a real, cooked meal? She can't remember. "How much does it cost?" She digs in her pockets for coins.

"It's free," says the man. "Everyone's welcome."

"But I'm not—" Ilona stops herself. "I'm actually trying to find someone. An older man, six feet tall, with curly grey hair. He plays a harmonica on the street sometimes. His name's Davy. Maybe."

The man watches her closely, as though looking for a secret mark or gesture. Her green coat, black wool cap, blue pants and beat-up hikers must pass some test, for his smile returns, if a little less broad. "I'm just a volunteer, for the supper, you know. Is this person a family member? How long has he been missing?"

"No, he isn't family and he isn't really missing. I just want to... to see him again, and talk to him."

The man leans closer to her. "Has this person been causing you trouble? Maybe you should contact the police."

"Oh, I've had it with the police."

She turns her back on the man and walks toward the counter where a couple of women are serving the food. Two or three other latecomers have trickled in and watch eagerly as turkey, mashed potatoes and mixed vegetables are piled onto plates.

Ilona sidles up to the counter. "Hi there," says a woman with a pleasant, weary face. "White meat okay with you? We're out of dark. Gravy?" She passes the plate on to her vegetable-serving colleague.

The vegetable woman is getting something from another part of the kitchen. She comes back to the counter with a pan of brussels sprouts and looks up at Ilona, spoon at the ready. A smile appears on her face, vanishes and reappears. "Ilona?" she says. "Oh wow, I didn't..."

Shit! It's Trish! What the hell is she doing here? Hoping I'd turn up, that's what. So she can laugh at me. Let's get out. *Now.*

Ilona turns and scrambles for the door. "Wait, you forgot your supper!" says the first woman. A few diners look up, worried expressions on their faces. She must have sworn out loud and shocked them. Well too bad!

Outside, she relishes the cool, damp air and the wind. It's always too hot in those places. And she didn't want that food, dished up from steam tables, and the coffee from those industrial urns is never as good as the smell promises. They make you wash the dishes after, and tell you when to go to bed and when to get up, almost when to go to the bathroom, even. Besides, Davy wasn't there.

Ilona walks on. *Not me, not him, not now, not ever...* Cars swish by, their tires pulling the film of water off the pavement and replacing it in evanescent tread patterns. She passes a gas station, lurid yellow and blue lights glowing from the pumps, a lone cashier sitting in the glass-sided booth, like a parrot in a cage. A sign strapped to a lamppost wobbles in the wind. It shows a smiling car against a blue background, above it a few snowflakes and bright red letters: "Winterize now!"

Ilona stops and stares at it for a long time. *They spelled it wrong.* She looks again, shakes her head and walks on.

• • • •

1987

Davy phoned to tell me he'd finally finished classes and all his projects. "Just exams now," he said. "We should celebrate."

"Oh, Davy, I can't, not tonight. I'm going out with some people from one of my classes."

"Which class?" I thought I detected a note of suspicion in his voice.

"Just one of my Ed. classes. We're going for dinner at a restaurant in Kits." *Please don't ask me which one.* "Then maybe drinks somewhere. It'll probably be boring, but I've already said I'd go and someone's made reservations."

"Okay, well, what about tomorrow night? After that I'll be studying for my first one. Hot and heavy. I'll phone you tomorrow, okay?"

"Okay, fine. I'm really sorry about this, Davy." I hung up before he could say anything else.

I was going out, but not to dinner at any restaurant; and it was with people from a class, but not Education. Libby had invited all the Romantics to a BYOB bash at her place. "Everyone's coming," she said. Including Harold, of course. Including me.

I ransacked my wardrobe for something to wear. "Casual" parties were hard to dress for. You couldn't go truly casual, as in sweats, but it was better to underdress than to look like you had gone to too much trouble. In the end I resorted to those perennial favourites—the black sweater and the long denim skirt, with a big paisley scarf as an accent, tied over one hip. Underneath were a black lace bra and panties, purchased especially for the occasion, which made me feel sexy and daring. Standing before my mirror, I visualized sipping wine in a quiet corner and chatting with Harold. Or maybe someone else?

Libby's place was in Kitsilano. Walking to the bus loop, I was certain I would bump into Davy and have to think up more lies to explain why the mythical class dinner was so late—nearly eight o'clock. It was raining, so at least I could hide behind my umbrella.

The campus was wet and black, with puddles of reflected light under the avenues of trees. Nameless, sexless figures, alone or in small groups, hurried here and there, except for a couple sharing an umbrella, who drifted slowly along, obviously in love. I turned and looked at them after they passed, breaking the Don't Look Back rule I had set for myself years before. They're like the *Winterreise* guy and his girlfriend, walking across that green meadow. Except instead of an umbrella she would have had a parasol.

The music building loomed up on my left. For some reason the front doors were propped open and I could hear someone playing a cello inside. I stood and listened, arrested by the deep thrumming of the strings, the deliberate gravity of the music, even though I had no idea what the music was. I went inside and tracked the sound to its source. A lone figure on the stage of the recital hall was playing to the empty seats. White shirt, black pants, a mop of wavy blondish hair that flopped forward, concealing the player's face. Thin fingers moved rapidly over the strings on the neck of the instrument as the other hand guided the bow. I stood and listened, feeling myself vibrating as though I was being played, safe in the embrace of one who knew all of me.

It was a message—something wonderful is about to happen. (*Soon you're going to see him, soon you're going to be with him.)* I was filled with an intense excitement. The night was full of magic. I slipped out of the hall and ran the rest of the way to the bus loop, humming to myself.

There was no liquor store on campus, so I had to buy my bottle of wine on the way to Libby's. The walk was longer than I expected, and the party was well under way by the time I got there.

Libby lived on the main floor of one of those big old three-story houses so typical of Vancouver. I didn't know then that her parents owned it and Libby lived rent-free in exchange for "managing" the other three suites.

The front door was ajar. A jumble of boots and shoes nearly filled the entry way. I took a deep breath and decided to plunge right in. This should be easy. I knew these people, didn't I? We had something in common.

Except a lot of extras were there, friends or significant others of people in the class, plus other friends of Libby's and their friends. Music blatted from the living room. (Definitely not Schubert; more your Depeche Mode). Bodies shimmied and jostled to the beat. I couldn't recognize anyone in the dim light. I was about to rescue my boots and flee, when someone came up from behind me and touched my arm.

"Hey Ilona! You made it! I'm so glad you're here." Goody smiled down at me from a cloud of lily-of-the-valley perfume. She was never so effusive in class; looking at her flushed face, I decided she was more drunk than not. "Corkscrew and glasses in the kitchen," she said, noticing my liquor store bag, and nodding toward a doorway down the hall. "Have fun!" Then she melted into the living room crowd.

In the kitchen, I found a few more familiar faces. As usual, the talkers had congregated there. Everyone had a drink in hand, and I decided the faster I equipped myself with one, the better. A huge array of bottles in varying states of emptiness stood on the counter. I found the corkscrew and managed the uncorking operation successfully, despite the fact that one of the corkscrew's arms had come off at some point and had been reattached with a piece of wire, making it lopsided. There were no more wine glasses left, but I found some tumblers in a cupboard and filled one up. I drank the wine down like medicine (fast, fast, fast relief from social constraint!) and refilled. Halfway through the second glass, the end of my nose began to get ever so slightly numb, and I felt myself relaxing. I laughed loudly at a not terribly funny joke told by a guy I had just met, and was rewarded with an invitation to dance.

We proceeded into the living room, where I parked my glass on an end table and joined my partner on the floor. We danced, if five minutes of energetic jiggling could be called that. There was no hope of a conversation, though, so as soon as was decent I left him and set out in search of more interesting company.

It took me a while to find my drink. Several other glasses of the same type had joined mine on the end table, and even though I was pretty sure mine was the one closest to the lamp, I could have been wrong. In fact, I'm pretty sure I picked the wrong one. Whatever was in the glass was stronger than wine, but I was feeling reckless and drank it down anyway. The alcohol, I reasoned, would kill any germs.

I circulated through the living room, glass in hand, weaving around bobbing bodies, even getting drawn into a dance with an insistent someone for a minute or so. This time I didn't set the glass down, and my partner, perceiving its empty state replenished it from a flask he pulled out of his pocket. "This'll put hair on your chest," he said thickly. What an idiot, I thought, and raised the glass to him in a gesture of thanks and farewell.

Next thing I knew, I was in the front hall again, lost in the land of boots and shoes. No one there but me. I fortified myself with a slug of the fiery liquid in my glass (what was it, anyway?) and considered my options. I'd done the living room and the kitchen scenes. Bedrooms were out of bounds, at least until you found that special someone, and I was still looking.

Then I discovered a little room across from the kitchen, a breakfast nook or something, and there was Harold, legs stretched along a settee, smoking and talking to someone who sat in a chair with his back to me. A brandy bottle and nearly empty glasses on the table between them suggested they had been there for some time.

"Hi, Harold," I said. "You've found a peaceful haven from all the sound and fury."

He turned his bony face my way, at the same time brushing the ever-flopping hair out of his eyes. "Uh-oh, don't tell me Libby sent you to round us anti-socials up and return us to the herd." Without waiting for a reply, he said to the other, "We've been discovered. This is Ilona Miller—a fellow Romantic."

"Ilona. That's an interesting name." The stranger turned and regarded me lazily, as though he had all night to check me out. His eyelashes were the longest I had ever seen on a man, concealing eyes of an indeterminate colour. His hair was black and reached nearly to his shoulders. But his features were strong—long nose, big mouth, square chin. "It's Hungarian, isn't it?"

"What? Oh—my name." I had been so busy staring at him that it took me a few seconds to connect the question with his first remark. "I don't really know, actually. I think my mom saw it in a book or something and liked it, that's all. And you're—I'm sorry, I didn't catch your name."

"He's an actor; they don't have names, only roles," Harold interjected. "You could call him Bruce now, or something else next week, depending."

"Or you could call me Julian." He pulled a chair over for me and I sat down, ignoring the piqued expression on Harold's face.

"Would you like a drink?" Julian asked. It occurred to me fleetingly that brandy might not be a good idea on top of everything else I'd had to drink, but I waved the thought aside. If brandy was his choice, it would be my choice too. I gave him my glass. "Thanks, I would."

"Names are important but mutable, fortunately," he said, pouring an inch of golden liquid and handing it to me with a smile.

"What do you mean?" I asked. *Oh shit, that sounds stupid.*

"Well, a name that's unusual or unintentionally funny can be hard to live with. Say your name is Bruce Barker—you're a seen as a bit of a dog, maybe. 'Arf, arf,' everywhere you go. So maybe you change it to something better, like—oh, I don't know—Julian Harker. Makes perfect sense to me, but some disapprove. Or pretend to." He gave Harold a sidelong glance.

I was about to reply when Goody, Libby and two other women burst in on us. "There you are, Harold!" Libby exclaimed. "Ilona, how selfish of you—two guys all to yourself. Okay, let's bring 'em back alive, girls! Come on, out of here, all of you—back to the party! Dance, dance, dance!"

And the four of them danced around us, pulling at our arms and laughing. It was clear there would be no resisting them. I leaned over to Julian and murmured, "Dance with me?" On any other occasion, I wouldn't have done that, but tonight was different. Tonight I felt carefree and light as a soap bubble.

"Sure," he said, getting up. I took his hand to make sure he didn't get lost on the way to the living room, where the party pulsed and throbbed harder than ever. The crowd made close dancing the only option, no matter what the music.

He was taller than Davy, and stronger. I slipped my arms around his waist and smiled up at him. I was dizzy and happy, and nothing else mattered.

• • • •

I woke from a dead sleep to a pounding on my door. "Phone!" someone shouted. "Third time, and he won't leave a message!" I dragged myself out of bed. I had to sit down again as the floor and my stomach lurched in opposite directions. My head thumped and ached. I nearly collapsed back onto the pillows, but one thought got through the fog and made me get up again.

It might be *him*.

I propelled myself down the hall and picked up the phone. "Hello?" My voice sounded as head-plugged and nerve-scraped as I felt.

"Ilona? It's Davy. What's wrong? You sick or something?"

Shit. Davy. "No, I'm fine. Why are you calling so early?" I was shivering in my nightie and had to lean on the shelf with the phone book to keep from falling over.

"Since when is two in the afternoon early? How about if we meet at—?"

"Davy, can I call you back later? I'm not really—"

"There is no later." He sounded surly. "Jesus, Ilona, you know after today I'll be studying all day, every day, except when I'm actually writing the fucking exams. This is our last chance to get together, and I'm really getting the feeling you're not into it."

His voice was like coarse sandpaper scraped over a sore. "Actually, Davy, I think it's over," I heard myself saying.

"What's over?"

"Us. I don't think it's working any more." I took a breath and kept going. "And besides... there's someone else."

"Someone else? What do you mean, someone-fucking-else?"

I'd never heard Davy use the f-word so much. This was a revelation. "I'm seeing someone else. Besides you, I mean. So I don't think it's right for me to keep going out with you."

"Jesus, Ilona, that's pretty heavy..." His voice got hoarse. "Hey, don't you think we should get together and talk about this before—?"

"I don't really have a lot more to say." *Besides, I have to pee.* "I don't see any point in getting together. We both have exams. Let's just agree that it's over."

"But it's not over! Not for me! Shit, Ilona, it's like you've just kicked me in the gut and you expect me to say, 'So long, it's been good to know you?' That's stupid!"

I couldn't believe how whiny he sounded, like a little kid who didn't want to share a toy. I was cold, I was sick and now I *really* had to pee. "Davy, I'm sorry, but that's just the way it is. Goodbye."

He gasped. He really did. "Wait, Ilona—tell you what, maybe after exams. How about if we get together at home, over Christmas? How about that?"

"I don't think that would be a good idea."

"Jesus Christ! Who is this guy, anyway?"

"Sorry, I've got to go. Bye, Davy." I hung up, gently, and headed for the bathroom.

It was only later, in the shower, while I was lathering up my hair, that I remembered—I still had Davy's CD player, and I couldn't give it up.

11

I dreamt
Of hearts and kisses,
Of bliss and ecstasy.

2007

The night of December 21st is the longest of the year. The sun sets by 4 p.m. and will not rise again until after eight the next morning. Even then, it will probably be obscured by clouds.

This is also the time for some of the major holidays of the year, both sacred and secular. In the dark streets, people scurry about feverishly, full of stress and anticipation, decorating, socializing, consuming and fretting. Coloured lights twinkle and glow, giant inflatable figures are hoisted in suburban front yards, to jiggle and jitter in the gale-force winds. Artificial lights nearly succeed in negating the solstice.

Not for Ilona. She is in her own solstice. She does not decorate, shop or entertain. She walks. She sleeps. Sometimes she dreams.

When you sleep a lot, long and deeply, Ilona realizes, you discover a secret country, with its own geography and history. You travel within it, returning to specific places in different dreams.

There is the city of wide streets and solid, imposing buildings of pale stone and many windows. The buildings are connected by walkways, tunnels, squares and courtyards. Occasionally, crowds hurry through them; in other dreams they stand silent and empty, with the sterile perfection of architects' models.

Near the edge of this city, there is a small street of modest houses, shaded by old trees. The houses contain secrets and conspire with one another to keep them.

The countryside beyond is broad and varied. A wild river rushes through a canyon whose steep, gravel banks hold precariously to the angle of repose. Occasionally there are wide flats, with small trees and shrubs. The river flows through them, full of dangerous pools and currents. Far from the river is a region of wooded hills through which runs a two-rutted, winding road. Its destination is a mystery, veiled in vague terror.

Somewhere is a high hill, grass-covered and dotted with densely branched conifers, like large Christmas trees. At the summit dwells an incomprehensible power, splendid and terrible.

Ilona drifts through this interior landscape, from city to country and back again. She hurries down streets and corridors, climbs stairs, leaps from windows with a sickening rush and lands unscathed. She meets strangers, acquaintances, parents and friends. Sometimes she is filled with a terrible sense of urgency, emergency and catastrophe. From these dreams she is happy to wake and return to her small, circumscribed outpost of reality. Other dreams leave her too quickly, dissolving into coloured fragments, blowing away like dust, leaving behind only faint residues and intriguing mental aftertastes.

In a state halfway between sleep and waking, Ilona thinks, weaving strands of dream and memory, groping through layers of dead years to grasp and pull them into the present.

Dimly comes the realization that the dream-city is a university campus, one of the sprawling campuses of the west, its buildings linked by covered walkways and open spaces. The countryside, however, is like nothing she has ever known. Those secret-keeping hills and twisting roads are far removed from the flat farmlands on which she grew up (which were, nevertheless, bordered by hills and distant mountains). And the street of little houses? It means nothing. And yet, there is some link, some aspect of her waking life which elicits in her the same emotions as those hills, that street.

What if the hills were covered with snow, Ilona? The white landscape, the black trees, the grey, rutted road going on and on without a destination. Yet it is the only possible road...

And the street? She has seen so many streets, has followed them in her endless walks. Rows of houses, rows of trees, dormant gardens, dozing cars, people walking dogs, dogs walking people, sniffing at tree trunks. She has seen so much since she started looking for Davy.

Davy. If it's really him; she still doesn't know. All she knows is that she has to find him and look him in the eye.

If she can't find him on the streets, maybe there's another way.

Davy's father had owned the feed and seed business in their home town. Ilona's father had dealt with him regularly. While their families weren't exactly friends, they were acquainted. Davy's father was dead, but his mother was still alive; at least, she had been when Ilona had moved away. Her own mother had taken such an interest in obituaries, surely she would have mentioned Mrs. Dawson's passing.

She still has the old phone book. Why she kept it is a mystery, or just another one of those silly, sentimental habits. She looks up "Dawson." There are four listings. How would his mother be listed? Ilona scrutinizes each name. "Dawson, David, Mrs." seemed to be the most likely possibility. Davy had told her he was named after his father, whose nickname was "Dave."

Ilona picks up the telephone. There's a dial tone, so it's still connected. She can't remember the last time it rang.

She dials and waits. Four rings. Five. Six. No answer, and no answering machine either, it seems. Just as she's about to hang up, there's a voice.

"Hello." An older woman, out of breath.

"I… I'd like to speak with Mrs. Dawson, please."

"She can't come to the phone right now. She's resting. Who's calling, please?"

Now that the speaker has caught her breath, her voice is mature, officious. A nurse-like voice. Again, Ilona nearly hangs up. Oh, don't be stupid! Talk to her!

"My name is Ilona Miller. I'm trying to track down an old... friend, Davy Dawson. I was hoping to talk with his mother."

"Oh. Well, she's resting now, like I said. But I'm Davy's sister, Doreen Hill. What did you say your name was?"

Doreen. Of course—his older sister. "Ilona Miller. I knew Davy in high school. And afterwards too, in college. But I sort of lost track of him." *Ha, that's the understatement of the year. You lost track of everything. You were derailed, in fact.*

"Ilona... Oh—you're that girl! What the hell do you mean, you're trying to find Davy? You ruined his life!" The officious voice has become strident.

"I don't understand. I ruined Davy's life? How could I have done that? I haven't seen him since... since I don't remember when. Years and years." *Or maybe just weeks and weeks, eh?* "I need to... tell him something."

A heavy sigh from the telephone. "Geez, just what I need... Look, I can't talk right now. My mother just woke up and I have to... She gets upset when the phone rings at this time of year. How about if you give me your number and I'll call you back some day when it's a better time?"

"All right. Thanks, Doreen."

After relaying her phone number, Ilona puts down the receiver and sinks back into the couch cushions. How did I ruin Davy's life? I thought I only ruined mine. I guess that's one more reason I have to find him.

• • • •

1987

The Eleventh Song: "Frühlingstraum" (Dream of Spring)

This song is a major turning-point in the cycle, where the protagonist thinks for the last time of his faithless fiancée. There is a fleeting reference to her, perhaps, in the nineteenth song,

"Täuschung" (Illusion), but this is the last song that dwells explicitly on love and romance.

The music demonstrates three different states of mind. At first, the protagonist dreams of springtime and love. This is represented by a pretty, tinkling tune on the piano, sweet and nostalgic. It is interrupted by a harsh chord representing the crowing of a cock, which awakens the dreamer to cold, dark reality. After a few moments, he slips back toward delicious sleep, but the melody now is full of sorrow as he considers the pathos of his situation. It is easy to visualize him, lying on a narrow bed in a poor inn, slipping in and out of sleep, gazing at the frost-patterns on the window...

He has been walking for days, to the point of exhaustion. Walking and walking. Putting one foot in front of the other, then again, and again, and again. The road stretches on ahead, up a little hill, is lost to sight on its far side, reappears beyond a copse of trees, and then vanishes in the distance. The ground is frozen iron hard, and a thin layer of new snow fills the ruts made by wheels and the impressions of horses' hooves and the boots of travellers on foot, like him.

He has avoided other people, sheltering at night in barns and the cramped huts of charcoal burners. Despite his weariness, he finds it hard to get to sleep, because of the cold. When he awakes in the night, his sorrow and bitterness are always there to greet and torment him. At least when he is walking, the physical exertion keeps him warm and the ever-changing scenes occupy his mind.

A sleet-storm nearly finishes him, and that night he seeks out an inn in a little town. The room costs more than he can afford, it is mean and cold, but at least it is out of the weather and away from the eyes of others. For one night at least he can sleep in peace and truly rest.

He sleeps, and dreams of a summer morning, with soft breezes and cuckoos calling. She has finally been permitted to go out walking with him, and her little gloved hand rests on his arm. He nearly wanders off the path a few times, because his eyes are fixed on the curve of her cheek, the flutter of her lashes. He is intoxicated by her nearness, her scent, the reality of her presence.

There is no one nearby. He leans closer to her, opens his lips to say the words.

A harsh, grating sound interrupts. Again. Again, louder. He opens his eyes, sees the cracked and dirty floor boards; on them slouch his battered boots, with his rucksack and walking stick lying nearby. He lifts his eyes to the dim squares of the window panes. The cock crows again and is answered by the croaking of ravens, probably on the roof just above his head. Below, in the inn's yard, a man shouts and another replies. Wheels rattle on cobblestones and a dog barks.

He groans and rubs his eyes. The room is cold and he can feel the itching of some new flea bites from the blankets he has slept in. "Come on," he says to himself, "time to get up." But he can't bring himself to leave the warm cocoon of the bed. Not just yet. His head falls back onto the pillow.

He gazes at the window, telling himself he will get up when it brightens to full daylight. Then he sees the glass is covered with leaves and flowers of frost, intricate and beautiful. They are like the leaves of acanthus, or like feathers and lace—the feathers in her hat, the lace of her gloves.

He smiles. Even here, in this wretched place, he has found her beauty again. Even now, when he knows he's a fool.

He falls asleep, the smile still on his lips.

He takes her hand in his, kissing it through the thin lace. He turns it over and presses his lips to her wrist. The glove does not cover the skin there, and he feels its warmth with his lips, and the tiny pulse of life in the blue veins.

She gasps and tries to pull her hand away, but not very hard. The slight effort subsides and suddenly her fingers are touching his face, lightly, tentatively. "Please..." she murmurs.

He puts his arms around her waist and draws her toward him. He kisses her cheek, her lips and throat, one sliding kiss that goes on and on, there in the shadow of her parasol, which surely must be swaying and jerking, signalling to any busybody within sight that something is going on. But his girl—ah! she isn't struggling, isn't trying to push him away—

• • • •

That's how it was, all right. Except there was no parasol, no lace and no watchers. And I didn't have to pretend to be a pure, spotless maiden. I kissed Julian with as much fervour as he did me. More, even. I held his face in my hands, dug my fingers into his hair, all the time hearing the voice of his namesake in the back of my head: "*Von Herzen und von Kussen / Von Wonne und Seligkeit.*" *Wonne und Seligkeit*, that means bliss, rapture. Oh yes.

• • • •

The cock crows again, and another joins in. Then they are both drowned out by the hollow racket of empty beer barrels being rolled up a ramp into a wagon, and the shouts of the men doing the rolling. He groans as a sharp knock sounds on the door of his room, followed by a voice. "Get up in there, you! Time to get out or pay for another night!"

But his eyes close again. The dream is gone now, beyond recovery, but a residue of its sweetness remains, like traces of honey in an empty bowl that once brimmed with it. This time, the landlady sticks her ugly face into the room and shouts into his ear. "All right, all right," he mutters. He sits up and looks once more at the frost flowers on the window. But they are melting already, turning grey, turning to water.

••••

I looked up from the paper. One a.m. Shit! My plan was to write for half an hour as a break from studying for the next day's exam—Ed. 354, Curriculum Design. And here it was, an hour and a half later. Well, I had finished another section, intended to illustrate the emotions generated by the combination of Müller's words, Schubert's music and Northridge's voice. I had started the paper in the true, objective, academic style, but had decided early on that what I had to do was not just write about Romanticism, but actually make the reader experience it. What I hadn't realized was just how all-absorbing this would be. My habit of writing with the music drilling into my brain (thanks to the headphones and the "Repeat" function) made it especially intense.

Intense. Like the other night.

It started with a lovely blur of talking, drinking, dancing and flirting, of noise, music and smoke, and ended with sex. With Harold's friend Julian, whom I'd never seen before that night, but who obviously was there for a reason. For me.

Everything I did felt right, including asking Julian to drive me home. Harold insisted on tagging along, even though he lived in the West End, and I was on campus, miles away. "I'm halfway between the two of you," Julian said, "so we'll drop Harold first, then I'll run you out to campus. Perfect."

It was perfect, all right. That's how I remembered it.

All the way to the West End, making a kind of giddy, bantering small talk with the two of them, I kept thinking how I couldn't wait until Harold was out of the car. Harold, whom I had found so interesting not so long ago. Now he was just an obstacle. But he introduced you, I reminded myself. Without him, you would never have met Julian.

That name had to be more than a coincidence. It wasn't common in Canada, for one thing. I studied his profile surreptitiously while Harold was telling a scandalous story about someone called Binky. Long, straight nose, high cheekbones, good chin, lots of hair (but black, not light brown)—he even looked like Julian Northridge. Well, a little. Not a real resemblance, but the same type.

We dropped Harold in front of his apartment building (did he really say, "Be good now, kiddies!" giving me a glare that would have struck me to the heart if I hadn't been feeling so carefree?) and turned around. Halfway across the Burrard Bridge, with dark water below us and twinkling lights all around, Julian reached out, picked up my left hand and kissed it. Then he twined his fingers with mine.

"Do you sing?" I asked.

Instead of saying yes or no, he sang the refrain from "Scarborough Fair." "I can't remember any more," he said.

The song wasn't right and his voice wasn't right either. "No, no," I said. "That's not what I meant." What the hell—I cleared my throat and sang. "*Fremd bin ich eingezogen / Fremd zieh' ich wieder aus / Der Mai war mir gewogen / Mit manchem Blumenstrauss*. Oh shit, I can't remember any more either." And I started to laugh.

But *he* sang it. Yes, he did! I heard that voice, the one true voice, as clearly as I ever I did in my room, with Davy's headphones over my ears. Julian Northridge's voice. I heard it as we drove over the bridge, with the twinkling lights all around. All the way through, to the last line, "*An dich hab' ich gedacht.*"

"Bravo!" I said, applauding. "You're wonderful!"

"I think I'm a better actor than singer, actually." And he gave me Romeo's speech from the balcony scene, the whole thing, ending with "That I might touch that cheek!" And he did it, running the backs of the fingers of his right hand so lightly over my left cheek that it felt more like a breeze than a touch. Then he took my hand again, and was silent.

I couldn't think of anything to say after that. It seemed wrong to go back to small talk, and suddenly I felt as though my head was about to go into orbit while my stomach sank down and down. Don't you dare get sick! I told myself.

Suddenly, I realized we weren't travelling west along Broadway toward campus, but south. "Where are we going?" I asked.

"Somewhere you've never been before," he said. Yes, he said that; I think he said that.

Or maybe it was, "To my place." He kept his eyes on the road while he spoke, then gave me a quick glance through those remarkable eyelashes. "Do you mind?"

"N... no. No, I don't." I elbowed down the part of me that tried to butt in. You only met this guy tonight! He's a total stranger! And what about Davy?

He turned off onto a winding side street. I could see big houses and wide lawns, but after a few more turns I had only a hazy idea of where we were. Julian pulled into a driveway, parked the car and helped me out. My lack of balance was a surprise; he practically had to hold me up while he gently closed the car door. "Ssh," he said. "It's late."

He led me to a side door, unlocked it and waved me into a dimly lit space. I saw a couch, a desk, a minimal kitchen. Typical student digs, but his caution had raised a flag and I was about to ask him if he had a roommate. I didn't get a chance, though. He came up behind me and spun me into an embrace so intense and purposeful that I forgot everything else.

Then we were in his bedroom. It must have been his; who else's could it have been? I had no time to look around, but I knew it was a bedroom because it had a bed.

Julian unwrapped my coat and enfolded me in a swaying embrace. Hearts and kisses, bliss and rapture. If she hadn't sent him away, that silly girl—*I* wouldn't have—this is how it would have been for her. A velvet-dark room, private, warm, and secret. Perfumed pillows. Oh—lily-of-the-valley. He kisses my neck and fumbles with the tiny buttons of my dress, while I laugh and tell him to hurry, hurry. Then I am naked, skin to skin with him. Our two fires become a single conflagration as we melt into one another and fall onto a bed as soft as a cloud. He plays me like a piano, and I sing my delight. Our joining goes on and on, spinning me into ecstasy, as he ravishes me for hours of *Wonne und Seligkeit*.

I must have dozed off, only to be brought back to a utilitarian reality by someone shaking my shoulder. "We have to get you home now, Ilona." The voice echoed strangely. "Get you home... home, get you home now, Ilona... lona... lona." I shook my head to clear it, but was stopped by an unbelievable dizziness and pain. Julian—it must have been him, who else? (except I can't remember what he looked like then, or what he was wearing) handed me my clothes, all bundled up. I struggled into them, found my way to the bathroom somehow, peed for what seemed like an eternity (and it hurt when I wiped; what do you suppose that meant?), rinsed my hands under cold water, splashed some on my face, dried off with a towel that smelled like strangers. Then someone (Julian? It had to be) took my arm and led me out to the car again. It was still dark outside. I had to concentrate on putting one foot in front of another, carefully, carefully, don't want to fall, do you? Then I was in the car, and we were moving.

Suddenly, there was my residence, and I was getting out of the car, lurching for the door. "Are you sure you'll be okay? I'll call you later."

Ah. Those magic words. "I'll call you later." Except I hadn't given him my phone number. Or had I? And did he say "later," or "tomorrow?" No matter, here's my key in my pocket, here's the keyhole. Got it. Now to my room, and now to bed, and now to bed, and now to bed.

12

When storms were still raging
I was not so wretched.

2007

The twenty-fourth of December is solidly overcast with a sullen little rain, but overnight the air pressure increases. Clouds lift and thin, helped by a brisk westerly breeze. On the twenty-fifth, the sun rises unimpeded from the sea and floats into a blue sky decorated with a few fluffy clouds.

It is inevitable that once the business of gift opening is finished and breakfasts, simple or elaborate, are eaten, the thing to do is go for a walk in the sunshine. Men, women, children, and dogs leave their homes in droves and head for parks and beaches.

Ilona is out too, but not on a Christmas morning walk. She has no such ritual, especially not this year. She is out cold, the result of incautious self-medication the previous evening—a couple more of the purple pills washed down with wine considerably younger than they, but no less potent. She sleeps late, oblivious to the arrival of brunch guests in the apartment above hers. The silvery fanfare of women's voices fails to wake her, never mind the more subdued rumble of men exchanging greetings. A baby cries, festive tunes gush out of small but powerful speakers, a coffee grinder whirs, a dishwasher sloshes and hums. Ilona hears none of it.

Noon comes and goes. The neighbours and their guests go out for a walk, except for the couple with the infant, who go home.

Maybe it's the silence that wakes her. Absence is the air she breathes now, her natural environment. Emptiness speaks to her and she is always prepared to listen.

She sits up in the rumpled bed, which now resembles the sleeping place of an animal, rather than the centrepiece of a well-dressed bedroom. The decorator details, pillow shams and cushions, are piled in a corner, along with the suit Ilona tossed there after her last job interview, weeks ago.

Ilona rises, goes to the bathroom, rinses her face and dresses in what has become almost a uniform—jeans, turtleneck, sweater. For once she's hungry, probably because she slept so long, but there is nothing edible in the fridge and not much anywhere else. Time to go grocery shopping; she can't remember when she last did that.

She sits down to make a list. In the old days, she would plan a menu for the week and buy accordingly, but that seems silly now. She eats when she's hungry and hardly cooks at all, except for coffee. The list is short and basic—bread, cheese, apples. Foods for the wanderer. She puts on her coat and heads out.

With the blinds always closed, she hadn't realized how bright the day is, and immediately feels like a shucked oyster, out on the street. *Just like that spring, isn't it, 'Lona?* Way too bright. And there are so many people! Couples, families, dog walkers. She's pretty sure it isn't Sunday. She hasn't forgotten the dynamics of the street, and there shouldn't be this many just-out-for-a-walk pedestrians at this time on a weekday. She thinks some more, and it finally hits her—it must be Christmas Day.

That explains all the happy, happy people. There they are, full of breakfast and togetherness, anticipating turkey and more togetherness. And it's a gorgeous day in paradise to boot—just nippy enough that folks with new knitted hats, mitts and scarves actually need to wear them. *Have yourselves a merry little Christmas.*

But will the grocery store be open? It isn't, and she has to go across the street and up a couple of blocks to a smaller, more expensive place, not much more than a convenience store. She gathers together the items she needs, throwing in a box of Kraft Dinner and a can of diced tomatoes. KD chez Miller—after all, it's Christmas.

The kid at the cash register gives her the usual funny look. She's getting used to it, knows it from both sides now. She used to wear it herself, not so long ago, when she saw strangely-dressed, aimless people on the streets, people like her present self, who don't always know what day it is. People whose Christmas dinner is made by Kraft.

As Ilona emerges from the store, the sun drops below the line of fir trees on the horizon. The sky is still blue, but the light has taken on the deep golden quality of late afternoon. "The day is ending," this light says. "Hasn't it been wonderful? And if not, it's too late now. Maybe tomorrow. Maybe next year."

Is it too late to find Davy? I need to do that before I'm done. Find Davy and tell him... something important.

The trouble is, she isn't sure what that something is. Ever since she first saw Davy downtown, when she could still pass for a normal person, she's known there is something about him that is significant to her. It's taken her a while to put the pieces of the puzzle together, even to realize that there is a puzzle. And there are some important pieces missing. The woman she talked to on the phone, Davy's sister Doreen, probably had a few of them, but the biggest missing piece was Davy himself.

What would she say, if he was in front of her right now?

"Hey, Davy, what are you doing and how did you get here?"

"What happened to you, back then?"

When was that, anyway? We were in high school together. And after, in college. No, university. Other kids went to college. Davy and I went to university.

Then what happened?

Climbing the hill toward home, grocery bag in hand, Ilona again wishes she had brought her sunglasses. Not because the low winter sun is in her eyes (because now it's behind her), but to keep off the looks of the people she meets. Their peering eyes, their judging expressions. "There goes another weirdo. A bag lady with a bag."

Too bad it's such a nice day. If it was raining and blowing all these nice people would stay home and I wouldn't have to see them, or they me. There are sun people and rain people, and they don't mix well.

A little girl in a stroller looks at her seriously with big, dark eyes.

"I'm a rain person," Ilona mutters under her breath, and turns away.

The child smiles.

• • • •

1987

I didn't want to go home for Christmas. Once exams were out of the way, all I wanted was to lose myself in Schubert and my paper—listen, think, dream, write. My dreams were vivid, and many of them involved him—Julian (what was his last name? Barker or Harker?) Now it was him I saw when I listened to *Winterreise*. It was he who walked endlessly through that snowy landscape. When I listened to Julian Northridge, I saw the other Julian's face in my mind—his black hair hanging into his eyes, his gold earring, the dark stubble on his chin, the curl of bitter irony on his lips.

I delayed my departure as long as I could. As long as the residence offered meals, as long as the libraries were open, I lingered. I spent hours in the Music Library, or in the labyrinthine stacks of the Old Main, reading about Schubert and Müller and their world. I pored over maps of Vienna, dreamed over prints in old books showing rustic Austrian scenes. There were those mountains, heaths, villages, groves, and Schubert's beloved brooks—flowing, babbling or lying still and frozen under snow.

The last couple of days, there was hardly anyone in the library, only a few staff and me. I wandered aimlessly through the stacks, picking up whatever books caught my eye, whether because of their titles, their bindings, their sizes or shapes. The most interesting ones I carried back to the study carrel I had adopted as mine, all alone at the far end of the second basement level, tucked behind a pillar and private as a self-contained little room. I thought of it as a kind of monk's cell, and toyed with the idea of camping out there after the residence closed down for the holidays. I could live on granola bars and fruit juice, bring in coffee in a thermos. I could sleep under the table in blankets and a pillow smuggled from the residence. The idea of being alone in this world of books was intoxicating. I pictured myself reading and writing in the small hours by the faint glow of an oil lamp.

In the end, I had to admit the idea was at best impractical and at worst a bit crazy. The entire campus would be closed and abandoned on Christmas and Boxing Day, and I couldn't think of a plausible excuse to explain my absence from home on the Big Day. The last thing I wanted was to have my Mom report me to the cops as a missing person.

Strangely, I didn't pine for Julian. My memory of our night together was perfect. It nestled in my mind the way a glass sphere rests in the palm of your hand. I could retrieve and examine it whenever I wished. That was my main reason for wanting to spend the holidays alone. New memories are more durable when there aren't a lot of people around to interfere with your thoughts.

As for the real Julian, he was out there somewhere. In January we would circle back toward one another, like a pair of planets. He'd said he would call. That was enough.

I spared no more than a fleeting thought for Davy.

I got on a bus for home on December 23rd. After a bit of dithering, I left the manuscript of my paper and most of my books in my residence room. I took with me only the photocopy of the texts and translations of the *Winterreise* songs and a book by Dietrich

Fischer-Dieskau tracing Schubert's life through his songs, with advice to would-be performers. These would be enough to keep the flame alive. By this time, reading the *Winterreise* texts inevitably triggered my own personal "Play" button.

My mother met me at the bus station. It was strange, but I didn't recognize her at first. Who was this woman with glasses and curly dark hair starting to grey, and why was she smiling at me like that? Oh—it's my Mom! Weird. Once I clued in, I was surprised that she looked pretty much the same as she had at Thanksgiving. It seemed way longer than two and a half months since I'd seen her.

I put my stuff in the back of the truck and climbed into the passenger seat. As we followed the familiar roads from town to our farm, we had the Homecoming Conversation. I knew the script and delivered my lines convincingly.

Mom: Well, exams all done?

Me: Yes, I finished a couple of days ago. (Five could be called a couple, couldn't it?)

Mom: Any idea how you did on them?

Me: Hard to say at this point. Okay, I think.

Mom: Well, I'll bet you're ready for a break. Dad and I have missed you.

Me: Umm. (At least they don't give out report cards at university, with comments like "Ilona is a bright student but rarely contributes to class discussions. She needs to focus more on social interaction with her peers." Those always got Mom worried and launched her into another me-improvement project).

Mom: Just think, only four months left before graduation.

Me: Umm.

Mom: Aren't you getting excited?

Me: Not really. There's all of next term. Then I have the practicum and final exams.

Mom: Maybe you'll be able to do your practicum here at home. Wouldn't that be great?

Me: Sure, except the placements don't come out 'til February or so. I don't really know.

Just then, Mom abandoned the script and took off on a tangent, with a funny little smile on her face.

"I hear you've been getting together with a friend from high school."

I was genuinely puzzled. Who could she mean? I ran through my small list of girl friends from high school and came up empty. None of them had gone to university.

Mom gave me a quick look, still wearing that smile. "I ran into Margaret Dawson in town a couple of weeks ago and she told me Davy said something to her about the two of you being... friends."

"Really?" I didn't know what to say. It was the last thing I expected to be talking about with my mother. I should have known better though, small towns being what they are. My lack of "dates" in high school had been another of her big worries; little did she know that the last thing I wanted was her and Dad scrutinizing any boy who came to take me out. I was actually relieved that I managed to make it through high school without that ordeal.

Mom looked at me again as she stopped the truck at the last intersection before our place. The little smile was almost gone.

"I hope I didn't get it wrong," she said. "You and Davy are... going together, aren't you?"

"Not... exactly," I said. "We did go out for a while, but lately we've sort of drifted apart. We were both so busy at the end of term, and there were exams... So we're not really—you know—together."

The little smile had been replaced by a little frown. "Oh, Ilona, I'm sorry to hear that. Come to think of it, Margaret did say that Davy seemed upset about something and she was worried about his exams. Will you be seeing him over the holidays? Maybe you can patch things up. He seems like such a nice boy."

Come on, Mom—you met him maybe once? Five years ago, at least.

"Oh Mom! I don't know."

"He's in engineering, isn't he? I'm sure that's what Margaret said. His final year, too, just like you. I guess he'll be looking for a job soon, won't he? Or do engineers have to do a practicum too? Is he going to be staying in the area? That would be nice, if he got a job in the Valley—"

"Mom! Stop butting into my life, will you? I don't know what Davy's plans are and I don't care! Didn't I just tell you I'm not going out with him?"

This happened every time. Fifteen minutes with my mother and I turned into a crabby teenager. Thank God we were rolling down our long driveway, toward the diversions of homecoming. There was Skipper the dog, running out to the end of his chain, barking with excitement. There was the barn with its rooster weather vane, slightly off kilter since a big windstorm a few years ago. There was Dad, coming out of the barn, wearing his red and black checked jacket and a Buckerfield's baseball cap. I was home.

I wondered if Davy had told his mother about lending me his CD player.

13

There's no letter in the mail for you.
Why then this strange surge of hope,
My heart, my heart?

2008

In January, an enormous area of high pressure establishes itself over the North American continent and generates deep winter, even though the days are lengthening imperceptibly. On the coast, the direction of upper air flow alternates between westerly and northerly, and the weather fluctuates between wet, warm and stormy and cold, bright and calm. Everyone has something to complain about every other week.

At least once per winter, cold air flowing down the fjords and river valleys from the interior of British Columbia meets warm, moisture-laden air from the Pacific. Snow falls, and nearly everyone complains, except children sprung from school and the few adults who love snow.

Some people are nearly oblivious to weather, but Ilona is not one of them. Every day, when she gets up (no matter what time it is), she opens her curtain—carefully, carefully, because you never know—and peers out to get a feel of things outside.

First—is it dark or light? Cloudy or bright? Bright days are a challenge. She prefers the world blunted and dulled. On grey days, she knows she can be nearly invisible. The sun brings out her shadow and makes her blink nervously. Dogs snarl at her and small children become afraid when they look her in the eye.

Ilona sits in her living room and looks at the large pile of mail that has accumulated. She finds a bag and begins to sort. Most of the envelopes and flyers end up in the bag for disposal. She sets aside bills and any communications that look official, "for future reference." One that she opens immediately is from the property management company to which she pays her rent. It contains a notice of a ten per cent increase, effective March 1st. Happy New Year!

Well, that's that. Even if I still had the job, this would be a problem. So I guess I'm out of here by March.

She sits with the letter in her hand, while on the wall a grid of yellow light falls through the partially opened venetian blinds, elongates and moves slowly toward the corner of the room as the sun prepares to set.

The phone rings, making her jerk and drop the letter. Shit! She hasn't heard it ring for so long that the sound has become an alien one. She picks up the receiver. "Hello?" Her voice is rusty from disuse. She clears her throat and tries again. "Hello."

"Is that Ilona? Hi, I'm Doreen Hill. Davy Dawson's sister. Happy New Year!"

Easy for you to say. "Oh, uh, same to you."

"Sorry I wasn't able to get back to you sooner," Doreen Hill continues. "We had quite a to do here over Christmas. My Mom got really sick. She's in the hospital now and we just don't know how things will turn out."

"I'm sorry to hear that." *Right, okay, that's the right thing to say.*

"Well, she's over eighty, so what can you expect? We're taking it one day at a time. But I've been thinking you and I need to talk. About Davy—why he took off like that."

Davy took off? When? "I'm sorry, Mrs. Hill. When I called you before Christmas, I was hoping you—your mother, actually—could tell me something that would help me find Davy. I haven't seen him in years—not since December 1987."

"Oh boy..." Doreen sighs heavily. "I guess that means we have to go back to the beginning." There's a moment of silence, and then her voice again. "As far as we could tell, everything was okay with Davy until Christmas of 1987. That's when he went off the rails."

Christmas 1987. That was the start of it for me too. "What do you mean?"

"I told you—he took off. Was supposed to come home for Christmas, but didn't turn up. On Boxing Day my folks got a phone call from him, from Brandon, Manitoba, of all places. He said he had to hit the road, wouldn't be coming back here or to university. Mom and Dad tried to argue with him, but he wouldn't listen, just hung up. We didn't hear from him again. Dad had to go get his stuff from his dorm room. He'd left everything behind, except the CD player the folks gave him for his birthday. We never found out what happened to it. Maybe Davy gave it to someone. Turned out he hadn't written his exams or anything. He just gave up, in his final year. He'd always had straight As, too. We couldn't understand it."

"I see," Ilona says.

Doreen goes on as though she hasn't spoken. "It worried Mom nearly to death. She kept going over and over every detail, trying to figure it out. The one thing that stuck in her mind was that Davy had told her just a little while before that he was going out with you. She had an idea that he fell apart and went away because of something you said or did. That's why I said what I said when you phoned before—that you ruined his life. If I was wrong, I'm sorry. But now I've been thinking maybe you can tell me something. Were you and Davy going together?"

The telephone is a dead weight in Ilona's hand. "Mrs. Hill. Doreen. I don't think I can help you. Maybe you know—I got sick about then. Davy and I, we were friends. But I can't tell you anything else. I was in a... hospital all that spring, and I don't remember much from that time."

"Yeah, I can understand that, I guess. Oh well, I was hoping—"

One last thing. "Wait—can you tell me—what happened to Davy? After that, I mean. Where does he live now?"

Doreen doesn't reply immediately, and when she does, her voice is no longer friendly, but tired and strained. "Didn't you hear me? He went away. He never came home again. We phoned the police and reported him as missing, but nothing came of that. It nearly killed Mom. She always gets into a state at Christmas, waiting and hoping he'll come back. He could be dead, for all we know."

He would be so lucky. "I see," Ilona says again. "I'm sorry. Thanks for your help." And she hangs up.

I think I know where your brother is, Doreen Hill. I think he roams around Victoria, picking up bottles and cans and playing a harmonica. He looks like he's living rough. And I'm going to find him, because I need to tell him something. Only I don't know exactly what it is, or why it's so important.

Ilona picks up the letter from the property management company again. *I'm jobless and soon I'll be homeless too. Homeless and hopeless. This is, this is, this is your life.* Methodically, she tears the letter into strips and tosses them into the air, letting them flutter to the floor around her feet, like crazy confetti.

She lies down on the couch, pushing the "keep" pile of mail onto the floor. She stares at the tree outside, its shape just discernable through the blinds, following the upsweep of its naked branches, the purposeful way each one departs from the trunk and takes off in its own direction. Her eye keeps returning to that point of division, its solid inevitability.

I went away to university, for my final year. I remember thinking that next spring I would graduate. But it never happened. Something else happened instead. Then the hospital and Dr. Polansky...

University in the fall. Hospital in spring. In between was winter.

• • • •

1988

The day before I went back to university, my Dad and I had a Talk. Dad wasn't much of a conversationalist. He liked being with friends and family, especially at Christmas, but usually he listened and watched everyone else enjoying themselves.

That day, for some reason, he wanted to talk. He asked me to come for a walk with him to look at the new blueberry plantings at the far end of our land. We put on coats and boots and started out.

"So how's school going?" he asked, after we had splashed and squished a hundred feet or so down the muddy farm road.

"Okay, I guess."

"Enjoying your studies?"

"Yes. Mostly. You know, it's too bad our family forgot how to speak German."

"Why?"

"Well, I'm taking this course, on German Romanticism, and writing a paper about some music by this man called Franz Schubert. The composer, you know. He wrote a whole lot of songs, and they're in German, so it would have been great if I knew the language."

He smiled at me. "And here I thought you were going to tell me you met some romantic German fellow."

"Not exactly." I felt myself blushing and broke off a stalk of dry grass from a clump at the side of the road.

"Not exactly German, or—?" He was still smiling.

"Not German, no."

"But romantic?"

I threw the piece of grass away and looked him right in the eye. "Yes," I said. "Very."

"Well, that's nice." He looked a bit embarrassed and cleared his throat. "It's just that, I've been wondering if you're okay."

"What do you mean, Dad? Sure I'm okay."

"You look sort of... thinner, maybe. You're not on some sort of diet, are you?"

"No, it's just that I've been busy with school and stuff. You know, exams."

"And that romantic fellow too. What's his name?"

"Julian."

"No last name?"

"Oh Dad! It's Northridge. No, wait—Harker. Julian Harker."

"Are you sure?" He was looking worried again.

"Yes! I just got mixed up for a second. I know two guys named Julian, you see."

He put his hand on my shoulder and gave it a squeeze. "If you ever need any help, Ilona, just call us and come home. Don't forget that. Your mom gets... well, she gets worried about you. But she means well. I hope you realize that."

Yes, I thought, and she put you up to this, didn't she? I could hear her saying, "You talk to her, Carl; she never tells me anything."

Nice try, Mom. "Sure I do."

I was so glad to get back to university it was almost indecent. All the other times, it was hard to leave home, almost like the first departure all over again. It would take a few days of classes and assignments to wear off my homesickness.

But this time, I couldn't wait. I longed for the campus, its wide avenues lined with bare trees, its mossy corners, the smell of ocean and decaying leaves. This was my zone of struggle and excitement, the place where I lived my life. The thing I was creating was there, and the materials for that creation—the voice of Julian Northridge and the actual, living self of his namesake, that other Julian (Harker or Barker? I should have written it down.) Surely by now he must have tried to contact me.

Except he hadn't. There was no message waiting when I got to my room and threw my backpack onto the bed, along with an extra bag stuffed with Christmas sweaters, pj's and books. My manuscript lay on the desk where I had left it, the capped pen on the topmost page, notes and books surrounding it in a ragged constellation. I had been thinking about it all the way from the Valley on the bus—my protagonist's relentless, doomed journey through the winter country, his feet on the snowy earth, his mind in darkness.

I sat down and reached for the headphones, pressed the magic button. The voice I had longed for welcomed me back while I reread the whole thing. I wrote three more pages before I unpacked my stuff.

• • • •

The Thirteenth Song: "Die Post" (The Mail Coach)

He has walked all night, because it was too cold to sleep. At least the wind was at his back, which made it easier to keep going.

Now he is in the square of a little town. The sun is just rising. For a few precious pennies, he buys a loaf of bread hot from the oven. The woman in the bakery gives him a cup of milk to go with it. He sits down at the foot of a statue of a man on a horse, because the sun striking the stones warms them ever so slightly.

He eats half of the bread, drinks the milk and dozes off. It's not a peaceful sleep, because he knows by now that sleeping in public during the day usually attracts the attention of someone official who tells him to "move along, now." But surely a few minutes won't matter. He is so tired, and the sun on his face is so good.

He wakes suddenly, not because someone is prodding him with a boot, but because of the rattle of wheels and the merry sound of a horn. He starts up, grabbing his bag and stick, ready to run.

It's only the mail coach, from the town he has left behind forever, the town where until recently he was so happy. He stands and watches it turn and stop in front of the inn on the other side of the square. People are hurrying over to it, eager to see if there are any letters for them, to meet the alighting passengers or simply to talk with the driver.

He starts toward the coach, a strange, happy feeling in his breast. Maybe—oh, maybe! Then he stops. "No," he says, out loud. "Don't be a fool. There's no letter for you. How could there be? Never for you." A couple of boys look at him and snigger. But he stands and waits just the same, until the leather mail bag is empty.

The small crowd disperses and the coachman goes into the inn for a drink, leaving the coach and horses in the hands of his helper.

He can't resist. He goes over to the fellow. "Came from _____, did you?" he asks. The man looks up from adjusting the harness. He has a cast in one eye, which gives him a sinister expression. "Yes, left last night. Had a cold trip, I'll tell you. He'd better bring me out something to warm me up." He jerked his thumb toward the inn.

This coach rolled through the streets she sees every day, he thinks. Maybe she looked out of her window last night and saw it go by. I could write a note, ask them to take it to her...

He laughs and the man looks at him strangely, because he hasn't said anything funny. "No," he says, turning away. "What would I say, in my letter? 'Remember me? How is it with you? Engaged again? Congratulations and good wishes, my dear! Perhaps it will turn out better this time, eh?'"

Still laughing, he leaves the square and the town, seeking once more the empty fields and the road, which goes on and on.

• • • •

Classes resumed and I still hadn't heard from Julian. I had no idea what his schedule was like; maybe the drama program didn't start at the same time as the others. The second day there was an empty seat next to Harold, and I took it.

"Happy New Year, Harold. How was your Christmas?"

"Same to you." He barely glanced at me. "It was okay, I guess. How about you?" But he didn't look interested.

"The usual. I'm glad to be back here. How's your paper coming?" I couldn't think of a way to ask about Julian without admitting I hadn't seen or spoken to him since the night of Libby's party. And then there was the uncomfortable fact that I wasn't quite sure about his name. Most uncool. I needed an excuse for a casual reference that might elicit some information.

"I've done some reading," Harold said. "Made a few notes. Don't tell me you're finished."

"Not quite." I had no idea how close I was to finishing. It was a journey with no end in sight, and that was fine with me. "I've run into a problem."

"Oh, what's that?" Harold, I knew, was always interested in people's problems; they were part of his conversational stock-in-trade.

"Wilhelm Müller, the guy who wrote the *Winterreise* poems, was part of a group that wrote and acted out plays for fun. Home theater, you know. But I can't find out any more about that. Was it very common in 19th century Vienna? I need to find someone who knows about theater history."

"Sorry, can't oblige. Not my field."

"What about that friend of yours—the actor who was at Libby's party?"

Was I blushing? Could Harold tell how important the question was to me?

He gave me a blank stare. "Actor?" he said, coldly. "Is that what he is? A bad actor, then. Why don't you ask him yourself? The two of you were getting along like a conflagration that night, by the looks of things." He turned away and started to talk with Maria, who was sitting on the other side of him.

The next few weeks, I was sure something was up. Harold, Libby, and Goody weren't talking to me. It was as if they had all had "Drop Ilona Miller" on their lists of New Year's resolutions. When I greeted any of them, they emitted monosyllabic replies and suddenly realized they had to be somewhere else. And it wasn't just them; several others in the class began to treat me like a leper. I tried not to be paranoid, but I could have sworn that at least once I interrupted a bunch of them talking about me. Why else would they have backed away from each other when they saw me, suddenly chattering in loud, artificial voices?

It was a while before I realized that they had all been at Libby's party.

In my Education classes, the situation was the opposite—I was the one who wasn't interested. I had to force myself to go, at least to the most important ones. The rest I attended sporadically at best.

I spent long afternoons alone, reading, thinking or working on my paper, stopping at intervals to stare out the window at the abstract shape of a tree in front of the brick wall that surrounded my building. I became deeply familiar with the pattern of its branches against the white sky, the pictures they made—the boot, the shoe, the fat woman, the cracked egg, the VW Beetle, the water-carrier, the phallus. They were party to my thoughts, the words I wrote and listened to, the melodies, the voice.

As I listened to his voice now, I found myself whispering the words, shaping them with my lips and tongue, as he must have. I breathed along with him, inhaling when he did, pushing out my breath at the end of a line, eventually singing along with him in a voiceless murmur.

In the evenings, I walked. I wandered the campus with Schubert's tunes in my head, accompanying the rhythm of my steps. More than once, I found myself by the building that housed the Drama Department. I even sneaked in to watch rehearsals of some play the students were putting on. But I never saw him.

14

They say your hair can go grey overnight,
But I don't believe it.
Mine hasn't yet, through all of this long journey.

2008

Cold air pools in low-lying areas, and if it contains sufficient moisture, frost forms on objects and surfaces. The moister the air, the thicker the frost, sometimes like a growth of white fur.

Such a frost, like fog, transforms the landscape, makes it strange and special. It ornaments the mundane—chain-link fences, leafless shrubs, dead grasses. And like fog, it is evanescent. The sun clears the horizon, the temperature climbs the necessary few degrees, and ice becomes water, sparkles, drips, disappears.

All evidence of the frost is gone by the time Ilona is on her way downtown. Clump, clump, clump she goes, in her old boots. Move one foot, move the other foot, right, left, right, left, go, go, go. She doesn't want to, but she has to. She's under orders.

Last night, she had another talk with herself. Late, when everything was quiet, she lit a candle and took it to the oval mirror with the gilt frame. It was the kindest of all her mirrors, but even it, even in the soft candlelight, showed her a woman very different from the one who used to check her appearance on the way to the office. Her hair had grown out of its style and hung in heavy hanks, mostly grey. Her eyes were like wary animals protecting their caves of refuge. Had her nose grown longer too? She tried smiling, but the resulting facial spasm was not reassuring.

She was turning into someone else.

The stranger spoke. "Well, you haven't had much luck tracking down Davy, have you?"

"No..."

"You need to try something different. Doing the same thing and expecting different results—you know what that is, don't you?"

"Yes..."

"I figured you must have learned that much, anyway. So listen up. If anyone knows about your pal Davy it would be social service agencies, charities, welfare. Those outfits. You just go downtown and ask them about him."

"I don't want to."

"Why not?"

"I don't like those places. And I don't like asking questions. Not of strangers."

"Lady, everyone's a stranger now. Don't you know that?"

"Those people think they know better. They'll try to make me do things I can't. They'll talk about making better choices and creating solutions and putting together a plan. I know it and I don't want to listen to that crap."

"Can't blame you." A grin showing teeth like a pair of saw blades. "But you don't have to get all worked up. All you need to do is ask if any of them knows a guy like Davy and where he hangs out. Either they'll tell you or they won't. See, they don't care about you. They won't try to fix you or make you look for a job or whatever it is that's giving you fits these days."

"They might. They probably know the unemployment insurance people. The ones that were spying on me."

The Other didn't look sympathetic. "What a mess you are! Who would have guessed you'd turn out like this!" She leaned out of the mirror and tugged on a strand of Ilona's hair.

"Don't do that!" Ilona blew out the candle and the vision vanished in a blur of smoke.

The Social Services Department is in a large, shiny building on the eastern fringe of downtown. It sits uncomfortably between two old brick churches, like a smart, lacquered girl flanked by tweedy matrons. Evidence of some of the clients is visible on the sidewalk—a shopping cart containing empty bottles and sodden garments.

Ilona walks up the shallow steps to the door, enters and looks around the foyer. A sign directs her to the second floor and a large, brightly lit office where a substantial counter separates the clients from those who serve them. Beyond it is a landscape of upholstered dividers defining the personal workspaces of the staff.

Ilona stands and looks, remembering. Once, not so long ago, she had a little domain in a place just like this. Once.

"May I help you?" A woman has materialized behind the counter. She is wearing office clothes, her hair is smooth and her face has the correct expression of bland helpfulness. An official name tag identifies her as "Donna, Client Services Assistant."

"I hope so." Ilona approaches the counter and rests her forearms on its edge. Donna steps back, ever so slightly. "I'm looking for someone. An old... friend. I wonder if you can help me find him."

"I'm sorry, we can't provide personal information. Does your friend work here?"

"No, no—he doesn't work here. It's not like that. He's a—I think he lives on the streets. I've seen him—but not for a few weeks. I thought you might know something about a person like that."

The woman smiles; at least, her lips (carefully painted a cranberry red which clashes with her burgundy-tinted hair) shape themselves into something that is commonly called a smile. "I'm sorry," she says again, "we don't keep a list of street people, if that's what you mean."

"But he'd be a 'client' of yours, wouldn't he? Your name tag says you assist clients. He'd get a cheque or something every month. Or is it more often? So you'd have him registered, wouldn't you? His name is Davy Dawson. David Dawson, maybe. Unless he's changed it."

Donna sighs and moves her shoulders as though she is trying to shrug off a burden. "The cheques are distributed in a different building," she says, clearly trying to maintain an even, patient tone of voice. She picks up a piece of paper and a pen and writes something, then pushes the paper over the counter. "You could try there. Nine o'clock every second Wednesday. I'm not sure if it's this week or next. Your friend might show up."

Ilona starts to turn away, but something happens mid-turn. Maybe it's the woman's choice of lipstick, or the imperfectly disguised condescension in her manner. She turns back and leans right over the counter.

"It could happen to you too, you know," she proclaims. "Don't imagine you're safe, just because you've got this job. I had a job, just a few months ago. Now I'm being kicked out of my place, because I can't afford the rent. So don't look so smug, you bitch! This could be you some day!"

She digs her fingers into her hair, spreads it out on either side of her head and thrusts herself forward, goggle-eyed, nose wrinkled, tongue protruding. "Don't cry for me, Belladonna!" she sings.

The woman lurches back with an exclamation. A man approaches—youngish, pudgy, with glasses and thinning, no-colour hair. "What's going on here?" he asks, looking quickly from Ilona to his colleague and back again.

"I don't know," Donna says. "She was leaving and then she... freaked out. Maybe we should—"

"Relax, honey," Ilona says. "I'm about to go. I'm getting out. Leaving the building. That's what everyone wants us to do, isn't it? Well, all you nice people, have a nice day."

She raises her hand and brings it down in front of her own face, like closing a window. Then she turns, flinging out the hand in a gesture of farewell, and walks out of the office. Not too quickly, not too slowly. That's right—make the most of your exit, but get out before they call the cops. The policeman is not your friend, remember?

Outside, the air is cold and clean, and she breathes deeply, trying to get rid of the hot, dizzy feeling. She walks half a block before she looks back to make sure no one is following her.

"Well, you really let them have it!" says that new voice inside her, the one that goes with the reflection in the mirror. "Way to go, girl! 'Don't cry for me, Belladonna!' Ha-ha! That was a good one, all right."

"I don't know about that," Ilona mutters, zipping up her coat and pulling on her knitted hat. The wind is cold and her hands are freezing, but she's either lost her mitts or left them at home. She can't remember, and feels panic coming on.

It's like that time when she left something in the truck—a suitcase or something like that—and she was crying, telling her Dad she had to go back and get it, and he was holding her by the arms, saying, "No, you and Mom go and get you checked in. They're expecting you. I'll get your bag." Then he hugged her and when he pulled away, she could tell that he'd been crying too.

When? When was that? It was spring, wasn't it? The sun was shining—so bright, so harsh. We went for a long drive in the truck and they were taking me somewhere. Then he left. He left me there. Then a few months later, he was dead.

Ilona stops, right there on the sidewalk, and lets the tears come, and a howl of grief.

• • • •

1988

Mona Lang started us on a new section of the course: The Legacy of German Romanticism, how it is viewed in the present day, in the light of present-day sciences. Psychology, for instance: "Of course, it's almost impossible to psychoanalyze or diagnose someone simply from letters, diaries, or other writings, but attempts have been made. Schubert, for example, had a dark side; his friends often said he was two people in one body—their convivial companion and a melancholy misanthrope. From this, scholars have speculated that he may have been manic-depressive."

Lang also noted the large number of Romantics who died relatively young, some by suicide. Schubert's friend (and, according to some, his lover), Johann Mayrhofer, was a perfect example—an antisocial, moody individual who eventually killed himself, after contemplating the act for years.

"Death," said Frau Lang, "was, as you should know by now, an old friend of the Romantics, a major preoccupation. They wrote poems to death, sang songs about death, wrote novels in which death is almost a character. Think of Werther, think of Schubert's song about the gravedigger who longs for the grave."

This was for a long time accepted as just the way the Romantics were, Lang explained. But beginning in the late 19th century, and especially in the 20th, psychologists and others began to inquire into the state of their collective mental health. "Several explanations have been put forward," she said. "They range from drugs, such as hashish and opium, to a kind of collective self-hypnosis, to manic depression."

"How can they be so sure about something like that?" I asked Harold as the class broke up. "How can you diagnose even one person from stuff they wrote? Especially a hundred years later?"

"Well, it's just a theory, isn't it? One nobody can prove or disprove, so what does it matter? Hey, I've got to run. See you, Ilona."

I'd been hearing that a lot from people in the class since Christmas break. "Got to run, Ilona. See you later." Harold, Libby, Goody—all of them had to run, more often than not. Well, what did I care? To Hell with them. They were probably jealous that I was well into my term paper while they hadn't even started.

But Julian Harker hadn't phoned, and I hadn't managed to track him down anywhere on campus. That bothered me, but not as much as it might have if I hadn't already captured a part of him, that night we spent together. I had extracted a piece of his essence—the topography of his features, the texture of his hair, the trajectories of his movements, his fingers on the steering wheel, on the gearshift, on me. I was a mould into which he had poured himself, and his image remained in me forever.

And his voice was the voice of the other Julian, Julian Northridge, an Englishman otherwise unknown to me. I knew what he looked like, although the pictures that accompanied his recordings seemed different from one another in subtle ways; they almost seemed to be of different people. I had no idea what sort of person he was—arrogant or shy, opinionated or secretive, scholarly or bombastic. I didn't know what he did in his spare time, where he went on holidays, what kind of car he drove, whether he liked dogs or cats (or parrots?), what he liked to eat and drink, how much time he spent with his children, how he behaved toward his wife, in public or (especially) in private. I knew a few skeletal facts about him, that was all.

But I knew his voice intimately, from the bright timbres of the vowels to the precise punctuation of the consonants, the momentary harshness of "*ach*" and "*nach*." So many times now he had taken me through the entire course of Schubert's winter journey, from embittered sanity to the place beyond the village where the organ grinder plays endlessly his futile melody. He had instilled the words into my ears with his breath, until they were embedded in the nerves and circuits of my brain, part of me forever.

To that voice, and the body I had known briefly but intensely, I added the poetry of Wilhelm Müller and the music of Franz Schubert, and constructed a whole man. I didn't even have to close my eyes now, to see him...

• • • •

He walks along the street of yet another little town—this one barely a village. The pavement is poorly maintained, full of pits and irregularities. Beyond the huddle of buildings he can see a mill, and on the far side of the bridge over the millstream, a few more houses, then the road—narrow, rutted, going on forever.

Aside from the mill, the biggest building is an inn of some sort. It's the only one with glass windows. He approaches and peers into one of them. It is dark inside, but as he draws back, he sees his own reflection in the small panes. Yes, there are his nose and eyes as he remembers them, the unsmiling slash of his mouth, all surmounted by a thatch of grey hair. (Two days before, he had exchanged his hat for a loaf of bread and a sausage).

"It's grey!" he thinks. "It's been that long, then!" "And so hard!" his heart replies. "A long, hard journey, but surely soon over."

Wearily, he runs his hand over his face, brushing back the grey hair. "Soon over," he mutters. He is old now, and looks it. But as he lowers his hand, he can see in the reflection that his hair has become black again. Hoarfrost on it had made it look grey. All that's left now is water that drips from his fingers.

"Not yet, by God!" He shoulders his pack again and turns his back on the window, the inn, the village. "I have endured so far, how much is left?"

• • • •

I had to get out and walk. That was the only way I could find Julian. He had told me he walked the winter nights. If I wanted him, I would have to do that too.

The campus was huge, with plenty of wooded areas interlaced with trails, forming a buffer between the academic community and the city beyond. It was easy to slip out of the residence building and into this urban wilderness.

The night air was damp but not particularly cold. It had rained much of the day, but now there were only random drips from the trees and bushes. At intervals I caught whiffs of a strange, sweet perfume from some winter-blooming plant.

Out of the corner of my eye, I saw a shape moving in the direction I intended to take. A jogger, maybe. The campus was full of joggers. But no, it wasn't running but walking, quickly, purposefully. Man or woman? Too tall for a woman. A man, then, dressed in dark clothing, with dark hair. Longish dark hair.

He was already a dozen yards away from me. If I wanted a better look, I had to hurry before I lost him, but I had to be careful that he didn't see me unless I wanted to be seen.

I quickened my steps, keeping a fifty-foot buffer zone between us. He moved so fast I had no trouble doing that; in fact, I had nearly to run at times, so as not to lose sight of him. All the while I was trying to decide if it was really him—Julian. There was something about the way he moved that seemed familiar, but he was only a faint black shape against the night, so I couldn't be sure.

It wasn't long before we had left the civilized part of campus behind. There were no lights here, and since I was totally concentrated on keeping my quarry in sight, I suddenly realized that I was, for all practical purposes, lost. I could just make out the path before me from the channel of grey sky above, flanked by black trees. It twisted and turned, so I no longer knew if he was still there, moving steadily forward to a destination known only to himself. It was quite possible he had slowed down or stopped, even realized he was being followed.

What if I came around the next corner and he was standing there, waiting for me? What if it was Julian? What if it wasn't? I stopped, not sure what to do next.

A wind sprang up, showering down a fresh patter of rain. Ahead, three tall firs thrust into the lightless sky—their tops black hieroglyphs on a grey ground. Propelled by the wind, their branches began to gesture and sway. The movements, simple at first, became obscure and dense, vaguely threatening. I averted my eyes and hurried on.

That was the only time I was afraid.

I kept walking, I don't know how long, or where. I saw no one. Whoever it was I had followed, he had turned off, doubled back, vanished. Once, a rustle startled me as an animal, a small, panicked shape of cat or raccoon, ran across the path and into the bushes. And then I was on a road again, one with a paved sidewalk. A street light cast its weird orange glow on my surroundings, including a weeping birch tree. Looking up into its twiggy branches, I saw a halo, almost a tunnel of light formed by the reflections from the dense tangle of wet twigs. I had never noticed this phenomenon before. It was as though the tree had chosen to reveal a secret to me.

A few paces farther, and I knew where I was, surprised that I had come so far from my point of departure.

The street was empty. No one else was there.

15

Crow, do you intend quite soon
To make a meal of me?

2008

There are winter days when nothing happens—no rain, no wind, no snow, no sun. Featureless grey stratus covers the sky. The air is still and damp, the light even and dull, the sun a spot of diffused brightness behind the clouds. Late in the afternoon, perhaps, the edge of the cloud layer opens to the west and the sun shines a lurid orange farewell before slipping below the horizon.

Most people have nothing good to say about such days. "It's so dark! Where's our sunshine?" they complain. But a few among them feel otherwise (even though they may not admit it). The absence of sun means they don't have to squint or cover their eyes; the absence of wind is sweet and calming to the nerves. On such days, they walk unoppressed under the grey sky, savouring the scents of woodsmoke and decaying leaves.

Time doesn't matter any more, Ilona thinks. Time is for other people. I can do what I want, when I want. (And the barely suppressed corollary: Until I can't do anything at all, ever).

It is nearly dawn, and she is far from home. Home—the few hundred square feet for which she pays nearly two dollars per square foot each month. The place she goes to when she is exhausted, hungry, or fed up. The place where she goes to ground. And also the place where she feels trapped, with her possessions standing stupid and mute, never moving from their places.

Restlessness drives her out. As soon as she decides to go—it doesn't matter where—the anxiety is allayed. It's replaced by an almost pleasant sense of urgency as she pulls on extra socks and sweater, laces up her boots, shrugs into her coat, finds gloves and a knitted cap. Then there is the moment of opening the door, closing it behind her, locking it. The mute, stupid things, the unanswered questions, are locked in (but they will still be there when she gets back), and she is off.

Nearly dawn, still dark, but with the slightest brightening in the eastern sky. A heavy raft of clouds lies on the western horizon. The bluffs overlooking the strait are nearly deserted—only a pair of early-morning joggers in the distance, and the inevitable dog walker, already heading home, the dog loping along contentedly by his or her side. Gulls circle in the ever-present breeze and crows flap noisily among them, their perpetual adversaries and companions.

Ahead, the ground falls away into a kind of hollow, where a section of the bluff must have collapsed long ago. The official trail leads around it, but a scuffed and eroded path scrambles straight down, through the wild rose bushes and wind-dwarfed oaks, a short cut to the rocky shore.

Nowadays, Ilona usually spurns short cuts of any kind. She is in no rush to get home, or anywhere else, but she wants to avoid the joggers, who are fast approaching, sleek in their elasticized garments, heads bobbing, feet moving in perfect synchrony, encased in expensively engineered shoes. These are the type of people that always give her funny looks.

Ilona scrambles down the side path just in time. It's steep and she has to grab onto branches and exposed roots to keep herself from going into an uncontrolled slide. At the bottom is a tangle of driftwood, and then cobbles, pebbles, and sand. It is light enough now that she can almost distinguish the colours of the stones—mostly grey, black, and nearly white, but she knows that some of the greys are really greens and purples, and the pale colours include tans and dull pinks.

Finally, she is clear of the logs and rocks. A strip of beach lies between her and the water. Nearby, a flock of crows jostles and pecks, while others flap and hover in the air above, encircling a human figure who stands with its back to Ilona, scattering pieces of torn up bread for the birds.

The figure is short and sturdy, wearing clothes similar to Ilona's, except that her woollen cap is bright red, and her boots are truly formidable—high, lace-up jobs, like those an old-fashioned lumberjack might have worn.

The woman seems to sense the presence of someone besides the birds. She turns around, making the nearest crows rise into the air and flutter away. She studies Ilona intently, and then paces toward her.

Moments pass. A long time, it seems to Ilona, during which the woman becomes more distinct, as though coalescing from the departing darkness. Then she speaks. "Nice morning. You're new, aren't you?"

"New? Me? I'm not sure I—"

"New at this game," says the woman. "Life in the raw. Welcome." She laughs and spreads out her arms in a gesture that takes in the whole beach.

"Do you feed the crows here every day?" Ilona asks.

"Nah! Special treat today. Crows are tough, they don't need anyone to feed them. I get a kick out of it is all."

The crows have returned and peck away industriously, ignoring both their benefactor and Ilona.

"People don't give crows enough credit, that's what I think," says the woman, emptying the last of the bread from a plastic bag. She stuffs the bag into her pocket. "Okay guys, that's all for now," she says. The crows ignore her.

"Crows pick up a lot of garbage, you know," the woman remarks. She begins walking along the beach, and Ilona falls into step beside her. "Anything edible. They've always done that. Back when, they used to help clean up dead bodies, after battles and stuff. Now it's just French fries and sandwiches kids throw away." She laughs again. In the growing light, Ilona sees that the woman isn't much older than she is. She looks weathered and tough, with leathery brown skin and black hair streaked with grey hanging below the red wool of her cap.

"We're like crows too," the woman continues, in no hurry to leave the subject and apparently not caring whether Ilona is listening or not. "We pick up bottles and cans—anything that can be cashed in. If we could make money by picking up paper and plastic and shit like that, we'd do it, and there'd be way less garbage around. So what're you doing here?" She gives Ilona a sudden hard look with eyes the colour of root beer.

"Me? Nothing. Just walking."

"Well, you don't fit the pattern," the woman says. "I could see it, right off the bat. This time of day, you get your dog walkers and joggers, that's all. And us, of course, but I've never seen you before."

"Who's 'us'?" asks Ilona.

"Us. Outside folks. We live under their noses but they don't see us. And that's fine with me. I'm mostly invisible, unless I want 'em to see me, that is."

"Invisible? Sometimes I think I am too, actually," says Ilona. She laughs for the first time in weeks. Months, even.

"Hmm." The woman looks at her again. "Maybe some day. But you have a lot to learn first. You look pretty soft to me."

"So how did you learn?" Ilona asks. "And what kinds of things do you mean, anyway?"

"Everything. How to keep dry, how to make a fire, how to kill a rabbit." She whips an object out of her pocket. "See this slingshot? I made it myself, and I can bean a rabbit at twenty feet with this baby. Lots of rabbits around, if you know where to look. Up at UVic, on the campus—it's lousy with them. Bag a rabbit and roast it, you got food for two, three days. Get some extras from the food bank, greens from the parks, you got it made. Then you've got to know where to get a shower, where to do your laundry. You need cash for that; that's where the bottles come in. Where to go for a free meal, free cup of coffee. All that stuff. And mostly, you've got to know how not to attract the wrong kind of attention."

"How did you learn all that?" Ilona is still awed by the slingshot and the casual talk of rabbit hunting.

"By doing! That's the only way. When you have to, you do it. Either that or give up—die, or get mixed up with cops or drug dealers. Or social workers, even worse. Dying is better than that, if you ask me, but living is best, if you can call your own shots." She laughs and brandishes the slingshot. "Hang out at the library, read the newspapers and the books, use the computers. Find out where there's free food. Go where you like, do what you like. No one tells me what to do."

"I guess you're right, I have a lot to learn." Ilona looks at the woman—her boots, her clothes, her leathery face. Has she ever seen her before? Then she has a thought.

"I wonder, have you ever seen... Do you know a man who plays the harmonica? He's six feet tall, about my age. His name's Davy."

"Maybe." The woman looks at her with a gleam in her eye. "Maybe I know a guy like that. Why do you ask?"

"I think he's a friend of mine, who I haven't seen in years. Davy Dawson. I've looked for him downtown, but no one seems to know him."

"Hmm." The woman looks sly. "Davy Dawson, eh? Maybe he doesn't spend much time downtown. Have you thought about that?"

"Oh—you do know him!"

"I didn't say so, did I?" That sly look again. "Maybe I do and maybe I don't. You wouldn't find me downtown most days, I can tell you. Well, suppose I see him? Is there something you want to tell him? A message for Davy?"

"Yes. Tell him this, please. That I'm sorry for whatever it was I did, back then, to ruin his life. Twenty years ago."

"Sorry! Oh, don't be too sorry. Sorry never gets you anywhere except sorrier. Especially if you can't even remember what it is you're sorry about. That's what I say. But hey—it's your message. And who are you, anyway? Who is it that's so sorry?" Her root-beer eyes look at Ilona mockingly.

"Ilona. Ilona Miller."

"Ee-lo-na. Funny name. But I guess I'll remember it. Ilona Miller. Twenty years ago. Now she's sorry. The mills of God grind slowly, eh? Bye, Ilona, see you again, maybe."

She walks away, goes around a projecting ridge of rock, is suddenly lost to sight as though she never was. Ilona sighs, turns, and prepares to scramble up the bank where joggers, dog walkers, and others are out in force.

• • • •

1988

Now he is weary, even to death. It's been a long time since he had a good meal or slept anywhere better than a barn or sheep-shed. Fresh snow falls almost every day and he can't stop feeling cold.

But he has acquired a companion. A crow joined him as he was leaving the last town, and has followed him ever since. Every now and then it flies off to the trees or fields near the road, and he thinks he's seen the last of it, but a few hundred steps along, there it is again, fluttering overhead, gliding low and landing in front of him, only to take to the air again as he gets closer.

He begins to talk to the crow. It's a female, he decides, although there is no way to be sure. She is like all the other crows he has ever seen, with her shiny, purple-black feathers, black beak, black feet, small, gleaming black eyes. She is competent and capable, picking up grains and seeds in the fields and along the roadside, getting along in this winter country as he no longer can.

"What is it you want from me?" he asks the crow, as she lands a short way in front of him once more. "Do you think we're going to travel together? But I don't know where I'm going, only where I've come from. And I'm not going back there." His throat contracts suddenly and his eyes fill with tears. He had thought he was done with this foolish weeping, and wipes them away angrily with his sleeve.

"I wouldn't bother, crow, if I were you. Unless... Of course! You know, don't you, that soon it'll be the end for me. Then you can have a feast. All right, when I'm dead, I'm yours for good, sweetheart. Take my eyes, take my heart. You, at least, will be faithful to the grave, ha, ha!"

• • • •

There was a guy who had been auditing the German Romanticism class, a friend of Harold's. He'd attended pretty regularly for a while and then gradually tapered off. He'd been to only one or two classes in December, none at all in January. But he had been at Libby's party, and he was reputed to be psychic.

His real name was Leonard something, but Harold always called him Aardvark, and eventually everyone else did too, even Mona Lang. He was tall and fat, almost grotesque, with a big, round head and eyes that looked like poached eggs behind thick, steel-rimmed glasses. His lips were thick too, framing a mouth full of big teeth. Everything about him was big and weird. His hands were always doing something to each other, like puppies fighting.

Aardvark was said to be highly intelligent, a genius in fact, but afflicted with some sort of disorder that made it impossible for him to concentrate. So he had become an eternal student, drifting from class to class, never completing the right combination of courses to get a degree. His parents were reputed to be quite rich, and must have seen the university as a safe haven for their son.

In class he would hold forth in long, rambling monologues, full of words like "paradigm" and "Ur-text," with his eyes fixed on a point on the blackboard, or maybe beyond it. I always lost the thread of his argument after the first few sentences, and just sat and watched him the way you would a natural phenomenon, like a thunderstorm or a volcano erupting.

Once I overheard Goody telling Libby that she had asked Aardvark to "read the cards" for her, and that everything he had predicted had happened. "What cards?" I asked. Even though this was before they put me in the deep freeze, I guessed I had overstepped some boundary, because both of them looked annoyed at my butting in.

"Tarot cards," Goody said. "It's a kind of fortune telling thing. He does palms and tea leaves too, and I heard he can find lost things. Not sure how he does that, though."

He can find lost things. I knew Aardvark liked to hang out at Zoot's Cafe, a self-consciously seedy, black-walled establishment on the fringe of campus, furnished with cast-off couches and chairs, decorated with posters and strings of Christmas lights. It served dark-roasted coffee before it became popular and herbal teas of exotic provenance. The music was obscure, alternative rock, and the muffins were mostly inedible, despite the healthy intentions that went into them.

I found Aardvark there on my third try, slumped on one of the old sofas, arguing with a thin, frizzy-haired guy in a purple tee shirt. At least, I assumed that's who Aardvark was talking to, even though he appeared to be addressing his remarks to a Che Guevara poster on the wall opposite him.

I placed myself right in front of him, so he couldn't help but see me. "Hi Aardvark, how's it going?"

The guy in the purple tee shirt pulled on a sweater, grabbed his backpack and left, as though my arrival was a chance to escape.

Aardvark didn't seem to notice. "...there'll always be philistines who don't get it." Then he blinked. "Oh, hi," he said. I must have come into focus by then.

"I haven't seen you in German Romanticism lately," I said, mostly to give myself context. "Did you have a good Christmas?"

"You could say so," he replied. "But I wouldn't."

"Oh, I'm sorry," I said, hoping I had picked up the right nuance. "I think the last time I saw you was at Libby's party, back in December. Just before exams."

Aardvark put the tips of his fingers together and studied the ceiling. "What a party that was!" he said, finally. "Were you there?"

"I sure was! Don't you remember?"

"Fragments." He rubbed his forehead theatrically with his thumb. "I retain only fragments. But are they the crucial ones, that's the question."

(Groan). Don't get him started. Get to the point.

"Hey, Aardvark," I said, "I wonder if I can ask you a favour."

He sloshed me a look. "Like what?"

"Well, I've heard you can... find things for people. Things they've lost, by using... psychic powers."

He grinned, showing his tombstone teeth. "Yeah, maybe. What is it you've lost?"

"I'll tell you the details later," I said. A group of people had come in, and I didn't want an audience. "How about if you come to my room tonight, about seven? I live in residence." I scribbled the name of my building and my room number on a scrap of paper and handed it to him.

"Done deal," said Aardvark, and stashed the paper in his shirt pocket. "I'll see you anon, Ilona."

I was surprised that he remembered my name, and even more surprised when he actually turned up, almost on time. My first thought—Oh shit! My second—finding Julian, that's what this is about.

I waved toward my bed, which I'd disguised as a couch with a bunch of cushions. But I sat in the chair in front of my desk. "How about some tea?" Tea seemed like the correct drink for a psychic session.

"Do you have green? It clears the channels." He stretched out on my bed, looking way too at home.

Fortunately, I did have a few bags of green tea. When it was made and poured, Aardvark looked at me through the steam rising from his cup. "So what is it you've lost, Ilona?"

It was disconcerting to have him look right at me for once. Maybe he felt safely camouflaged by the steam.

"I need your help to track someone down," I said. "Can you find people? Or just things?"

"If it resonates in the world beyond, it can be found," Aardvark intoned, flexing his hands in a way that looked painful. "Except that people cast shadows that can obfuscate their trail. Okay, first you need to light a candle."

I found a candle and placed it as directed, on the floor between us. I lit it and turned off the lights.

Aardvark's face looked even weirder lit up from below by the candle. "Sit on the floor across from me," he said, moving his bulk from my bed and assuming a cross-legged position with some difficulty. "Closer. That's right. Now, give me your hands."

I was nervous of being so close to the candle, and to him. I had to inch even closer to put my hands in his comfortably. I hoped his were clean; they were certainly hot and sweaty.

"Close your eyes," he said, "and concentrate on the object... the person you want to find."

That was easy, even in my awkward position. The memories came almost too readily, in a hot, bright freshet. Julian's face—the ironic curve of his lips, the abundant hair carefully arranged, the small gold earring, the way his hands gripped the steering wheel, the way the "ch" sound caught in his throat a little, the hardness of his body—oh yes!

My face was hot, whether from the candle or from blushing, I couldn't tell.

Aardvark's guttural voice broke into my thoughts. "I can't hold it steady. It keeps slipping away. Something's blocking the signal, for sure. It's almost like I'm getting a double... Wait—I think I've got it. Not on campus, that's for sure. East, it leads east."

Well, "not on campus" pretty much meant eastward, if you left out Vancouver Island. I could have told him that. Or if you started in Hawaii. Or Asia. This was ridiculous. I tried to pull my hands away from his, but he tightened his hold on them. "Wait. I need to concentrate. Give me something to work with. Feel those feelings, think those thoughts."

We sat there for what seemed a very long time. I tried to visualize Julian's face, but found to my horror that I couldn't. I would have it, but then it would be Northridge's features that came to mind, or those of the man in the scenes I had written, who was a combination of them both. Then I got worried that I was too close to the candle and my hair or clothing would catch fire. I opened my eyes and gazed at the flame. That seemed to empty my mind, and sure enough, I heard his voice, singing of ice and snow and wind. I was almost startled when Aardvark spoke again.

"Strange. Very strange. He's all over the place, this guy. A real shapeshifter. You're going to have to make a great journey to find him. Go east, young lady, go east. Through wind and rain and snow. To the Old World. Climb every mountain. And just maybe you'll start out in... Shaughnessy. That's certainly the picture I'm getting. But no, it's shifting again. Damn it, it's gone."

He dropped his hands, and I gratefully pulled mine back. I was surprised to see that the candle had burned down to a stub.

"What did I say?" Aardvark's magnified eyes looked at me, puzzled.

"Don't you remember? Something about starting out in Shaughnessy, but I'd have to go to Europe too, or instead. That's the Old World, isn't it? Then it slipped away."

"Shaughnessy, eh? Well, well, well," he chuckled. "Lucky you, maybe. Who is he, anyway?"

I smiled. "What makes you so sure it's a he?"

Aardvark wagged a finger at me. "Come on, I wasn't born yesterday. But I won't tell." He looked smug.

"Oh, well... it's someone I met at that party, actually." For some reason, I wanted to tell him that. Then I wished I hadn't.

"Oh, what a party that was! But I didn't actually see you there." He picked up his mug and took a gulp of tea.

"I was there—I told you! I was in another room talking to Harold and... a friend of his. Then I was dancing until... oh, I don't know, until late."

"Good old Harold. Yeah, I saw him, talking with some guy. Black hair, earring, a real Mr. GQ type, with a touch of Conan the Barbarian. Right up Harold's alley, I guess. I didn't see you, though. Not for a long time. And I don't remember you dancing. Oh, wait—" He thumbed his forehead again and pushed his glasses higher with a forefinger. "I dimly recall Harold remarking that his friend had gone off with some girl, much to his chagrin. I offered my sympathies but I don't think he valued them. I would have demonstrated more interest, perhaps, if I hadn't found just the right comfy chair and bottle of Scotch. Inertia set in. And later, much later, there was—this is extremely dim—there was a bit of a flurry about some girl... lots of talk about whether to take her to Emergency, but in the end someone just drove her to someone else's place to recover..."

"I don't know anything about all that," I said. I was tired and my head was starting to ache. Maybe Aardvark was remembering some other party. "I was talking to Harold and his friend, and then Libby and some others came in and made us all go out and dance. So we did. And after, Harold took me home." No need to tell him everything.

"Hmm. Okaay... except Harold doesn't have a car. He's a slave to public transit, which distresses him deeply."

"Okay, so his friend drove us both." I got to my feet, feeling stiff and awkward. "Thanks for doing this, Aardvark. Do I owe you anything?"

"No, my dear." It took him a while to get up. "No silver must change hands, but one kiss will suffice, my pretty one. Right here."

He offered his cheek and pointed. I kissed it, feeling silly. He put his arms around me and kissed me on the mouth. (Oh gross! Kissing Aardvark!) But he let me go, and was out the door almost before I could say goodnight.

16

Ah, and if the leaf falls to the ground
My hopes fall with it.

2008

One storm after another spirals out of the Gulf of Alaska and jumps on board the jet stream for the eastward ride. A pool of cold air rolls over the region, with no plans to leave. It greets the surges of moisture gleefully. Snow falls at higher elevations, and sometimes at lower ones too, causing consternation or delight among the human population, before dissolving into rain.

Grey is the colour. Sea, sky, mountains, trees, streets and buildings assume varying degrees of greyness. Gone are the brilliant days that prevailed at the turn of the year. When the wind blows, the cold bites, and it blows a lot. The streets are littered with plastic bags, dead umbrellas, and branches from rudely pruned trees.

Ilona watches two plump raindrops that cling to her window. A series of squalls, propelled by westerly winds, have brought horizontal rain, dashing it against the glass like a handful of pebbles thrown by an impatient lover.

"Come out, Ilona, come out and play! We're out here, where things are real, where things are wet and wild and cold. The gulls and crows are out here playing. You come too!"

I'll be out there soon enough. No need to rush things. She turns her attention to the two drops on the glass. They're sitting side by side, like a pair of race cars waiting for the flag to drop. Surface tension holds their shapes intact. One of those little miracles of Nature that aren't miraculous at all, like Jesus bugs skittering around on the surface of a pond. Surface tension, that's all.

The drop on the left swells, sags, lurches downward and stalls. The other plumps up a bit, creeps down an inch or so, slithers sideways and stops. Then it suddenly streaks down three inches.

"If the drop on the right hits the bottom first, that means I won't have to move out," Ilona says. "I'll get my act together, find another job, get back into things."

But if the other drop wins? Then what?

"Then I guess I won't do those things, and I'll have to move to a room in some dump, and eventually I'll be down and out. Like Davy. Like that woman who was feeding the crows."

Lady, if you think I'm down and out, you'd better think again.

Where did that come from? It's almost as if the crow woman is in the room with her, root-beer-coloured eyes glaring accusingly.

"Well, you're not exactly a model citizen and taxpayer, are you?"

Neither are you, honey. When are you going to admit it?

Ilona shakes her head. "Go away. Get out."

The drop on the right is still creeping downward, but also sideways. "Go drop go!" Ilona cheers it on. She eyes the left-hand one, willing it to stay where it is, but it's getting that plump ready-to-roll look again, and sure enough, it does another two-inch zip. Now it's a whole inch ahead of the Right Drop, the Drop of Salvation.

The right drop slithers sideways again and collides with another, smaller drop that was just sitting there. That makes it swell, sag, and slide straight down.

"Hurray!" Ilona sits up to get a better view. Her drop, the drop that means a return to the old, good life, is now two inches ahead of its rival, the Evil Drop of poverty and failure. The Good Drop is more than halfway to the goal, the bottom of the window pane. "Come on, you can do it!" She absolutely cannot interfere, by tapping on the glass, for example. That would break the magic.

Magical thinking, Ilona? Do you often indulge in that?

This was a new voice. Definitely not the crow woman. But not really new. She has heard this voice before, heard way too much of it—cold, authoritative, ironic. A white-coated voice. Twenty years later, it's still there. Doctor knows best. *You're sick, Miss Miller.*

"But look, the right drop has slipped down another three inches! It can't lose now! The other one's just sitting there. Soon everything will be okay again. Tomorrow, for sure."

Is this magical thinking? I used to tell myself—if I see an eagle, today will be a good day. If I see seven blue cars, he'll phone. If that cloud moves away from the sun in the next thirty seconds, Mom and Dad will be happy.

Sometimes it worked.

But lots of times it didn't, right?

"Sure, but what's wrong with omens? We don't understand everything about how the world works. Didn't someone say that the flutter of a butterfly's wings can trigger a storm half a world away?"

Oh, I can see the face now, that goes with the voice—a smile on thin lips above a cleanly-shaven jaw. Muddy brown eyes with crinkles around them. The lips smile, but the eyes are cold. "I think that was meant as a metaphor, Ilona. Do you know what a metaphor is?"

"Yes, Doctor, I know what a metaphor is. If I say you *are* a snake, that's a metaphor. If I say you're *like* a snake, it's a simile, and if I say you are low, reptilian and repulsive, it's the truth."

"All right, Ilona, you've made your point." His expression didn't change, but I did see a faint pink in his cheeks, and congratulated myself. Not that it made any difference.

But now something is happening. The right drop hits some invisible obstacle on the glass—a bit of spider's web, maybe, or a speck of dirt, and swerves to one side. As though cursed, it slips swiftly to the edge of the pane and stops dead two inches from the bottom. The other drop, encouraged by its rival's defeat, descends a crucial two inches, captures a small stationary drop and plummets to the goal.

You've lost again, dear. You're a loser, for sure.

A loser. That's her, all right. Carl Miller's much-loved daughter is a loser. And Carl, her father, is dead. In part because of her, because of the stress of finding out that his smart, college-educated daughter, on whom all his hopes were pinned, was actually a loser, and crazy. Instead of going to her graduation ceremony, he was visiting her at the Pine Valley Centre once a week. Visiting, worrying about her, wondering why, why, why? And all the time he was trying to run his farm. No wonder he had a heart attack and died.

"What's the point?" Ilona asks her messy, dusty room, the rain-smeared window, the dead plants in their pots. "What's the point of this? It's so stupid! I'm just taking up space and going through the motions. If this is the way my life has to be, I don't want it!"

Now the dismal scene blurs again as the useless tears come. She wipes them away and sits with her head in her hands, eyes closed. She is spinning off the planet, in free fall.

The public library has a copy of *Final Exit*. She'd looked it up before cutting off her Internet service. She'll go and borrow it and take action. For a full minute, she worries about what to do with the book afterward. She won't be able to return it. That makes her laugh, one of those rough, shaky laughs like an engine misfiring.

Then another thought, like a big rock that she'd forgotten about, sitting in the middle of the room. Davy.

Oh shit, who cares about him? Let's just get on with it.

"I care. I have to. He's the last person I owe something to. I have to find him and tell him the truth. Then I'll go."

• • • •

1988

You can go a long way before you realize it. Say you're climbing up a long, steep hill. You look at it from the bottom and it seems impossible, but you get started, put one foot in front of the other, again and again and again. Then you stop and look behind you and it's shocking how far you've climbed. Or you swim out from shore and look back to see everything receding and small. Can you ever make it back there?

That's how I felt by the latter half of January, when I realized I hadn't been to an Education class in weeks. I hadn't even bothered to look up the results of my Christmas exams. My notes and texts from those courses might as well have been written in Chinese for all they meant to me.

Reading Dietrich Fischer-Dieskau's book on Schubert's songs, I found that someone who had preceded me had left her mark. In the chapter on *Winterreise*, many paragraphs had been underlined in fine, light pencil, using a ruler. The person had also made notes in the margins, in tiny, delicate, Chinese characters—clusters of dainty pencil strokes whose meaning I could not read, but which were intriguing just the same. A girl from Hong Kong or China had read this book, read it carefully and thoughtfully, because like me, she wanted to understand. I touched the characters with a forefinger, as though I could absorb their meaning through my skin. How long ago, I wondered, had the unknown girl made these marks, and where was she now? Did she still listen to Schubert, or had she forgotten everything once the course was over?

In fact, by the end of January, I had even stopped going to German Romanticism. The last time I'd been in class, Lang had been droning on about the rise of the middle class and political movements in Austria and Germany in the 1840s. I didn't care about that stuff. I needed every moment to immerse myself in *Winterreise*, so I could finish my paper. I had to do the necessary research, not always in books and libraries. For some of it, I had to go deep inside myself; for the rest, I had to find Julian Harker (or was it Barker?). It was as though a December storm had blown him to me, like a leaf torn from a tree, and then whirled him away.

Maybe he was walking through his own winter, somewhere. (But not on campus, Aardvark said). I could see him so clearly sometimes, the very attitude of his body as he stood in front of a copse of trees near the road, watching the last few leaves that clung to the branches and trembled in the breeze. Yellow and orange, they fluttered brightly against the dull colours of the bark and branches, like silly little hands waving goodbye to hope.

And oh! I wanted to catch him before the last one fell, and he with it, his last hope annihilated. Before he and the leaf dissolved into earth and water, fragments of cellulose and humic acids, I would break the cycle, clasp him to my heart, give him a reason to live. Because down the road, far ahead, beyond sight, was the fatal signpost to the grey road at whose end, by a haze-shrouded, lonely light, stood the *Leiermann*.

In January, while the rain fell outside and my fellow students toddled off to their classes, came back, went to meals, came back, went to the library, came back, went away for the weekend, came back—I stayed in my room, plugged in, wired up, swapping discs. Baritone, tenor, tenor, baritone, returning always to the tenor, like coming home. I trolled the twenty-four songs again and yet again, as though by repetition I could conjure him from the air. Him. Or him? The man of sorrow or the man who carried sorrow like a knife in his boot? At night they stalked my dreams and I hunted them in turn. *Him*. There was only one. But which one?

There was a place on the campus—probably still is, since I don't think they would build anything there (or would they?)—a rose garden, just below the highest point of the west end of campus, with a blue view of mountains, sea and sky. The rose beds were laid out in a lawn surrounded by big, fat rhododendron bushes, with a few trees (cedars, maybe?) here and there. You climbed down a set of steps from the viewpoint and there were benches to sit on. I had heard it was a popular place for proposals, and more. Very romantic.

On this Sunday afternoon, no one was there but me. It wasn't a romantic sort of day—sky grey and shot through with a dusty light, a cold wind funneling out of the Fraser Valley, laden with the resentments of dwellers in cold inland places, getting their own back at Lotus Land.

I didn't need to admire the view, so I went down the steps to get out of the wind. The rose bushes stood in their beds, like people who found themselves naked at a party, stiff and ridiculous. Here and there, a dull, leathery green leaf, insect-nibbled at the edges, clung to its twig, but there were buds on some of the plants.

Roses in January? I went over to have a closer look. A dark red bud was at the stage where you would expect it to open the next day, if it were June. I could see it had been in that state for a long time, months probably, since the last warm days, when the sun had encouraged growth and life. Then it had grown cold. Frost had settled on the tightly furled petals, and even though it melted the next day, something had changed. The bud was sealed shut, unable to open, doomed eventually to shrivel and dry and fall to the ground. It had endured in this arrested state through the ever longer nights and dull days of rain, through more frosts and repeated thaws.

What was inside? Petals, layer upon layer, protecting the inner sexual parts of the flower, which now would never feel the form of the questing bee, would never swell with developing seeds and become a rosehip. (Never mind that someone might have picked it before it got to that stage.)

I shook my head. *Silly, silly thoughts, Ilona!*

Or were they? Because wasn't this rosebud trying to show me something? Wasn't it just like me? I was lost in a hopeless search for someone who wasn't there—Julian Harker-Barker-Northridge, Franz Peter Schubert, the homeless wanderer, Wilhelm Müller the poet-librarian. Which of them was I really looking for? Müller's words and Schubert's music had created the image of the wanderer.

Northridge's voice had brought him to life for me, and I had found something like its physical embodiment in Julian Harker and fused it with something in myself. Then I had lost him, and I needed to find him again to finish whatever it was that I had begun.

I reached out and grasped the stem with the mummified bud. I bent it and it broke, but not before a thorn slipped into the end of my finger, jabbing it painfully and drawing blood. I pulled the mangled stem free of the bush and sucked my finger, tasting salt and metal mingled with the bitter, green sap.

Back in my room, I put the rose bud in a glass of warm water. The wood of the stem was green—surely it would revive in the warmth of the room, would open and bloom after all?

But it didn't. Three days later, frustrated, I tried to pry the petals apart with my fingers. Even inside, their edges were brown, their substance thin and spent. I persisted, seeking the centre, the heart, the secret. Was there anything left?

In a way there was. Curled in the heart of the furled rose was a little worm-like thing. Awakened by the warmth of the room, disturbed by my probing, it began to wiggle and twitch. Disgusted, I threw the rose on the floor and stomped it flat. Then I picked it up and tossed it out the window.

17

Dogs bark, chains rattle;
People sleep in their beds,
Dreaming of things they do not possess.

2008

The jet stream wobbles and wiggles, climbing northward, slipping southward, sometimes splitting in two. Near the end of January, in a southward perturbation, it snares warm air from the vicinity of Hawaii and shuttles it northeastward with a great fanfare of rain. "Another pineapple express," say the weather forecasters, almost apologetically. It rains steadily for nearly twelve hours. There is minor flooding here and there; in low-lying areas, basements are swamped, despite overworked sump pumps. After nightfall, the rain tapers off and finally stops. Trees drip, drains gurgle. Fog creeps secretly, bringing with it the smell of the sea to mingle with the night scent of winter-blooming honeysuckle and the ever-present base note of moldering leaves.

Ilona uncurls from her nest on the couch. All day she has been restless, alternating bursts of pacing with attempts to rest and relax. Just as she starts to doze, her brain churns up another unwelcome morsel: "Poor judgment, bad attitude, unrealistic expectations, resistance to change." There seems to be no end; it's as though she has broken open a piñata of negative assessments and they spill out, plaguing her like gnats.

She opens the door and sticks her head outside. It's dark, quiet, calm, and strangely warm. A good night for walking. Maybe all those nasty little epithets will stay behind. Maybe she can escape them by replacing their thin, buzzing voices with the soft, measured thuds of her boots striking concrete, harmonizing with the interior lub-dubs of her heart. If she returns before dawn, maybe she'll be able to sleep.

Out again. Going out. How many more times, before it's the last? Never mind, quick step now—one, two, one, two, one, two, get out, get lost, no more, no me, all gone.

So Davy doesn't spend much time downtown, she thinks, remembering what the crow woman said. Well then, I'll go somewhere else. She turns right instead of left, to the crest of the hill instead of its downward slope. Up and over, and then down the east-facing side. Cars swish by and once a bus, garishly lit, with a few lone figures slumped in the seats, going somewhere. She passes one or two other walkers, but doesn't look at them or speak. She must stay focussed on Davy. "I'll find you yet, you slippery devil," she says. A couple passing by on her left look at her, then at one another, and then back at her. Ilona doesn't reciprocate.

She keeps to the main street, past apartment buildings and a few shops. A real estate office. A restaurant. A bank. A drugstore. A coffee shop. A place selling used furniture. A dry cleaner. Then more apartments and houses that look rented. A few balconies and roofs still wear Christmas lights, which look seedy and irrelevant, even though they are exactly the same lights that were so magical several weeks ago. Christmas trees lie on their sides near garbage cans, clinging remnants of tinsel testifying to their brief, spent glory. The hands that placed these strands of tinsel were the same ones that carried the trees out and dumped them here.

It grows late. Ilona walks through a region of prim bungalows, each one with its patch of lawn, its shrubs and trees, tended or unkempt. Matching urns and gnome figurines, groups of pots or wooden half-barrels containing slumped and tattered remnants of summertime plants. Wreaths hang on a few doors, sagging into tired-looking ovals.

Another tiny shopping plaza under a solitary street light. The shops (a grocery, a butcher shop, another dry cleaner, a hairdresser) are closed, but a bare tree stands before them, festooned in lights—blue, all blue, those new-style lights that glow rather than sparkle. It's as though the air in their immediate vicinity has absorbed the colour, and clouds of it hover around the bare branches like a blue mist.

Ilona stops and looks. So blue. So strange. She stares and stares while minutes go by, becoming aware that her back is stiff and her feet feel hot and spongy. She has walked too far—but not far enough.

Then she sees him—or her, perhaps; it's impossible to tell. Someone is there, on the other side of the blue tree, close to the butcher shop. Lumpish in a shapeless coat and baggy pants, the figure appears to be doing exercises, an idiosyncratic form of calisthenics—flip arms up and over sideways, bend from the waist until the hands nearly touch the ground, then jerk the body upright, shake the head, up with the arms again. Repeat. Repeat. Repeat.

Ilona watches. Surely this must be another of what she now thinks of as the Outside People. She wonders if this person knows Davy and could tell her where to look for him, but she does not want to ask a question of someone engaged in such a bizarre activity. The longer she watches, the less she wants to speak to this person. If she were to interrupt them, what kind of face would she see? What kind of eyes? She moves on.

Now she is climbing yet again. Near the top of this hill stands a pair of stone pillars, flanking a road which goes off at an oblique angle. A portal? It is much darker there, under a roof of tall trees. Illuminated globes line the road, leading away into the distance.

Ilona stands for a moment, thinking. Then she enters.

In short order she concludes that the gateway is no meaningless whim. It has significance, because she has entered a different world. The boulevards are wider, the houses set farther back from the road, many obscured by tall hedges or shrubs. Circular driveways and *portes-cochères* are not uncommon. Over everything lies a deep hush which carries a hidden meaning: the people that live here are different, because they are rich.

They have more space and therefore more privacy. No discarded Christmas trees can be seen here, no strollers or clotheslines. Not even in daylight, and certainly not now. There is only the pavement curving away, and the line of iron lamp posts, each one surmounted by its glowing globe. Trunks of trees, also marshalled into rows, vague shapes of shrubs, looming facades, the occasional illuminated window.

These are far apart, like wayward beacons. Here the cold light of a kitchen fluorescent, there the curtain-muffled glow of a table lamp, elsewhere the kaleidoscope flicker of a television in a dark room, or the bright, concentrated rectangle of a computer screen.

Insomniacs of the world, unite!

Otherwise, nearly everyone is asleep, lying in the dark beneath fluffy duvets and designer sheets, sunk in deep sleep or travelling the eye-twitching trajectories of dreams, in which desires, fears and anxieties are strained, processed and recompiled for assimilation into the mind's unknown country. When their dreamers awake, the dreams dissolve, leaving behind faint traces of themselves; soon lost to the demands of the full bladder, the crying child, the affairs of the waking world.

A dog barks behind a high hedge of laurel, behind a double iron gate with sharp points, which sports a small metal sign bearing the discreet but distinctive logo of a security company. Another dog responds from across the street. Ilona hears a scramble of paws on concrete and the rattle of a chain, then another burst of barking, nearer this time, and the counterpoint from farther away. She stands perfectly still for many heartbeats, but the barking is not repeated. A snuffle and the sound of the chain sliding tell her the animal has returned to its kennel. Silence ensues.

Ilona steps off the sidewalk and into the middle of the wide street. She paces along, goose-stepping elaborately, waving and bowing to the silent houses, the dogs and their sleeping owners.

"Good night, sleep tight, don't bite," she mutters, snorting a silent laugh. "You won't catch me, not this time."

The street proceeds downward, toward the road that follows the shore. Here, pairs of wheeled refuse containers sit on the boulevard next to each driveway, blue ones for paper, grey for garbage, and squat, wheel-less blue bins for other recyclables. "It must be Garbage Eve," says Ilona, peering into one of the small bins. It contains a few cans and jars, four large milk jugs and a fabric softener bottle. No wine, pop or juice bottles. None in the next six bins either. Strange; don't these people drink anything but milk?

"No, it's not that," she says aloud. "It's Davy. He's been here. He knows when a neighbourhood gets its garbage picked up and he comes by the night before to scavenge the returnables." She remembers the bottles stashed in the shed near her place. "He's just been here, I know it!" She breaks into a faster walk.

The road ends at the shoreline-hugging drive. Ilona turns right, leaving the houses and lights behind, and enters a zone of nearly total darkness where the road passes through a large park. The sidewalk slopes down into a foggy hollow. Her footsteps seem very loud, the only sounds in the world, inviting a response from the darkness—a word, a cough, a groan. Any second now, she will hear it, and what will she do then? Say, "Hi Davy, it's me!" But how will she know it's Davy and not some stranger?

Ilona feels panic approaching. Where is she, anyway? It's as though she has been transported to one of her dream-landscapes, in which roads go on forever. And now a large, white shape looms dimly on her right, across the road. Then she remembers—it's a war memorial, a female figure presiding over the names of the fallen. She makes herself keep going. Come on, now—walk, walk, steadily,

steadily. There's a light; not far from here is a sidewalk to a public beach.

She is exhausted. Climbing down the flight of concrete steps to the beach, she nearly stumbles and has to grab the iron handrail to save herself. Logs are piled in drifts above the tide line, and here and there grow clumps of beach grass. Ilona finds a hidden hollow and sits down. The night is relatively warm and the rain hasn't come back. A short rest would be good, before she seeks the homeward road. She curls up on her side, in the ancient position of the sleeper—or the corpse—and closes her eyes. The ocean makes small, irrelevant noises nearby, and maybe someone is playing a harmonica, far away...

• • • •

1988

After a month of fruitless speculation, explanation and investigation, I had a brilliant idea—I would find Julian Barker at home. I would track him down in the place he had taken me that night. It was where he lived; surely he must spend time there, even though he didn't seem to be on campus much. In fact, I was beginning to think he wasn't a student at all.

I lay on my bed for quite a while, thinking and making a plan. The main problem was that I had only the vaguest notion of where Julian's place was. I had looked in the phone book, under both Barker and Harker, without success, but I was fairly sure it was in Shaughnessy. We had gone south on Oak or Granville after dropping Harold in the West End. I clearly remembered tree-lined streets and big houses on big lots. Julian had parked his car close to the side or rear entrance to a large house, almost a mansion. Thinking about it, I was pretty sure there was a circular driveway. Big and rich in that general area meant Shaughnessy. And hadn't Aardvark said I should look there?

But where exactly? I had been in no state to notice or remember specifics, such as street names or house numbers, either on the way there or on the way back to campus. The only thing I was certain about was travelling south on one of those major thoroughfares, and then a right turn onto a residential street. That street curved and meandered, but we had not turned off it before we reached the house.

I closed my eyes and tried to reconstruct. He had sung something, hadn't he? I asked him if he could sing, and he did. "*Ich träumte von bunten Blumen, So wie sie wohl blühen im Mai.*" Was that really it? Did Julian Barker sing in German about flowers that bloomed in May? I had never been in a car with Julian Northridge, I was sure of that. Oh, but it didn't matter! Whatever he had sung, it was while we were on the Burrard Bridge. Where exactly had we gone after that?

I consulted a city map. We couldn't have followed Burrard, because it ended at Sixteenth Avenue, still in the strict grid pattern of streets, not curving boulevards. We must have gone via Granville. Left from Burrard onto Broadway, and then right onto Granville. What was at that intersection? Suddenly I remembered—the Aristocratic Restaurant, with its landmark sign from the 1950s. "Risty" and his monocle. I even recalled a hazy thought along the lines of "Wouldn't it be nice to stop in for a coffee?" Julian and I in a corner booth, holding hands under the table... But that hadn't happened.

The best time to carry out this plan would be at night. You didn't want to be caught loitering in Shaughnessy, casing the joint. Reconnaissance was best done under cover of darkness.

I went to supper late and made myself eat even though I didn't want to, because I would need energy and endurance for the night ahead. Afterward, I had a shower and carefully blew my hair dry so it looked like it had on the night of the party. I even put on makeup and the silver earrings that made me feel dramatic—a sun on my right ear and a moon on the left. As for clothes, the choice was obvious—black jeans, black sweater, hooded black jacket. I stuffed some cash and a few tissues in one pocket, keys in the other, and set off for the bus loop.

It was cloudy but not raining, ideal weather for an undercover operation. Two buses brought me to the zone of action. I began walking south, trying to take myself back to that other trip, to put myself into a state of mind where I would automatically recognize the right street when I saw it. But all I could remember was what came after. His hands, his lips, his voice...

The only thing to do was to check every likely right-hand street, until something looked familiar. I was pretty sure it was between Sixteenth and King Edward, which narrowed the possibilities considerably (unless I should have been on Oak after all, and my memory of the Aristocratic was from some other occasion, with Davy—but never mind!)

The rhythm of my footsteps on the pavement triggered the *Winterreise* thing in my head, and it was almost as if I were plugged into Davy's player, listening to Northridge one more time. "*Fremd bin ich eingezogen, Fremd zieh' ich wieder aus.*" Well, that was certainly true; in Shaughnessy I was *fremd* as all get out (until I found him, anyway), and it wasn't a place that welcomed the unlooked-for stranger.

I slowed my pace, but not too much. I wanted to look like someone who belonged here, out for a leisurely walk. It would have been better if I had a dog, of course. That was just about the only reason most people walked in a place like this, to take Fifi or Marmaduke out for a crap.

An hour later I was almost ready to give up. I had tried several streets, without success. A couple of times I thought I had the right place, but a closer look proved otherwise. The driveway was on the wrong side, or the house wasn't the right size. The worst thing was that the place I was looking for might be just around the next corner. On the other hand, I couldn't follow every damn street to its end. My feet were sore and I was getting tired.

One more, I said to myself. Then I give up.

A street branched off to my right, wide, curving, tree-lined. Just what I remembered (but also like so many streets I had already tried). I was pretty sure the house I was looking for was on the right-hand side. "Right and right and right," I muttered, hoping I wasn't in fact wrong and wrong and wrong again. It wasn't the first house; I knew that because I clearly remembered that we had driven along the street for a short distance. But only a short distance, maybe to the third or fourth house.

The third was obviously wrong, a big new place with acres of windows, all lit up even though it was nearly eleven o'clock on a week night. But the fourth... There was a circular driveway (with the obligatory Mercedes sitting in the middle, like an ad for the Secret of Success), and a secondary drive leading behind the house.

I looked around carefully. The place was dark. No one was visible, either on the street or at any of the windows. Luckily, the house across the street had one of those huge, stranger-excluding hedges. They wouldn't be able to see me. The cost of privacy: I can't see you, but you can't see me either.

I moved to the far side of the driveway and quietly made my way toward the back of the house. It was a Tudor-style mansion, of light-coloured stucco and dark wood, two stories high, with a steep roof and several dormers.

And yes, here was the paved area near a back door, a nice, solid door with a peep-hole, and a curtained window next to it. There was a faint light inside; I could just see the glow through the curtain. And here was the clincher—in the parking spot that obviously belonged to the ground floor suite was an older BMW. Julian's car. I had found him.

So what should I do now? Knock on the door? "Hi, it's me. Long time no see." I went a little closer. Brighter light spilled out of a larger window around the corner, illuminating the shiny leaves of a nearby shrub.

Without thinking, I went past the door, past the first window, to the other one, pressing myself against the wall. I crouched between bush and wall, wondering what to do next, especially since I had just discovered it was a holly bush. A couple of spines dug into my backside, right through my pants. Cautiously, I wiggled myself free and raised my head to look inside.

The view was partially obscured by a venetian blind, but the slats were angled so I could see into the room. Was he there? Was it really him? I was nearly faint with excitement. Would he look the same? If he was there, I would tap on the window and give him a surprise.

I leaned forward and turned my head so I could get the best view. Across the room and almost directly in line with me, someone was sitting at a desk. But it wasn't Julian. It was a woman. All I could see was her back, but the long, blond hair, gathered into a thick braid, was horribly familiar.

Goody. So that was why everyone in German Romanticism was acting funny around me! They knew. They knew that Goody had moved in with the guy that poor Ilona had fallen for at the party in December. And of course no one had bothered to explain any of it to me.

There she sat, right at home, a big stack of books on the desk in front of her, a mug of tea nearby. She was writing something, making notes or (what else?) working on her paper for the course. While I was lurking in the darkness outside, alone.

"You bitch!" I shrieked, and pounded on the window with my fists. If there had been a rock handy, I would have hurled it.

Goody stood up and whirled around. Now I had a perfect look at her, eyes round with surprise and mouth open—three circles in her face and her nose sticking out of the middle. The picture of guilt. Ha, ha! Gotcha!

We stood like that, looking at each other, but only for a second. The pulsing bleep of an alarm sounded from inside the house. Then a dog started to bark, a door slammed and people shouted. Goody turned and ran out of my field of vision. I thought she was yelling too.

I'd better get out of here. My legs felt weak and I was sure I was going to pee myself. But it was too late, because the dog (a big one; he sounded big) was coming around the corner. There he was, a large chunky dog, followed by a man in pyjamas. I tried to make a break for the front yard but a dense shrub on the far side of the window barred my way. I forced my way past it, only to meet a blank wall where the house front jutted out. Frantic, I turned to my right, but it was too late. The guy with the flashlight was already there, and the dog blocked a return by the way I had come.

The dog stopped just short of me, growling. "Stay, Duke!" the man ordered, directing a flashlight beam toward me. Light lanced into my eyes, blinding me. "Come on out of there!" he said, in a voice not much different from the one he'd used on the dog. The voice of a man used to commanding and being obeyed.

"I can't," I said, amazed at how hard it was to speak. There seemed to be no air in my lungs. "I can't see."

Duke was still growling at me but not coming closer, at least. The guy moved the flashlight beam down a couple of feet. "Okay, come on out now, please. Duke, come here."

The dog obeyed, giving me a lingering look, as though he would have liked nothing better than to knock me flat and sink his teeth in my throat. I could see two other figures behind Mr. Flashlight. "I've called the police," a woman's voice said.

The police must be perpetually ready for action in that part of town, because they were there by the time I emerged from the shrubbery. It was just as well, in a way, because I really wasn't up for a conversation with the heroic homeowner, or with Goody, who was hovering uncertainly behind him, along with the woman who had spoken. And I thought I could see some people coming up the driveway, probably from the lit-up house next door. Quite the little crowd I'd gathered.

There were two cops, of course—one young and the other old and crusty-looking. Just like in the movies.

They didn't get to ask the usual cop question ("What seems to be the problem here?") because Mr. Flashlight hustled up to them and said, "This... person was breaking into my house. She tried to break a window and that's what set off the alarm."

"I wasn't breaking in!" I began, but the older cop came over and said, "Come with me, please, young lady," in the kind of voice you just don't argue with. I realized the cops weren't interested in refereeing an argument between me and the homeowner. And I didn't want to see Goody, or talk to her. Leaving the scene with the cops was definitely the lesser evil.

I didn't make any fuss at all, just went to the police car and got in, as directed. It wasn't until considerably later that I realized I hadn't seen Julian.

18

My heart sees its own image
Painted in the sky –
It's nothing but winter,
Winter cold and wild!

2008

The storm front—yet another one—has passed, and the movement of air reorients once more, from southeasterly to westerly. The temperature falls and the wind whips up as air dragged eastward by the vortex of low pressure spirals inland. Clouds rise and thin, shredded by the wind. Stars appear in the rifts between the scudding cloud masses, pale with the approach of another dawn.

The wind wakes Ilona. Her eyes open to the infinite sky, rather than the familiar ceiling of her bedroom. Far above her, a gull wheels and drifts against the background of torn clouds, and its keening is loud in her ears, punctuated at intervals by the harsh retorts of crows.

Her entire body is appallingly cold and stiff. She wonders if she will ever be able to move again, get up, walk. And she has to pee. Carefully, she uncurls herself from the fetal position in which she spent the night, with her back pressed against a big drift log. She levers herself into a sitting position, trying not to put stress on her bladder, and looks around.

The beach is empty except for the inevitable joggers on the promenade. They aren't looking her way, being preoccupied with their own business, so she can do hers, right here. She fumbles in her coat pocket for a tissue, but before she can get on with it, a car appears, gliding slowly to the turnaround only a dozen yards away. A police car. Ilona stuffs the tissue back into her pocket, zips up her pants and leans back against the log, as though she's just admiring the view.

She fully expects the cop car to turn around and glide back the way it had come, beach patrol completed. But it doesn't. It parks at the end of the turnaround, right next to a "No Parking" sign. For a few moments, nothing happens. Ilona is about to get going, hoping the public washrooms by the playground (a long way off) are open, when the car's door opens and a cop gets out.

He crosses the sidewalk and stands for a moment, looking around. Then he comes toward her, walking with the swagger all cops seem to have. It must be part of the curriculum in police school. Swagger 101. Or maybe it's just the inevitable result of wearing a gun on the hip.

For a second, she has a nearly irresistible urge to run. "No, stupid!" the inner voice hisses. "If you run, he'll go after you for sure. Just stay put, talk nicely, but don't tell him anything."

A gust of wind sweeps her hair back, exposing her face. "*Die kalten Winde bliesen, Mir grad' ins Angesicht.*" (Where did that come from?) "Not now," Ilona says out loud.

The cop is right there. He's not as young as he looked from a distance. The beginnings of a paunch lurk under his uniform, and what she can see of his severely barbered hair is grey. His cop veneer is well-developed and firmly in place.

The policeman isn't always your friend. Remember that.

"Hello," the cop says. "Are you Joanne Hildebrand?"

"No," Ilona replies. "I am Winter."

"I see. Ms. Winter, have you seen anyone—?"

"Not Ms.," says Ilona. "Just Winter. I am Winter, cold and wild." And she smiles. In the sky behind the cop's head, a seagull executes a sweet aerial curve.

"Well, okay, it sure feels like that out here today," says the cop. "Are you out for an early morning stroll or have you been here all night? Are you lost, maybe?"

"No, I'm Winter." She laughs. "Okay, no more joking. I'm not lost. I was, but I'm not any more. Now I know where I'm going."

The cop looks patient and resigned. "You do understand, don't you, that loitering is an offense? And so is camping in public parks. In this municipality, that's still the law."

"Oh yes, I do understand those things. But what do you mean, 'camping'? I'm not camping. Do you see a tent? Wiener sticks, a fire pit? I was admiring the view, that's all." Another gust of wind whips her hair around; she wonders why the cop's hat doesn't go flying off—is the badge heavy enough to hold it down or do cops use some sort of secret glue to make sure their symbols of authority stay put?

"Ms.—ah, I'm just passing along some advice. Actually, I'm part of a search effort for a missing lady, Mrs. Joanne Hildebrand. Alzheimer's patient. She wandered away from home yesterday. I thought there was a chance you might have seen her." He flips open a notebook and reads from it. "Sixty years old, five feet six, 150 pounds, grey hair, red jacket, navy blue pants."

"All these wandering ladies," says Ilona. "Women, I mean. Wandering women. Does Mrs. Hildebrand play the harmonica, by any chance?"

The cop gives her a funny look. "I'm not sure I understand."

"I heard someone playing a harmonica. That's all."

"A harmonica. Here, on the beach? Would that have been last night?"

Ha, I know what you're up to. "No, it was this morning. I can't say what time, but it reminded me of a friend of mine."

"I see. Ms.—ah, Winter, I wonder if I could see some identification, please?"

"Sorry, I don't have any with me. See?" Ilona turns out her coat pockets and executes a slow pirouette. "I've just been out walking. I didn't think I needed ID for that."

"Technically, no, but you've refused to give a proper name, so—"

"Proper name? What's wrong with Winter? I had a friend called Summer once."

"And she played the harmonica, did she?"

"No, she played the tuba. Is there anything else you want to know? If not, maybe you'd better get back to looking for poor Mrs. Hildebrand."

The cop's face turns red. "You'd better watch it, lady. I might just decide to take you downtown."

"No thanks," says Ilona. "I have other plans."

"I'll bet you do. Just give me a minute, will you? Stay right there." He goes over to his car, opens the door, pulls out a radio and starts talking into it.

Ilona hears, but doesn't listen. She watches a couple of gulls flying and crows pecking at things on the beach. She watches a sailboat nearby and a freighter in the distance. The wind plays with her hair, flips her hood up and pulls it back down. She waits.

The cop comes back. "Checked up on me, did you?" says Ilona. "Thought maybe I ran away from Eric Martin?" Isn't that the way—if you don't fit the pattern, you must be an escapee from the local loony bin.

The cop blushes again. Or maybe it's just windburn. Surely he's too old to blush.

"I can give you a lift, if you like. Out to a bus stop or downtown, if that's where you're headed."

"No thanks," Ilona says again. *You can't fool me. Not again. I know your tricks.* The car's black interior with its glowing instruments. The radio voices, the bars on the windows, the unassailable authority. She's been there and seen that. Once was enough.

"Well, suit yourself, then." He turns and swaggers back to the car, climbs in and drives away.

The freighter slips out of sight. The sailboat sails. The gulls circle. The wind blows.

"*Es ist nichts als der Winter,*" Ilona murmurs. "*Der Winter kalt und wild.*"

• • • •

1988

The inside of the police car would have been interesting if I had been there as a guest, on a field trip or as part of an educational exercise. But I wasn't, so all I got was an impression of busyness and authority—the radio crackling and chattering, the reinforced glass, the bars between the front and back seats. Even the smell was unique—coffee and synthetic substances, and faint whiffs of something else, a dense black smell of sweat, fear, and defeat.

"Now may I see some identification, please?"

The cop wasn't smiling and he was totally calm. For him, this was just another night on the job.

I shrugged. "Sorry, I didn't bring any with me."

"Well, in that case, I need to know your name."

"Why?"

He sighed. "Miss, you were caught trying to break into a house. That's pretty serious stuff. Playing games with me isn't going to help you. It's too late for that. Now, what's your name?"

"I wasn't breaking into that house. I already told you that."

"All right, then—what did you do to set off the alarm?"

"I was looking for—looking for someone. That's all." I didn't know what to do with my hands. They kept shaking, so I had to hold on to them, one with the other. Then I thought that made me look nervous, so I let go and they started to shake again.

"Why didn't you just knock on the door and ask for this someone?" The cop wore a look of inexorable, deadly patience. He had all the questions, and all the right answers too.

"Because I wasn't sure if he—I hadn't seen him in a while and I wasn't really sure he lived there. I just wanted to look in the window first, and see if I was in the right place."

"But you hit the window." The cop's eyes were fixed on mine. I could see his short, dark eyelashes. He didn't blink. "That was what set off the alarm."

"I was just surprised, that's all. Surprised to see... someone else I knew. Not the person I was looking for." Suddenly I was exhausted and knew I was about to start crying. "Look," I said, dismayed at the sick, cowardly wobble in my voice, "no harm was done, so just let me go home, will you?"

"I'm sorry, I can't do that. You were trespassing on private property and appeared to be breaking into a residence. I have to follow procedures before I can let you go. So the more you cooperate, the better."

"I've told you everything. I came here looking for a friend. I thought this was where he lives. But I guess I was wrong. Or something. I didn't mean to set off these people's alarm and disturb everyone. That's all I can say." My voice broke on the last word, and I put my hands over my face.

The cop said nothing for what seemed like a long time. I felt the blood pulsing heavily in my temples and wrists and an electrical buzzing in my head. I had to get out of this. The cop seemed to be thinking it over; surely he would see what a waste of his time it was to bother with me. "Please..." I pulled my hands away from my face. He was writing in his notebook, but he looked up.

"Miss, I think I'd better take you downtown. You might feel more like talking there."

"No! No, please! If you lock me up, I'll die!" I tried to open the car door. I had to get away, to run as fast and as far as I could. I had to— But the door was locked, and there was the cop with that look of deadly patience and authority in his eyes.

"Take it easy. I'm not going to lock you up. We just want you to calm down so we can ask you a few questions, clear everything up. Look—I can call someone for you, if you like. Your parents or a friend. They can come and pick you up after all the paperwork is done. All we need to do is satisfy the procedure, assure those folks out there that their problem is being dealt with. Okay?"

"Not my parents. No way. Don't tell them."

"Well, how about a friend, then?"

So was I going to admit I didn't have any? Not any more. Goody was obviously an enemy; so was her pal Libby. Harold was in cahoots with them too. Aardvark? What a laugh. I didn't even consider any of the people I knew in Ed. They were on another planet. And it looked like Julian Barker/Harker didn't exist, not for me, anyway.

Fleetingly, I thought of Davy. And thrust the thought away.

"Okay, phone Mona Lang. She's one of my professors. Please."

The other cop must have climbed into the driver's seat without my noticing, because we were already underway. Another night ride, but so different from the one I remembered. The chiaroscuro of city lights was harsh and irritating, and the cop talk sounded totally alien. They might as well have been ant beings from Planet Blorg, taking me back to the mother ship to do experiments on me.

Halfway to downtown, I put my hand up to my right ear and felt no earring there. It must have fallen off when I was pushing my way through the shrubbery. "Oh shit!" I said.

"Excuse me?" The cop half turned toward me. I could see his bristly eyelashes again, and his left ear.

"I've lost my sun."

"I'm sorry—You lost me on that one."

"My earring. See, I've still got the moon, but the sun is gone. It must have fallen off back there, at the house."

"That's unfortunate."

I curled myself into a ball and tried to pretend I didn't exist.

19

Even mere delusion is a boon to me.

2008

In the second half of February, winter twitches in its sleep, turns over, and begins to dream of spring. After yet another weather system passes over the coast, dumping rain, comes a day of clear, mild weather. The sky is a tender blue, the sun is actually warm, bringing crocuses and the earliest daffodils into bloom. This is when coastal dwellers hasten to inform friends and relatives elsewhere in the country that it's twelve degrees outside and flowers are blooming. No, they emphasize, twelve *above*. They just cut the grass and are heading out for a round of golf—wearing shorts.

It's only five weeks to the vernal equinox. Sunrise is thirty minutes earlier than it was at the solstice, and sunset thirty minutes later. Because the trees are bare and will be for another three months, the growing light seems more intense than at any other time of year. Most people respond to it with unconscious gladness. A few, however, find it harsh and oppressive. Spring is not always happy, just as birth is not always easy.

Ilona gives in to a new compulsion to put things in order, to clear away excess, to clean. After months of indifference, such considerations assume a new importance. She is preparing for something, clearing for action, but she doesn't know exactly what the action will be. Whether she ever finds Davy (and increasingly, she feels him coming closer; almost every night she hears his harmonica from the edge of sleep), or whether the police will find a reason to track her down again, take her downtown, and (this time) not let her go. Or maybe one day will be *the* day, and she will set out on the longest of long walks.

Better make it soon, then, Sweetie, before it gets too warm.

Maybe this means she is finally embracing change, taking responsibility, dealing with it, reaching a state of acceptance, owning her stuff, sucking it up. She is still unemployed, and with her present attitude, unemployable. She is poor and getting poorer by the day. Soon she will have to give up her home. But she has to finish falling down before she can begin to pick herself up.

Maybe. In any case, Ilona cleans and sorts, dusts and wipes, vacuums and polishes. She defrosts the fridge and throws out all the spoiled food. She cleans the oven. On Garbage Eve, she puts all the papers, magazines and mail, opened and unopened, into her neighbours' recycle bins. She bags up all her career woman clothes and puts them into Salvation Army and Goodwill boxes. The useable things she has no more use for—electric can opener, chafing dish, rice cooker, television—she takes out by night to streets remote from hers and leaves them on boulevards with signs attached. "Free. Help yourself." Windfalls for strangers. She dusts her books and arranges them neatly on their shelves. She washes curtains, shakes mats, fluffs cushions. When she finishes with a room, it looks neat and spare, no longer lived in. Perfect.

On one of the sunny days of faux spring, Ilona goes out to her patio garden. She hasn't paid it any attention since last fall, except for checking for signs of Davy's presence. The narrow beds are full of dead petunias and marigolds. Each pot contains a drooping, desiccated plant corpse, and some have fallen over. Dead leaves are piled in brown drifts under the bench, between the pots and against the fence. Ilona stands just outside the patio door, blinking. The bright sunlight makes the scene especially dismal.

She goes back inside and returns with a pair of sunglasses and a couple of garbage bags. Her gardening gloves are still in the outdoor storage box, along with shears and other hand tools. She puts on the gloves and pulls up dead plants, stuffing them into the garbage bags. She rakes up the dead leaves, except the ones that are rotten and crumbly; she lets those lie on the soil, but removes the curled up dry ones that will not stay put.

Under the leaves are crocus buds, already hinting at their individual colours—yellow, purple and white. Daffodils and tulips are sprouting too. She had forgotten about them last fall and hadn't applied their dose of fertilizer, but here they are anyway, preparing to bloom. They don't know any better.

Next, Ilona deals with the pots. She dumps them out and levels the soil onto the beds, treating it like mulch. She hoses out the pots and stacks them neatly near the bench.

When all is done, Ilona sits on the bench admiring the results of her work. The clusters of bulb foliage stand out against the freshly disturbed earth. The dead things are gone and the little garden awaits spring and new growth.

Ilona wonders what the new occupant will choose to plant.

She goes back inside, washes her hands and walks through her bare, tidy rooms, imagines an echo, imagines how she might have gone on living here, changes she might have made—new colours, cushions, curtains. How the lamps might have shone out a brighter light.

Ilona shakes her head and smiles.

• • • •

1988

They actually did put me in a cell, but didn't lock the door. I guess it wasn't a very busy night. A female cop came and asked me questions, some of them the same as those the other cop had asked me. They must have thought that being interrogated by a woman would make me relaxed and cooperative, but they were wrong. I didn't like the look of her at all—tough and mean. Police uniforms never look right on women.

My main objective was to get out of there, so I took pains to explain that Mona Lang was a professor at the university (never mind that she was only an instructor, still working on her PhD). They wouldn't let me phone her myself, and before they agreed to do it, I had to give them my name.

They left me alone then, for quite a while, and this time they did lock the door. I suppose someone had to find Lang's phone number and follow all sorts of procedures before they actually made the call. I sat on the bunk and wondered if I was going to end up staying there all night. What if Lang had an unlisted number, or wasn't home? What if they phoned my parents after all? No, they couldn't—there were too many Millers in the book, and I hadn't told them my father's name, or where he lived.

After two hours, maybe more, the woman cop came in and told me my friend was waiting for me outside. That was all—they just let me go. I didn't even have to sign anything. (But someone did notify the university administration that I had been picked up and questioned, and those good people did have my parents' number.)

Mona Lang got up from a chair in the waiting area as the cop and I came out of the corridor that led to the holding cells. In sweat pants and a denim jacket, her hair bunched into a loose ponytail, she looked like a student. She also looked less than delighted to be in a police station after midnight. I was beginning to think I'd made yet another mistake.

"My car's around the corner," Lang said when we were out on the street. We walked along without talking, our footsteps loud on the pavement. At least, mine were loud; she was wearing running shoes.

"It's really good of you to do this," I said. Better get it over with. Grateful but not abject, that's the way. "Thanks a lot."

"It's okay, Ilona." She unlocked the passenger side of her car, an old Celica, and I got in. It took me a while to do up the seatbelt. By the time I got it we were under way.

"You live on campus, right?" Lang asked. Without giving me a chance to reply, she went on. "How about if we stop at my place for a cup of tea or something? You look cold."

I was surprised. "Sure, that would be great, if it's not too much trouble. I've been enough of a nuisance already."

"I think we need to talk." She kept her eyes on the road while she spoke.

"I guess so," I said. Talk about what? Of course I owed her an explanation for tonight. Then I thought of something else. "Have you had a chance to read my manuscript?"

I had given Lang a copy of my paper the last time I'd been to class, ostensibly so she could give me some direction. In fact, though, I was sure she would tell me I had already exceeded her expectations for a student paper. I had envisioned a cozy get-together, at a coffee shop maybe, where she would tell me I really should submit it for publication somewhere. Maybe that was what she had in mind.

"Yes, I've read it," she said, "and I do want to talk with you about it, among other things. I think it's time for that." She sounded serious. Again, I wondered if getting the police to phone her had been a bad idea. I didn't say any more, and neither did she.

Mona Lang lived in one side of a duplex about halfway between downtown and the campus. The house was old enough to have "character," with its wide window sills, hardwood floors, and hot water radiators. The living room was full of plants, books, overstuffed sofa, mismatched armchairs and a Persian-style rug. She waved me to a chair and excused herself. I heard kitchen sounds—clinks of china and metal, water running, and also a murmur of voices. Of course, Mona had a Significant Other. I remembered a rumour that he was a doctoral student in astrophysics. Or maybe just regular physics. I wondered if she would trot him out and introduce us, but she didn't.

"Coffee or tea?" she asked, leaning through the doorway. "I've put the kettle on for tea, but I can make coffee if you like."

"Tea will be fine," I said.

I looked around the room. Anything to keep my mind busy, so I wouldn't start thinking about how I got here. I felt like I was crossing a river on ice that wasn't quite thick enough. If I was careful and lucky, I'd make it across, but one false step would mean disaster.

Lang came back with a loaded tray—teapot, mugs, milk, sugar, spoons, napkins, even a plate with some Digestives. Everything you need for a session of Girl Talk.

I could tell her heart wasn't in it, though. She was trying to delay the evil moment by making a production of pouring the tea and fussing with the napkins. It was that bad, then. She hadn't said a word, and already the ice was cracking under me.

"Ilona," she said, when each of us had a steaming mug in front of us, "I'm not sure where to start." She thought for a moment. "I think you might... need some help."

Was that all? "I guess I do, all right," I said, relieved. "Thanks for coming to the police station. I just couldn't think of anyone else. It was such a silly thing, really—"

She held up her hand. "I didn't mean tonight. I think you may need professional help. Counselling, or... therapy."

"What are you talking about?" My stomach, which had relaxed since we left the police station, instantly knotted up again.

"Ilona, I've read your paper," Lang said, slowly. "It confirmed some... thoughts I've had since Christmas time. Your class attendance lately has been spotty and—"

"Just because I've missed some classes you think I need 'help?' Counselling? I don't get it, Ms. Lang."

"It's not just that. Hear me out, please. Erratic attendance, bizarre behaviour and an irrational paper. And tonight an encounter with the police. How about if you tell me about that first?"

I was still stuck on "irrational paper." "Irrational? How can you say that? What's irrational about it? It's a—"

"Ilona—wait. One thing at a time. Take a deep breath. Drink some tea. Then tell me what happened tonight. Just do that. Then we'll deal with the other things."

I felt a spurt of resentment. Who did she think she was, telling me to take a breath? But my mouth had gone dry and a sip of tea was welcome.

Lang was talking again. "Maybe 'irrational' isn't the right word. But what you've written isn't at all what I assigned. It's not an examination of social and cultural trends in 19th century Germany, but a kind of stream-of-consciousness fictional work. At least, most of it is. You started out well, but then something happened."

Well, she got that part right. Something did happen. "You said something about bizarre behaviour."

"Ah." She looked at the tea in her cup as though she expected to find an answer floating in it. "I have to say, this is all second hand. Some people from the class told me things."

My mind was racing. "Let me guess—one of them was Goody—Gudrun Appelt. And Libby Boyd. Am I right?"

She put the mug down and looked at me. Forced herself to look at me. "Well, you're not wrong. There was a party, wasn't there? Before Christmas."

"Yes, at Libby's place. I was there. But that's not where it happened."

"Not where what happened? Suppose you tell me your version."

"My version? Am I on trial here, or what? Okay, I went to the party and had a pretty good time. I probably drank a bit too much, but I wasn't the only one. I... met someone. He drove me home. And Harold Neville too. We dropped him off in the West End. After that—well, that's my private business." I felt a smile trying to start, and suppressed it.

Lang frowned, picked up her tea and drank. "Someone drove you and Harold home, you say. A man, is that right?"

"That's right." I heard a door shut somewhere in the apartment, and water running.

"That's not the way Gudrun and Libby remembered it. According to them, you were pretty quiet at the party—at first. Then you probably had quite a lot to drink and maybe some sort of drug too, because after an hour or so you became very... uninhibited. You approached several men in a sexual way. 'Came on to them big time' is how Gudrun described it. At least one of them accepted your overtures. At any rate, you and he spent some time in one of the bedrooms. The man was seen leaving the house, but you didn't come out of the bedroom. Eventually, Libby and Gudrun went looking for you. You were groggy and argumentative, but seemed otherwise all right, so Gudrun offered to take you home. Harold went along to help. You seemed more or less okay in the car, so Gudrun drove Harold home first, since he lives in the West End, I gather. Once the two of you were alone, though, you began acting in a way that indicated you were disoriented, maybe even hallucinating. You didn't seem to recognize her, for one thing, and you were singing in German, or maybe trying to get her to sing. It was hard to tell, because you were babbling incoherently. She didn't think going back to the party was a good idea, but she didn't want to leave you alone either. Also, she didn't know exactly where you lived and you weren't coherent, so she took you to her place."

"To... her... place." The ice cracked wide open, revealing black water.

"Yes. She lives in a suite in her parents' house in Shaughnessy. She tried to get you to lie down on her bed to sleep it off, but you... reacted as if to a sexual overture. She found that quite uncomfortable."

I was alone now, on my little ice floe. I didn't think I could speak, so I just nodded.

"In the end, she just left you there, on the bed. Eventually you went to sleep or passed out. She was afraid to leave you alone, so she sat with you for a while. You seemed quite agitated at times. Gudrun said you kept repeating someone's name."

Julian. Julian. Julian.

There was a little picture on the wall opposite me—a pretty Japanese scene of a bridge over a pond, a willow tree, a little house with a dainty lady in the doorway, welcoming a man. Were those water lilies on the pond, or birds? Lilies or ducks? I almost asked Lang, but then I remembered I couldn't talk, and why.

"So tonight," she was saying, "I gathered from the police that you'd been caught trespassing, somewhere in Shaughnessy. They said the property belonged to a Mr. Appelt."

So Mr. Flashlight was Goody's dad. It was his house, her apartment.

I had to get out of this. The less said, the better. Get the brain in gear. Drink some tea. Clear the throat. Find the voice. Talk.

"Ah, tonight was a big mistake. I went to see Goody to... explain about some of that other stuff. I guess I... had a sort of panic attack, and set off their security system. Then, when everyone came running out, and the dog was barking, and the police came, I didn't know what to say. It was such a disaster. I felt so stupid." I rubbed my hand over my face. "Look, Ms. Lang, I think I'd better go home now. Yeah, I've been under a lot of stress lately, and it probably wouldn't hurt to see someone, a counsellor, I mean. Thanks for putting up with me."

I could see she was relieved to be on familiar territory—grateful student thanks wise teacher for good advice. "That's okay, Ilona. I admit I've been concerned about you, but I wasn't sure what to do. Okay, I'll drive you home now."

I found my shoes and coat and put them on. Lang went off somewhere; I heard her talking and her man answering. "Just a bit longer," she assured him, and joined me in the hallway, putting on her shoes, shrugging into her jacket, picking up her purse and keys.

"There's one more thing," I said. "I'd like my manuscript back, please."

"Oh—of course. Wait a minute." She rushed off and came back with the familiar manila envelope. She almost said something as she handed it to me, but thought better at the last second.

"Thanks," I said, and tucked the envelope inside my coat.

We didn't talk on the drive to campus, until I directed her to my residence.

Well, I'd made it. But there was one final thing. "He sang to me," I said. "On the way to his place. He sang a song. I remember that."

Lang sighed. "I told you—Gudrun said you asked her to sing. Or maybe you did the singing, I don't know. Look, Ilona, it's been a long night."

"So what did she sing? Did she tell you that?"

"She did. It was 'Scarborough Fair.' Good night, Ilona."

I got out of the car. She put it in reverse, backed, turned, and drove off.

On the way from Lang's place, I had surreptitiously taken the moon earring from my left ear and put it in my coat pocket. Now my fingers found it there, squeezed it, crushing the points of the crescent hard into my palm.

20

Yet I have done no wrong,
That I should shun mankind.

2008

In late February, after several mild, sunny days, clouds and cold air return. The temperature falls and refuses to rise. The sky acquires the leaden quality that presages snow. When a moisture-laden weather system meets cold air yet again, it snows, even on the lowlands, even in February, even on the fragile blossoms.

Never mind, crocuses and daffodils, just because you've shown your pretty faces, that doesn't mean it's spring!

Ilona, worn out from her frenzy of cleaning and tidying, sleeps for a day and a night. When she gets up, she goes outside and looks southward at the mountain range across the strait. It's white with snow, the peaks icy and unreal against the pale blue sky. In the hills to the west of the city there is probably snow as well. Snow and cold. If she is to make her winter journey, it won't be on paper this time, but in reality, writing it with her feet in the snow, seeking the hidden paths that other travellers ignore.

But first, a shorter trip. She goes back inside, seeks for and finds a long-unused key, and proceeds to the storage area in the unfinished part of the basement. She moves several boxes and a bicycle someone has parked in front of the bank of locked closets assigned to each apartment. Hers has "#3" written on it in black felt pen. She wrestles briefly with the padlock, removes it, and opens the door.

There isn't much inside the narrow space—the empty boxes her TV and computer had come in, a broken toaster oven she'd stashed in here instead of throwing it out. And at the very back, the thing she has come for. The Box.

When she moved into her apartment, at the start of her new life, three and a half years ago, she put the box in here before she unpacked anything. This was the perfect place for it, outside of her living space, inconvenient, forgettable. She had carried the box here, deposited it at the very back of the closet, shut and locked the door. Leaning against the door for a moment, she appreciated its solidity and relished her victory. Then she went into the apartment to set up her new home.

But now it's time to bring out the box, to open it, to look inside. Ilona moves the empty TV and computer boxes, pushes aside the dead toaster oven with her foot, bends over and slides her hands under the box. It's heavier than she remembers. "Lift with your legs, not with your back," she mutters. There is a faint snapping sound as she straightens up and pulls it out of its bed of cobwebs. "Wouldn't it be just my luck, to get bitten by a black widow spider at this stage of the game?" She laughs.

She backs out of the closet, puts the box down, tosses the other boxes back in, and closes the door without bothering to lock it. Then she picks up the box again and carries it for the first time into her home.

There is an order to be observed. Ilona sets the box on the coffee table. She goes to the kitchen and finds the bottle of wine purchased for this occasion. Glass. Corkscrew. Remove cork, pour. All set.

Back in the living room, she places the glass on a side table and unpicks the knot in the cord which holds the box closed. Who tied that knot? It must have been her mother or father. Her Dad, probably. The cord was wrapped twice over and once around the box, neatly lashed to encircle and enclose it, keeping it shut and its contents safe. He'd packed away his daughter's things so they would be there when she needed them again.

"Except you never thought it would be twenty years, did you, Dad? Or that you'd be long dead by then."

The rope falls away. Ilona folds back the flaps of the lid. Underneath are layers of newspaper from February of 1988. Pakistan

Says Russian Withdrawal from Afghanistan Premature, Al Gore Hoping to Win Super Tuesday, Pat Robertson Speaks Out on Swaggart Scandal, Russians Beat Canada 5-0. The smell of stilled time wafts out, of paper decomposing, of cellars, of graves. She lifts the newspaper and sees a blue notebook cover. On it, her own printing. "ED 405."

She nearly shuts the box, but makes herself pick up the notebook. Under it is a red one, ED 410. Then a yellow one labelled ED 351. And under that one, a dark green cover (she had totally forgotten it was green) that brings a lurch to her stomach. This one's label is longer. "German Romanticism."

Gingerly, she picks it up, holds it for a moment, opens it. Her handwriting again, a scribble, "reaction ag. the rise of the bourgeoisie wh. was seen as stifling individual expression. Lang thinks conservatism inevitable in times of war or political unrest."

Time echoes and clangs. Twenty years ago or yesterday? Ilona closes the green notebook and lays it on top of the others she has removed. The next thing in the box is a manila envelope, slightly creased, its corners bent and turned up like the toes of old shoes. Faint discolourations, as of old water stains. There is no writing on it, but she knows it as she knows her own hand.

She picks it up and lets it lie on her lap while she stares into the box. Removing the envelope has revealed the textbooks which form the bottom layer of its contents. On top of them are three compact discs in their brittle, shiny cases: *Lieder. Die Schöne Müllerin. Winterreise.* Recordings of songs by Franz Schubert, sung by Julian Northridge. His face looks out from the box, multiplied by three. That face, that voice, those songs. Here they are, again, at last.

I wonder what happened to Davy's CD player?

But that doesn't matter, because she has her own CD player now, part of the appliances and amenities she bought three years ago to furnish her new home. Even though she got rid of her microwave and crock pot in preparation for her journey, she kept the mini stereo system. For just this moment.

Ilona reaches through the mist of tears that blurs her vision. *Winterreise.* The case opens easily; the shiny disc is cradled safely inside. Press the button to open the drawer, place the disc inside. Close the drawer. She pulls in a long, painful breath, presses the button with the triangle, exhales slowly.

Grave, deliberate notes on a piano, and then the voice, the one true voice, coincident with her outgoing breath. A stranger I came, a stranger I depart.

• • • •

1988

Mona Lang betrayed me, of course. I knew she would, by the way she waffled when I asked her to keep my encounter with the police to herself. (But Goody Appelt was right there when they picked me up, wasn't she, so how secret could it be?) Maybe Lang thought she was doing me a favour. She did give me a passing grade in the course, even though I never attended another class or finished the paper she had handed back to me that night.

She must have had second thoughts after she drove me home. I guess my demeanour didn't reassure her. "She's a seriously disturbed young woman," I imagined her saying to her man the next morning over breakfast. (Breakfast—coffee freshly ground and freshly brewed, drunk from bowls, with plenty of hot milk. Croissants from that great little bakery around the corner. Real orange juice in matching glasses. Mr. Astrophysicist nodding as Mona tells him about her problem student.) In the end, she must have convinced herself that contacting my parents was the Right Thing To Do. Or maybe she had to make some sort of report to the university administration and they did the contacting. It didn't help that I had done poorly on my Christmas exams and abandoned my Education classes.

Mom and Dad arrived at suppertime the following day. I had just emerged from the shower and was totally shocked to meet them in the hallway. I was even more shocked when my mother clutched me to herself, and then held me away and studied my face, her own all furrowed with concern, that worried-Mom look in her eyes. It was just like a bad movie. "They told us you had done something that involved the police. Are you all right?" Even that time-worn, stupid question. I wondered just how she had expected to find me—catatonic? In a straitjacket? Raving incoherently? Dad hovered behind her, looking uncomfortable, a cardboard box in his arms.

"What're you guys doing here?" *Shit.* I'd been planning to spend the rest of the night writing. I was glad to have my manuscript back. Now that it didn't have to be an academic paper, I was going to rewrite it without all the scholarly crap.

She ignored my question. "Where's your room? Let's go and get your things packed up. I've made an appointment for you the day after tomorrow. I was lucky to get it; he had a cancellation. Come on, don't just stand there!"

I should have resisted. Right there in the hallway, in my bathrobe, with my hair wrapped in a towel and people coming back from supper. I should have told them to go home and stop bothering me, that it was my life and I was living it the way it had to be lived.

But I didn't. I guess I thought it would be better to deal with them in private. I didn't realize that in public, where I could embarrass her, I had the edge. Once we were in my room, it was game over.

Mom started pulling stuff out of the drawers and finding my suitcases. Dad put my books into the box he'd brought. (Funny, when I first saw him standing there holding it, I thought he was bringing me an early birthday present. My very own CD player, maybe.)

It's not worth describing how we got from Point A, which was my residence room, to Point B, which was my parents' truck, to point C, which was the old home place. All that was by the by; what was really important was Point X, which was the psychiatrist's office, Point Y, which was the psychiatric facility where I spent that spring and most of the summer, and Point Z, which was the rest of my life.

That spring I wore sunglasses whenever I went outside. The light was intolerable, harsh, uncouth, needle-like, whether hazing a dusty window or jabbing laser-like into my eyes from chrome bumpers and trim on cars, or glassware and cutlery on a table. After the darkness of the lost winter, I felt as though I had been plucked and shucked. Day after day of bright blue skies, shot with that intense and hostile light. When clouds came, they were thin and high, diffusing rather than blocking it.

My desires were reduced to this: a dark room and sleep. I wanted to sleep and sleep. And to dream my own dreams.

Instead, I went with Mom (and sometimes with Dad) to endless appointments with a variety of "mental health professionals"—counsellors, psychiatrists, psychologists, maybe some others as well. I could never keep them straight. They did tests, the usual ones involving body fluids, but also tests of my perceptions, reflexes, mental functions, and pattern recognition abilities. I free-associated to beat the band. I answered all sorts of stupid questions.

Like this:

Q. Ms. Miller, how do you feel about yourself?

A. I don't. I mean, I don't think about that a lot.

Q. Well, let's get more specific, then. How do you feel about the past year?

A. Not so great, I guess.

Q. Why do you feel that way?

A. Because I didn't finish. I didn't finish my paper, I mean.

Q. Your paper. But surely there was more than one paper or project you left unfinished. Not to mention your final exams. You would have graduated this year, wouldn't you?

A. Yes.

Q. I'm curious about this paper you regret not finishing. Tell me more about it, please.

A. What's to tell? It was about Romanticism.

Q. But you were an Education major.

A. So what?

And so on, ad nauseam.

Another session:

Q. Ms. Miller, tell me about Julian Barker.

A. Harker. Maybe.

Q. Pardon me?

A. The name was Harker. Maybe.

Q. You're not sure?

A. Not entirely. But it doesn't matter.

Q. Why not?

A. It just doesn't.

Q. Describe him please.

A. Oh—he's gorgeous—black hair, grey eyes. And an earring. But he gets thinner and thinner, wandering around in the snow, sleeping in barns, not eating properly. Is that what you meant?

Q. Not exactly. That seems to be a different individual.

A. Well, it isn't. And how would you know anyway?

Q. Tell me about the man you had sex with after the party in December.

A. What do you want to know about him?

Q. His appearance and demeanour.

A. I've already told you—black hair, earring, tall, elegant. Gorgeous.

Q. All right, so who was wandering in the snow?

A. The stranger. He went crazy, you know—saw three suns in the sky. Delusional, obviously.

Q. You seem to be describing an imaginary character. Was he the man you were looking for the night you broke into Gudrun Appelt's house? Was he an illusion?

A. I didn't break in.

Q. All right. But you were looking for Julian Harker?

A. Barker. Maybe.

Q. Whatever. You were looking for him that night?

A. Yes.

Q. Tell me about him, please.

A. What do you want to know?

Q. What kind of person is he?

A. I have no idea.

(A sigh here, I'm sure.)

Q. Well, what does he look like?

A. Like an English schoolboy. All grown up, though.

Q. With black hair?

A. No, not at all. Light brown, I think. Blondish brown.

Q. No earring?

A. No earring.

Q. Anything else?

A. His voice is like water. Clear, you know. But like steel too—precise and controlled, like a fine instrument. Each song was finely crafted, a perfect miniature.

Q. Hold on, please, Ilona. This is yet another man you're describing, isn't it?

A. No, not at all.

You get the idea. I don't think they ever did. In the end, after I tried to run away several times, there was only one thing for them to do. I ended up in the Pine Valley Psychiatric Centre. There I learned (among other things) that ammonia smells like tears. And vice versa.

21

Are all the rooms in this house taken?

NOW I AM FINALLY READY. I have picked out the things I really need for the last walk. Everything else I have stripped away, thrown away, given away, or will simply abandon when I leave.

The days are longer now, which means the nights are shorter. There will be less time to learn the lessons. If I wait another month there will be more day than night and it will be warmer. Tempting, but if there's one thing I've learned, it's to avoid the obvious, easy choice. The hidden paths are steep and rocky. If the wilderness is my place, I must go there sooner rather than later.

I have spent the past two days looking through the box of relics and memories, listening, thinking, remembering, wondering. Now I am ready to close it, but first I must make a final accounting. In a way, I must finish that paper I wrote for Mona Lang's class, twenty years ago. Because now I realize something I didn't know then—the paper wasn't about German Romanticism at all. It was about me. I think if I had realized that at the time, things would have turned out differently.

If I let myself, I would blame my parents for the way I turned out. Or my teachers. But maybe they really couldn't see it. They didn't know who I was. The trouble with being abnormal in a way that isn't visible is that people assume you're normal and keep encouraging you into instances of failure. Even when you psych yourself up and tell someone in authority—a parent, a teacher—that you really can't do certain things, they don't believe you. You get the words out, you're anticipating the sweet relief of being off the hook at last, and what do they say? "Come on—try it! Try just one more time! Acts of courage have power. Every time you try, it'll get easier."

Ha.

In the end, you have only two options—fake it and fail, or rip off the mask and fall apart. That's what I finally did in the winter of 1987 and 1988.

My mother tried to fix me—oh Lord, she tried! She wanted to turn me into something safe, a woman who could always get a job, but a job that could be set aside when the babies came. She wanted me to marry a nice guy, settle down within visiting distance, and have those babies. She thought her efforts had paid off when I went into my final year of Education, especially when she heard that Davy and I were "going together." Degree. Job. Husband. Babies. Then maybe job again, to fill the empty hours. That was the program.

But I failed her. And really, she must have been half-expecting I would, ever since kindergarten and elementary school, where it first became evident that I had trouble fitting in. Maybe it was when she had to spend hours explaining to me why I had to go somewhere else for hours each day and be with people I didn't want to be with, doing things I didn't want to do. Or all those report cards with remarks like "Poor social skills" or "Reluctant to participate in team activities." Maybe it was all those times I'd run away and hide when they had company for dinner, instead of staying around and listening to stupid comments about what a big girl I was getting to be. Then there was the summer she registered me for summer camp, except she had to come and un-register me when they phoned and told her I tried to sleep in a tree instead of in the cabin with the other girls. And how I ran off to the woods instead of participating in organized activities. Didn't Mom realize what a betrayal that was, to send me away to strangers in summer? Summer was my happy time. Didn't she know that?

So maybe it shouldn't have been a surprise to her that I had a breakdown in my final year of university, just months before graduation. As though she'd been waiting for just such an event, my mother went into overdrive, dealing with the emergency. I would be fixed, even if it killed her. When I refused to cooperate with the doctors and counsellors she made me see, she kept looking until she found one who put me into the Pine Valley Psychiatric Centre for six months.

My parents drove me there on an April day, the first really warm day of spring. Winter was gone. New grass, indecently green, was pushing up through the old dead stuff and a mild breeze was blowing. Everything was bright and sparkling and stinging and painful. I wore my darkest sunglasses and a hat and still felt like a bug under a magnifying glass.

My father was worried about me, but I guess he didn't know what to do, so he went along with my mother and Dr. Polansky. While I was being admitted to the Centre, I could tell how uncomfortable he was by the way he kept looking around for the exit, shuffling his feet and fiddling with his cap (the blue one with "Buckerfield's" embroidered on it in red). But once I was checked in and assigned a bed, he couldn't seem to make himself leave. It was Mom who gave me a big, brave smile and said to Dad, "Well, honey, we'd better get going."

The Centre had routines. Every hour was scheduled. Maybe that was part of the therapy. Or maybe it was only to make things easier for the staff. Whatever the reason, it did make things easier for me. Once I realized I would have only specific hours for "therapeutic interaction," I knew when I had to nerve myself up to resist. The rest of the time was kind of like school—high school, that is. In that context I knew how to act the part of a Good Girl. I was on time for meals and activities, didn't do anything embarrassing (or revealing), replied when spoken to, and tried not to attract attention.

There are two things about the Centre I remember with pleasure. Two good memories: the laundry room and the "unstructured hour" every evening from eight to nine. The laundry was mostly automated, but some of us were given jobs folding sheets and towels and putting them on carts for delivery to the residential floors. The subterranean seclusion of the place, its cleanliness and warmth, were reassuring, and the precise, almost ceremonial movements were somehow calming.

Except for that ammonia smell. Memories, memories, memories of meeting myself in a haze of ammonia... or tears?

The unstructured hour was intended to promote socializing among the patients (or inmates, which was how I thought of myself). That was a joke, because it's hard to socialize with people who are lost inside themselves or dulled by "meds." Some watched television, or, to put it more accurately, fought over the remote control. Others wandered around the grounds. I would rather have slept, but we weren't allowed to do that except between 10 p.m. and 7 a.m. So I went to the so-called library and pretended to read.

They wouldn't let us bring our own books. Not me, anyway, but maybe I was a special case. No books, no writing materials and definitely no music of any kind. There was only a limited selection of reading material in the "library"—the National Geographic, a few news magazines, and the usual house and beauty stuff.

I selected a magazine and curled up in a chair near a window. Then, magazine strategically positioned, I closed my eyes and went inside myself. There was a little door, and I could almost always find it. I was not sleeping—I really was a Good Girl and followed the rules.

The sun through the west-facing window fell on my face. This was the only time that summer I enjoyed it. It was going down and soon would be gone, the harshness leaching away as the light became a rich gold. I leaned back and closed my eyes, turning the light into something else. Strained through the skin and blood vessels of my eyelids, it became an intense, glowing red. Then fuchsia, dark blue, tender turquoise, emerald, yellow, and orange. I amused myself by trying to induce these colour changes, but I could never figure out whether I really controlled them or if they just happened, moving through the spectrum by some unknown process.

Inside my closed eyes, the after-images of sunlight passing through the venetian blinds were like x-rays of ribcages, cheerful and sinister at the same time—broken black lines against blobs of vivid colour. I played with them, making them appear and disappear, trying to create skull-shapes above them, but without success.

Only I could see these things. They were hidden inside me. No one asked me about them and I didn't tell. I could while away the hour by experimenting with the after-images, making them longer or shorter, watching the shapes and colours change as the sun set and the light faded.

There were other diversions. I explored the geography of my teeth with my tongue, counting them, one side and then the other, uppers and lowers, pleased when they added up to the right number. I got to know each one individually, all the peaks and valleys, bumps and edges. I discovered that an interesting, metallic-tasting pain could be evoked by pressing certain spots on my gums with a fingernail. And I could nibble delicately on the insides of my cheeks, taking tiny bites of my own flesh without pain or apparent damage—a secret self-mutilation.

Another of my secrets was that sometimes I could still hear his voice. They might have confiscated my CDs and Davy's player, but they couldn't take the music out of my head. Sometimes, during those sun-shot hours in the library, it came back to me, not the whole cycle, but fragments. I never knew which of the songs would emerge from wherever they lived in my mind, but I always welcomed them. It was almost as though he came to visit me, to tell me he was still out there, in the winter country.

Then Dr. Polansky decided to try drug therapy. After that, I joined the rest of them in the TV room and watched the images on the screen flicker and dance.

Once my "meds" were worked out and I had "stabilized," I was released into my parents' care. Nice and neat. Except that the following winter my Dad died of a heart attack.

Well—enough of this chewing over of the past. As so many helpful people have told me, we must be proactive and move forward. So I'll say "*Gute Nacht*" to the past and think about the future. My future. Ha-ha.

In a short time, I will be leaving my apartment. I've thought about staying on even after I can no longer pay the rent, but what would that get me? Only the unwelcome attentions of the landlord and his hired guns—the rental agency, the collection agency, finally, the police. Or I suppose I could appeal to some social service agency and make myself into a "case," complete with "caseworker."

No thanks.

So what do I want? I have been considering my options. Just for laughs, tonight I've come to visit this cemetery by the sea. It's a nice piece of real estate, you have to admit. Of course, at night one cannot fully appreciate the view, but then, neither can the residents, so my experience is quite authentic.

Have I seen any ghosts? Only my personal ones. My mother, for example. After Dad died, she changed from a capable (if limited) middle-aged woman to an old, fear-ridden one. She never said so, but I know she blamed me for his death. The stress and shame of having a crazy daughter, added to the inevitable stresses of farming, did him in and turned her into a grieving widow. She sold up and moved to a little house in town, taking her daughter with her. Her crazy daughter, stabilized on "meds," who needed to live at home indefinitely. No telling what she might do if she was allowed to be on her own again.

Eventually, it was hard to tell who was looking after whom. In spring I got a job at Tim Lee's mushroom farm, and worked there for a few years. I liked that it was dim and out of sight. The other workers were mostly immigrants from different parts of Asia, without much English. That was fine with me; between "Hello" and "Bye-bye," they talked among themselves in their native tongues and left me alone. Eventually, I found it was safe to move out into the open again and worked on various farms, setting out broccoli and cabbage plants in spring, picking strawberries, raspberries, and blueberries in summer, pumpkins and those same cabbages in fall, following the circle of the year. It was hard work, but the repetitiveness was reassuring. It had a rhythm. My body worked and my mind rested in its cave.

My mother got a part-time job at Larry McKee's drugstore. She went there a lot, to buy my meds, and they struck up a friendship of sorts. She also did a little bookkeeping for a few small businesses. We lived quietly, as they say. After a few years I began to look like a younger version of her. Strangers who saw us on the street or in the grocery store probably thought we were a couple of funny old sisters.

Nearly seventeen years of that, can you believe it?

That brings us here, to this cemetery. It's as good a place as any, and better than many. Not that I'm thinking in practical terms, you understand. More the symbolic. Just about all the plots here are spoken for, anyway. Owned by their potential occupants, like those houses in the Uplands, with their gates and alarm systems. I would be trespassing and would have to be removed, like I was from Goody's house. I'd be "taken downtown" again too, and put through various "processes," no doubt. They won't drop me into a hole right where I lie, that's certain. But with luck, they'll never find me. I'll disappear, like Davy.

Joking aside, if I'm going to do it the way I want to, I'd better do it soon. Spring isn't here yet, but it's coming. And I'm not yet inured to going without things like hot water on tap, central heating and shelter from the storm. Hypothermia, they say, is possible almost any time of year, given the right conditions. But I'll bet those conditions are more likely to occur in February than, say, July. I don't want to have to mess with sleeping pills or firearms and I'm too much of a coward to do the big jump from a high place, or the little jump with a noose around my neck. The idea of thrashing around in deep water or on the end of a rope, witnessing the involuntary death-struggle of my body, fills me with horror. Sliding into a cold-induced sleep that lasts forever, that's my idea of a good final exit—relatively easy, painless, and dignified.

But why should I care about dignity any more? I've lost my job, my veneer, and what few "people-skills" I've ever had. I'm about to lose this little hole in the wall. I've nearly finished my metamorphosis into a bag lady, or something close—a "funny lady," a "weird woman," a "peculiar old dame." One of those sad beings that wanders around muttering to herself, occasionally raving at an unseen enemy or plucking at invisible slings and arrows. Just about every woman has a secret fear of ending up like that. I used to, and now I've done it. Welcome to my world.

It's pretty nice here in the cemetery. The wind is rising and every now and then the clouds rip open and show the moon, letting loose the *Mondenschatten* to keep me company, a whole revel of them, in fact.

Nearby is a grove of firs. They look fully dressed, compared to the oaks and maples, which are stripped and shivering, jiggling their branches like people too shy to dance, who stand by the wall, shifting from foot to foot. The firs, on the other hand, are dancing. They're right into it, undulating their horizontal black branches, each one moving in its own circle. The effect is one of constant, uneven but rhythmic motion, a self-absorbed, idiosyncratic trance-dance. The firs are oblivious to everything but the wind. They're dancing because they have to.

Oh, you trees, you *Tanne*, let me dance with you! Watching the whipping of your *Wipfel*, I know you are moved only by the blind force of the wind, that makes you gesture and mime. Your message is empty, alien and meaningless, but you go on and on, repeating the same cluster of jerks and shudders—and so will I. I may as well practice now, so eventually I can become what I really am.

I put my arms out, lift and circle, first one and then the other, then both at once. I raise and lower my feet slowly and deliberately, in the grave, steady pace of one with a long road to travel and no end in sight. Turn, step, turn again, raise arm, lower arm, raise the other, bob head, bend at the waist, swing around. That's it, that's it, Ilona, now you're doing it, no longer faking it. Listen to that music in your head, see it in the trees dancing with the wind, dancing to that harmonica someone is playing, far away.

Do it! Do it! Dance with the wind.

22

When my heart speaks in my breast,
I sing loud and happy.
I don't listen to its moans,
Moaning is so foolish.

IT'S COLD ENOUGH TO snow again—what a laugh that is, in late February! Well, who cares—I'll go out into the blizzard if I must, shake off the snow and come up laughing.

I was sprung from the Pine Valley Centre and went home with my Mommy and Daddy. Then Daddy died and Mommy and I went to live in a little house with lace curtains and no way out. Not for me, anyway. I took the pills that kept me a Good Girl, stayed at home and did what Mommy told me to. Mostly.

Seventeen years. My God, how did I endure it? The pills helped, of course. They insulated me nicely from myself and from everything else too. Nothing seemed to matter. I floated in my bubble through the little routines of each day, cooking, eating, washing the same dishes time after time after time—the flowered mugs, the plates with the green and blue stripes, the copper-bottomed pot, the cast iron frying pan. Cleaning the rooms every week, vacuuming the orange shag carpet (replaced in the '90s with a tasteful grey twill), mopping the linoleum, scrubbing the toilet. Trotting off dutifully to whatever job I was doing. One year blended into the next, TV sitcoms came and went, but the routines were the same, the house was the same, my mother and I were the same. Everything else was just beyond my reach. Everything else was what other people did—left home, had careers, travelled, had sex, got married, had babies, got divorced, had affairs, painted pictures, wrote books, took chances. Maybe tomorrow. Maybe never. It was all the same to me.

We never listened to music. There were the ambient TV show themes and commercial jingles. That was all.

Then my mother died. It was sudden. One winter she got sick and ended up in the hospital. She seemed to be getting better, but then she was diagnosed with pancreatic cancer and was dead in less than three months.

It took me longer than that to figure out that I was free. I was like an animal caged for so long it has forgotten the meaning of the open door. Besides, there were all the arrangements to deal with—death certificate, funeral, bank accounts, will. Not that it amounted to much of anything, but it took me a long time to get through it all.

Her death broke the years-long routines, shattered them, in fact. One of them was my pill routine—two in the morning, three in the evening. I forgot one or the other, eventually both. Forgetting became the norm. When everything settled down after the funeral, after all the officials and bank people and lawyers, minister, family friends and relations had done their bits and left the scene, I had time to sit and think.

Think. It's something we do too much or not enough. I had spent seventeen years not thinking, or feeling, for that matter. Now, without mother, routines or meds, my mind lurched into life and began getting ideas.

We don't have to live here, it said. We can go somewhere else and do something else.

I picked the Island because crossing the strait made the break seem more complete. And there was something exotic about the place—the rocky hills, the oak and arbutus trees, the pseudo-Englishness of Victoria—which seemed unique and exclusive. I needed to get away from the flat, mountain-rimmed valley with its ever-expanding network of highways and interchangeable suburbs. I wanted to live in a real place of my own choosing.

The sale of the house paid off my mother's meagre debts and left a little to spare, enough to get me settled in Victoria, in my basement suite (but a *nice* basement suite) on the hill overlooking the city, close to historic mansions and artsy-craftsy charm. I bought everything new to furnish my place, from curtains to linens to cutlery and china. Everything was new. Everything matched. Everything was mine.

I found myself a job, too. Or rather, a series of temporary fill-ins for maternity and other leaves in various offices. Over the next couple of years, I worked my way into a permanent job (or so I thought). The muffled days of pills and sitcoms were over.

Except I had brought some baggage with me, hadn't I? It was the kind of baggage you can't leave behind because it's part of you. Kind of like The Box. It had accompanied me from university to the farmhouse, to my mother's widowhood house. I didn't know what to do with it when I made my break to the Island, so I brought it along. It was, after all, neatly tied, self-contained, anonymous. I had a vague idea of its contents—stuff from before my breakdown. That was enough. I didn't need, or want, to open it.

Oh, now we come to the tricky part, the tricky part, the tricky part! Oh, now we'll have to face the facts, face the facts, face the facts, willy-nilly, yes or no!

What I didn't realize when I started my New Life, was that I was a broken person and always would be. Impaired. Odd. By the standards of this world, anyway. Eventually, it began to show. For instance, people hired about the same time as me were treated better and got ahead faster. All because I wasn't a social butterfly and ass-kisser, schmoozing with the boss, pushing myself forward, exaggerating my importance. It didn't seem to matter that I got the work done better and faster than all those self-promoters. But they got promoted and I didn't. In fact, after a year I began to suspect I had enemies in the office. And I was right, wasn't I?

Is that a rhetorical question, or do you want an answer?

So you're back, my dark sister! And I'll bet you have an answer, even if it is a rhetorical question.

Right you are! So—the reason you lost that job was because they needed to eliminate some positions, because of funding cuts. Downsizing, not firing. Remember, that counsellor told you not to take it personally. But what did you do—took it as personally as you could, that's what.

Okay, Smart-Ass, how can you not take something like that personally? That counsellor was full of shit. Maybe there were funding problems and a position had to be cut. But why did they pick *my* position? Why not Jean's or Charlotte's?

Maybe what they were doing was considered more important. How would they put it? "Crucial to the mission of the department."

Those two did exactly the same work as me, only I did it better. They could have gotten rid of them both and not noticed. No, it was me. They hated me because of what I am, the way I am.

Which is what, dear?

You know.

Maybe, but I want you to say it. In your own words.

I told you already. Broken. Dr. Polansky called it Social Anxiety Disorder, but what did he know? Really, the best thing would be to squash myself up and start all over again, the way I did with plasticine figures when I was a kid. It felt good to decide that some stupid, lumpish little effort just wasn't good enough. Squash, squash, squash in my hands and it was a primal mass again, pure potential. But it's not so easy to do that to yourself.

That's bullshit, Ilona. Sit down and listen to me. You are not broken and you don't need squashing into primal matter. Dr. Polansky and his pills got you onto the wrong track and now that you've had a few problems you're punishing yourself. Don't listen to those old voices. Listen to me instead.

So who are you, that I should listen to you?

I am Winter. I am you. I'm the one who's been there and done that. I know things. I know that you are what you are and shouldn't think you need fixing because someone else doesn't like things you do or say or think. Those people who tried to fix you, all they did was pin a label on you and give you a prescription. And look what that did—shut you up for seventeen years. Talk about being squashed! You're just coming alive now. Stand up straight and give yourself a shake, because there's a lot to do! You're lucky you have me as your *Gefährte*, your travelling companion. Together we'll burrow into the fabric of things, like a worm into an apple, and come up in a better place.

Like dead, you mean?

Maybe. There are no guarantees in real life. But before we're dead, we'll live, and learn a few things. In fact, we've already started doing that.

What sorts of things?

That the world is much larger and darker than most people will ever know. They trot along, happy when it's sunny, complaining when it's not. Don't they realize that the world—the universe, I mean—is mostly darkness? It's what you see when the sun is behind the earth, when you're not deceived by its glare. You see a huge darkness and tiny prickles of light. All those stars, those enormous clouds of pulsating gas, they're just tiny twinkles in the Big Black. Between them is Night, always. And Winter.

Agreed, this knowledge isn't what gets the baby changed and the mortgage paid and the degree earned. People are too preoccupied with their busy little lives to contemplate this stuff. But someone has to do it—astrophysicists, mystics, poets, philosophers (maybe, but they're a mixed lot). And people like us. Our job is to be what we are. You were diverted from that. It's taken you all this time to get back on track.

Get back on track? You're crazy! Here I am, a total failure, planning what might turn out to be my Final Exit, and you call it getting back on track!

Haven't you been listening, little one? Our track—the right one for us—goes through winter darkness, with only a moon-shadow for company. He knew that—little Schubert. That's why he was so taken with Müller's poems. He was positively ecstatic when he found the second batch, the *Winterreise* ones. They were just what he'd been looking for, whether he knew it or not. You've listened, you've read. You should understand by now. You have to go beyond the village. What do you suppose is meant by "*versteckte Stege Durch verschneite Felsenhöhn*" the hidden paths through snowy, rocky heights? You'll just have to get used to them, that's all. Like that crow-feeding woman. She knows them well, I'll bet.

That woman knows Müller and Schubert? I really doubt it!

No, silly! She knows the hidden roads, the night roads. And so will we, eventually, one way or another.

Where do they go, those roads?

I don't know, and I don't think it matters.

But what about the *Wegweiser*, the signpost? It points to "a road from which no man has ever returned." That has to be death.

Of course! But then, you knew that. Everyone goes down that road in the end, even all those nice, happy people.

But *we* see the road and the signpost. They don't.

Exactly. Now, enough of this talk! All you need to do is get going. Bang the door shut behind you and forget the past.

Not all of it, not yet. What about—them? Julian, whoever he was, and Davy. I've found Julian again, part of him, but I've never managed to find Davy, so I could tell him I'm sorry.

Sorry! After all these years! Why bother?

Because he thought I loved him, but I told him to get lost, I didn't need him any more. Not him, just his CD player, so I could listen to Julian Northridge.

Ha-ha! You're telling me you dumped old Davy-boy for Julian Northridge? Wowza! And anyway, Davy was happy to give you the player in exchange for sex.

Put that way, it sounds crude.

It was crude. Admit it.

No, it wasn't. It's more complicated than that. There was that guy I met at Libby's party. I thought his name was Julian. That he was... someone special. But he wasn't. He was just an opportunist. He got lucky that night, and I thought I did, but I was wrong. Davy was real, though, and it looks like he messed up his life after that, because of me.

Hmm. I wouldn't bet on that. Everyone has lots of chances to mess up their life. Don't waste your time on old regrets. Regrets are for losers. You're free now—no Mom, no Dad, no kids, no husband, no boss, no landlord. You can do whatever you want—sing in the park, swear in the street, kick sand on the beach, laugh like a loon, mumble like a pot boiling. Forget regrets!

But it'll be cold. And there are all sorts of people out there—strange people.

You'll be one of them! How much stranger can you get? Come on, stranger! Never mind danger. You're calling the shots now—be bold, put some swagger into it!

Jeez, are you really part of me? Where have you been all this time?

Hiding out, waiting for my moment. It was pretty hard to be myself when you were busy being a Good Girl, studying, writing papers on Curriculum Planning and the standardized test controversy, and even harder when you were doped up and zombie-ing through life. Or even when you were playing Little Miss Office Worker. But first chance I got, I took it, and here I am!

Great, just what I need, an imaginary pal who's a psycho.

Not psycho, if you please. Didn't you learn anything in the Psychiatric Centre? Avoidant, anxious, deluded, depressed, manic and paranoid, maybe. But not psycho. Whatever that means.

23

I saw three suns in the sky.

WHAT WAS THE THING that broke me and destroyed my life? What was it really—the final blow in the winter of 1987-1988? Not the encounter with the police, but the things Mona Lang told me—that the marvellous lover I had found, for whose sake I had dumped Davy—that he was an illusion.

So where did he come from? What was he? Now I can answer this question. I have walked a long road, a cold, dark road, and I know.

Many years ago, when I was about twelve, my parents and I drove to Edmonton for a cousin's wedding. It was February, not the best time for a road trip, but good for us farm folks, because it was the dormant season. I was excused from school for a week, and we went.

Once we left the fog-shrouded familiarity of the Valley, the weather grew colder and brighter, until on the eastern side of the Rocky Mountains, we found the typical prairie cold snap—harsh white and stark blue, with the sun an icy diamond hanging above the southern horizon. On the last morning of our outward trip, we left the motel early and drove out of night into the rising sun, from black to grey to blue to bright. The sun rose before us, flanked by two companions, two lesser suns floating above an iridescent layer of clouds in the pale blue distance.

I was entranced. "Oh look! Three suns! Weird!"

"They're sundogs, Ilona," my Dad explained, smiling. "Reflections of the sun in all those ice crystals up there. It's an optical illusion, that's all."

He explained it and I understood, but the three suns were still magical to me, hanging there in the sky. I wondered if they would rise in formation and set together that afternoon. But after an hour or so the sundogs faded and vanished. We drove into the city under the single, ordinary sun.

This morning I saw them again, rising from the sea. I was walking the beach at dawn, partly because I was hoping to see that woman again—the one who feeds crows and hunts rabbits with a slingshot. I wanted to ask her what she had done before and how she ended up living like that. She wasn't there, though, but the three suns were. The horizon was pale and fuzzy with high, frozen clouds and when the sun rose it had two others with it, just as bright but a little smaller. They looked inexorable, undeniable, but a mystery just the same. Were they angels or emissaries? I stood and stared, wondering if they would strike me blind, remembering.

There were two Julians. One was real, the other not. I suppose that's true, on the surface, but it's just as true that the first one wasn't real and the other most definitely was.

First there was Julian Northridge. Or, to be more precise, there was his voice. I listened to him sing *Winterreise* so many times that in my mind they became one—the poet, the composer, the singer and the man portrayed in the songs.

Chubby little Franz Schubert, with his curly hair and wire-rimmed spectacles, and the urbane Wilhelm Müller, librarian and man of letters, faded into the background. The man they had created with their words and music walked through a winter landscape of my imagination, with each step moving farther away from real, normal life. The only thing the songs tell us about his appearance is that he has black hair. In the fourteenth song, "*Der greise Kopf*," once the frost melts that made his hair look grey, it is black again. So—a dark-haired man. I brooded over that a lot.

Because in another way, he was Julian Northridge, whose voice had sung him to me and created him for me, brought him alive from the marks on paper made by Müller and Schubert. When I listened to his voice, I could see him. Not only the lonely figure on the snowy road, always alone, but the real man, the singer.

All I had was his recorded voice, frozen in time, and in a way, it was enough. Listening as I did, alone, with headphones, it was a very private experience, a strange, disembodied intimacy. He sang to me alone. Closeted in my room night after night, I absorbed his voice, knew it, loved it. All those consonant-rich German words came alive, over-enunciated in the technique of classical singing, the final t's crisp and distinct, the r's gorgeously rolled, the s's sibilant. The word *allein* was an arc, like a bent bow or an arching bridge, full of power and longing. *Elend* had an edge that could wound. *Dunkel* was soft and velvet-dark. The voice of Julian Northridge created for me a world I entered with gladness, a better, truer world, vividly coloured, where even grief is beautiful. I dwelled in that world long and happily, or would have, if I hadn't attracted the wrong sort of attention in my joy.

I had never seen him live or even on television. Nevertheless, with his voice in my ears and with my eyes closed, I did see him, his lips forming the words, the changing expressions on his face, the movements of his hands. He was there with me, in my private darkness.

But that was all. When the music ended, he was gone. He had no physical being for me once the air had ceased to resonate. Listening to him sing created longing as well as delight, a longing I did not know how to satisfy. I had no other point of contact with him, and never would. (In 1988, we had not yet been informed of the "six degrees of separation.") I lived in a different world from his—no, on a different planet. Once or twice, I entertained a notion to buy an airline ticket to London, England and go to one of his recitals. But what then? Did singers like him sign autographs? Did they have fan clubs? Groupies?

For a wild, fleeting moment, I imagined myself a Julian Northridge groupie—following him around Europe (by Eurail, bus, and thumb), showing up at his concerts looking thin and interesting in an increasingly shabby little black dress, its lace collar limp and askew, a fading rose on my breast. I would hang around near his dressing room afterward, hoping for a glimpse, a nod, a smile, or even a conversation.

(*Shit. I should have done it!*)

Instead, I told myself not to be silly. He was an Englishman, from a privileged background (I assumed), with an expensive education, a deep knowledge of classical music, part of a cultured, European milieu. What about me could possibly interest him? For that matter, aside from the fact that listening to him sing Schubert made me excited and weak at the same time, what would I say to him if I had a chance? I had feverish dreams in which I succeeded in meeting him, only to find myself tongue-tied, and what's more, wearing a nightie when everyone around me was in evening gowns and tuxedos.

A while ago, when I was working all this out, I decided to find out what Julian Northridge was doing now, in 2008. I was feeling energetic and hopeful (for once—what a surprise!) and I thought Why not? He had been so important in my life that I should know more about him. Maybe I would turn up on his doorstep one day after all, with a bagful of his CDs to autograph. "Hi, I'm one of your biggest fans—all the way from Canada! Twenty years ago, I flipped out over Schubert, and you!" Maybe seeing him in the flesh would do something wonderful to me, like a kind of benign shock treatment—turn me into a regular person, just in time. Maybe he would even sing for me—just one song, just for me.

I didn't have the internet any more, so I went to the Public Library and used one of their computers, feeling as nervous as though I was looking at pornography or bomb-making recipes. I thought everyone was watching me, but of course nobody was. I'm nearly invisible now.

Anyway, a few googles, and there he was—Sir Julian, he is now—fifty-three years old. He's lost that schoolboy look, seems rather gaunt and weary, in fact, but every inch the Englishman and cultural icon. He performs and records, teaches and hovers over the current crop of promising youngsters. All very fine and good, but he was a stranger to me. The magic, whatever it was, was gone. All right, you'll say, he was a lot younger back then; what's so romantic about a middle-aged guy with grey hair and lines on his face? Maybe, but there was more to it than mere looks.

I skimmed a few articles—his current projects, his thoughts on how this or that should be performed, his opinions on Music Today. When my thirty minutes were up, I got up and went home. By the time I got there, I'd stopped thinking about that stuff.

There's one thing I know for sure—Davy Dawson wasn't what I wanted back then. If he had been, it would have been so easy to quench my Northridge-inspired longing. But Davy was wrong, wrong, wrong. He was so much of my own time and place. There was nothing romantic about him—Davy with his short hair, his lingering adolescent acne, his tee shirts and jeans and running shoes, his technological enthusiasm and engineering ambitions. I couldn't imagine him wandering through a desolate winter landscape, contemplating fate and death. Not then.

Enter Julian #2.

I imagined someone elusive and bewitching, with longish, unruly hair and a thin, "interesting" face—long nose, shadowed eyes, expressive lips. His clothes would demonstrate a conscious sense of style, eccentric and individual.

I looked for him everywhere. At one time, I thought he might be Harold Neville, but he wasn't right either. He was too skinny and didn't have the necessary air of tragedy. (And besides, dear, he was gay. You didn't realize that, did you?) Without knowing it, I was looking for an idealized young Werther with the voice of Julian Northridge.

Did I find him? I thought I did, at Libby's party. But my memories are flawed, disturbed, and untrustworthy. I remember meeting someone wonderful and going somewhere with him—to his house or apartment, I assumed at the time—and having sex with him, passionate, glorious sex, romantic in all senses of the word. But Mona Lang told me something different, something sordid and ugly.

I tried to convince myself that nothing at all had happened, only my own romantic fantasy. But it was much more than a fantasy, that night. Drunk and possibly drugged, either by accident or deliberately, I was embraced, kissed, and touched by another. A man (a stranger, indeed) took me into a bedroom at Libby's place, had sex with me and left. Who knows what I did then? It may well have been something inappropriate. No doubt Goody and the others thought they were being helpful and doing the right thing when they hustled me off the scene and cleaned up the evidence.

That was the end of my Grand Romance. It was also the end of my university career. While my classmates were graduating, finding jobs, travelling, getting married, I was a guest of the Pine Valley Psychiatric Centre, and then a prisoner in my mother's house, kept on a soft but oh-so-effective chemical leash. It worked so well I barely knew it was there.

But that was then. What about now?

This morning, I stood on the beach, watching the three suns climb higher into the sky. I watched them, wondering if they would continue to move exactly together, or if one would fall behind or race ahead, like the raindrops on my window. Instead, the two flanking suns suddenly blinked out. They were gone as though they had never been and the ordinary old sun stood alone.

Well, what did you expect? They went *hinab*, that's what they did. Just like your two Julians, like your college career and your office career. I guess those were *die besten zwei*. Now you just have to get on with whatever comes before the final descent *im Dunkeln*, when *ist Alles zerflossen*.

Oh, don't you just love a good metaphor? So what is the final sun, the last, the inevitable, and how long will it shine for me? Not very long, I suspect. Bravado aside, I'm not sure I have what it takes, mentally or physically, to live in this world with no more insulation than my own skin and an old coat. I know others do it, but I'm not sure I can, unless they let me find them and ask them for help.

Find them—the slingshot woman and Davy Dawson, or whoever that man is, the one with the harmonica. I saw him downtown last fall, when I was a different person, and I think I've seen him, or evidence of his presence, several times since. I have heard his music faintly in the night. There is nothing left for me now, except to follow him.

There are signs in the sky. This morning, the three suns. A week ago, there was an eclipse of the moon. Today is the twenty-ninth of February, a rare day. This afternoon there is a halo around the sun, a glowing corona. It foretells rain, or perhaps snow, as it is cold and growing colder.

I am making my final preparations now, tidying away the last bits and pieces of my life here. I have gotten rid of the real superfluities; the rest can stay for my successor, whoever she is. (I am sure it will be a "she"; this is a woman's home). I will take only a few things with me—a change of clothes, extra underwear and socks, a tin mug, a pot, a skillet, a knife. Matches. Candles. Aspirin. A rope. Davy's red glove. I wonder if he still has the other one? Maybe that's how we will recognize each other.

I will shut the door behind me and go, creeping away softly, so as not to disturb my neighbours upstairs. They will not see me leave. And I will write *Gute Nacht* on the gate, of course.

There, beyond the village,
Stands the Leiermann.
With his frozen fingers
He plays as best he can.

• • • •

Barefoot on the ice,
He totters here and there,
And his little coin plate
Stays forever bare.

• • • •

No one wants to listen,
No one looks at him,
And the dogs are growling
At the poor old man.

• • • •

And he lets it happen,
As it always will,
He plays his hurdy-gurdy,
And is never still.

• • • •

Oh, you strange old fellow,
Shall I come along?
Grind your hurdy-gurdy,
And I'll sing my song.

• • • •

When I was researching my *Winterreise* paper, I found (in the book with marginal notes written in Chinese) a list of Schubert's possessions at the time of his death. It is absurdly pathetic, almost laughable in its meagreness. This was the entire property of a man dead at age thirty-one, by most standards a failure.

Three cloth evening dress coats, three frock coats, ten pairs of trousers, nine waistcoats.

One hat, five pairs of shoes, two pairs of boots.

Four shirts, nine scarves and handkerchiefs, thirteen pairs of socks, one sheet, two coverlets.

One mattress, one pillow, one blanket.

Some old music books.

The total value of these things was 63 florins. Even without knowing what a florin in 1828 Vienna would be worth in today's terms, I could see that Schubert's estate was pitifully small. It also included many outstanding debts, which had to be settled by his family and friends.

And of course there was his music, which was not included in the list, being already in the keeping of friends and family members, some of whom actually knew it for the treasure it was.

And here I am, nearly two centuries after his death, in a similar state of poverty (but without Schubert's achievements), preparing to set out on my own winter journey, whose ending I cannot foresee.

It is not permitted to know what will happen. We take to the road, ignorant of its length or the terrain we must cross, the burdens we must bear, the discomforts we must endure, the dangers we must face. We—the gatherers of darkness, the keepers of sorrow. We walk the boundaries, absorbing these things so the happy people may continue to be happy. They know nothing of us, which is as it should be.

I see this now. For years I avoided being what I am, because it is hard to serve this fate. I know I cannot choose the time for my journey, and that I must find my own way in this darkness. But ah! it would be good to find a companion who is more than a shadow.

What companion can there be? A tree, a river, a crow, a falling leaf? Inhuman and indifferent (as distinct from merely different). For Schubert and Müller's man, as for me, there can be only one human companion—the *Leiermann*, or, in my case, Davy Dawson.

This is my final reckoning, like that list of Schubert's clothing and linens. (One sheet. Only one. And thirteen pairs of socks!) I must lay it out clearly and plainly, holes, thin spots and all.

I ruined Davy Dawson's life when I dumped him the day after the night I spent with Julian Harker (or whoever he was). Davy must have tried to go on, attending classes, doing assignments, participating, memorizing, absorbing, synthesizing. But he couldn't. Part of him was mortally wounded, and everything seemed pointless. So he left the university. Maybe he explained it to himself as a little break, a holiday (right—just before Christmas exams!) Maybe he just wanted to go home for a few days, but then realized his family would get at him. "What's wrong, Davy, why are you here, what about exams? Tell us. Tell us. Tell us everything." He realized that would make it worse, so he just didn't get off the bus. Or maybe he did get off, but instead of phoning home to tell them he'd arrived, he headed for the highway and stuck out his thumb.

You just keep putting one foot in front of the other and eventually you're somewhere else.

Not far east of the town in which Davy and I grew up, the river valley narrows and becomes a canyon, miles long, cutting through rugged and beautiful country, the division between the Coast and the Interior. The gateway to the canyon is a place called Hope.

Davy, I think that all those years ago, you passed through Hope and went beyond, into winter. There would have been snow on the ground, and true cold, rather than the mild chill we call cold on the coast. Who knows what hardships you experienced, and how you dealt with them? Every step you took changed you from the naïve student you were to a *Wandersmann*, the man of many journeys I saw last September on the steps of the red brick church, playing your harmonica while strangers jostled and ignored you.

Did I start you on that road, with the words I said when you phoned me on the morning after the party? Remembering what your sister told me a few weeks ago, I think that's likely. I have thought about it a lot, these weeks, and this is what I have seen—a young man who is studying a profession that will lead to a respectable career, financial independence, and a certain prestige. He has a girlfriend, someone he knew in high school as a friend, because they had things in common—interests and attitudes. Now they are lovers. If he looks ahead a few years, he sees them married, he working as an engineer, she as a teacher. Their first apartment, first house, first child. Life unfolds as it should under the blue or clouded skies that arch benignly above them.

But suddenly, just before Christmas exams in their final year, she dumps him for no reason. This was the last thing he expected, and even though his expectations may have been naïve, this is a body blow from which he cannot recover. The only thing he can do is run. Home, he thinks—the place to which all wounded creatures run, but once he is on the road (the bus boring its way through the December rain, creating its own cloud of road spray), he realizes he can't face the explanations he will need to make, or even the sympathy of his family.

So he keeps going. Beyond Hope, beyond his money, beyond his dreams of happiness, following the winter roads to places where he isn't known. He does what he needs to do to stay alive. The months pass, the years pass; one day, he wakes up and knows it's too late. What he is now he will always be. He hardly ever thinks of her any more, the girl who set him on this course. But in a way she is part of him forever.

I am sorry, Davy. Now I can say this, because now I stand at the place where three roads meet and I know things I didn't then. I am sorry for the pain I gave you, but I really can't say I wouldn't do things exactly the same way, make exactly the same choices, if I had a second chance. Just like the man created by Wilhelm Müller and Franz Schubert.

I tell you this because it's the truth, and I am at the point now where there is no point in saying anything except the truth. People who understand music say that the works Schubert wrote in his final year of life are full of great serenity and peace, that they breathe acceptance and the joy that follows it. I hope you have found that, Davy, and I think I am about to, because I am going to set out on the Road while it is still winter.

Unlike you, I will not go eastward through the Valley, to the interior. My road will be a shorter one, along the seashore, down streets I have known in the days and nights. Perhaps at some point I shall seek the unfrequented heights, the stony chasms. It doesn't really matter. For both of us, there is only one road.

Unlike you, Davy, I did not manage to escape the benign clutches of my parents. To keep me safe they put me into a box in which I was happy to live for nearly twenty years. No, not happy, merely stilled and stalled. Then the box broke and I went free, but I was still myself, the self I was when I told you I didn't want to see you again.

Your rivals—there was only one, although he was a shape-shifter and took multiple forms, passing from one to the other without telling me. I was merely the axis around which they revolved, coming up now here, now there, wearing their different masks.

Julian Northridge, the Schubert singer—beautiful and remote, transmitted through pure sound and a few pictures, lived and grew in my imagination until I projected him outward, visited him on some stranger at a party, who took what I gave him and promptly disappeared. All I had left was false memories, broken hopes and the disembodied voice. That, at least, was true—the one true thing.

Tonight I got out the CDs again—*Winterreise* and the rest, the Beautiful Girl of the Mill and the collection of *Lieder*. It didn't matter which one I started with; I played them all, start to finish, sitting on my couch and listening. That's where it was, the magic, and that's where it remains.

I listened to them all, and just like all those years ago, I could see him as I listened—not Sir Julian, burdened with years and honours, but the romantic young man whose voice captivated me twenty years ago. His young voice, captured and frozen, preserved for me. Neither that man nor that voice exists any more, except in the disembodied form of recordings.

What if I had never heard that voice, Davy? Would you and I be married now, with 2.5 children, a house in the 'burbs, an old dog and a country club membership? Who knows? Who cares? That's not how it turned out.

But I don't really know how it ends, do I? It's not over yet. Because I'm about to get going on the last phase, the real phase. I will go through this door for the last time and turn my face to the road. I even have a *Wanderstab*, a stout stick of water-seasoned wood I picked up on the beach. It will serve me well.

Some (not you, of course) may wonder why I need to do this. All that happened was that I lost my job. I'm only forty-three years old. I could find another job. I could "get help," talk to a counsellor, see a psychiatrist, get myself back on track, back on "meds," get retrained and reshaped.

No. I won't do any of that stuff. Some people might, but only if in doing it they would be acting in concert with their natures. I went against mine all my life, except for those few months in the winter of 1987 and 1988, and now. "But it's so bad!" some will say. "It's so unnecessary—to live on the street like a bum, maybe end up dead—frozen or murdered."

Yes, the *Leiermann* could have thrown away his hurdy-gurdy and gone to work for one of those villagers snoring into their pillows, dreaming of pleasures old and new—but he didn't. Davy, you could have pulled yourself together, gone back to school, finished your degree, gone on to design bridges, married a nice girl, bought a house. But you didn't. Schubert could have stuck with teaching and composed in his spare time, but he didn't. He was a grasshopper—partying and singing when he wasn't spinning music, instead of providing soberly for the future. He paid the price too, dying young and impoverished.

So yes, I know it'll probably be bad. And I say, "Bad, perhaps, but right for me."

It's dark now, and still snowing. There are two inches on the ground and more to come. The air outside is blue, the glowing blue of snowlight. It's time to go. I have everything I need, in this rucksack, this pack on my back—clothes, food, a tin cup, a sleeping bag, soap, toothbrush, towel, matches, a knife. And my old manuscript too. I may as well keep it. No one else has any use for it, and maybe I'll even finish it some day, when I know how the story ends—under a bridge, writing with a stub of pencil by lantern light.

The door stands open to the night, but I have left the key under a stone by the front walk. The lights are all on, shining a path out to the sidewalk. Nothing moves outside, except me, and those like me. *Lustig in die Welt hinein, gegen Wind und Wetter!* Davy, I'll see you out there, I know it. You will play your harmonica, and I will sing.

• • • •

After midnight, the snowfall lessens and stops. A few tardy flakes drift lazily down, sparkling in the golden light slanting from the open door of the ground floor apartment.

One who looks in sees that the place is tidy, impersonal, abandoned by its inhabitant, like a shell found on the beach. But there is music within. A voice, a piano. The words are in German, precisely enunciated, the melody riding the vowels, punctuated by the crisp consonants. Again it begins the cycle—*Fremd bin ich eingezogen, fremd zieh' ich wieder aus*—sounding into the night.

The stranger looks, listens, turns and leaves. The footprints of his departure overlap those of his approach. Together they obliterate the single faint track already there.

• • • •

Finis

Afterword

THE BRIEF QUOTATIONS from the twenty-four *Winterreise* songs that open each chapter are for the most part taken from Richard Wigmore's translations (cited below). Exceptions are the first and final songs, for which I supplied my own interpretations.

While writing this novel, I listened to several different recordings of the *Winterreise* cycle.

Winterreise. Franz Schubert. D. 911.

Ian Bostridge, tenor. Leif Ove Andsnes, piano. EMI Classics, 2004. 7243 5 577902

Russell Braun, baritone. Carolyn Maule, piano. CBC Records, 2005. MVCD 1171

Matthias Goerne, baritone. Graham Johnson, piano. Hyperion, 1997. CDJ33030

Peter Pears, tenor. Benjamin Britten, piano. Decca, 2000 (originally released 1965) 289 466 382-2.

I discovered these two recordings of *Winterreise* only after I had finished writing the novel:

Alice Coote, mezzo-soprano. Julius Drake, piano. Wigmore Hall Live, 2013. WHLive0057

Le Chimera Project: adaptation [of Schubert's *Winterreise*] for bass-baritone, clarinet, trombone, accordion, violin, piano, and hurdy-gurdy. Philippe Sly, bass-baritone. Analekta, 2019. AN 2 9138.

• • • •

Books I read or consulted. Some citations are incomplete because I did not always write down the publication details. The books were borrowed from my local public library, and they are apparently no longer in its collection.

Schubert, Franz. *The Complete Song Texts: Texts of the Lieder and Italian Songs.* English translations by Richard Wigmore.

Fischer-Dieskau, Dietrich. *Schubert's Songs: A Biographical Study*. Translated by Kenneth S. Whitton.

Gammond, Peter. *Schubert.* London: Methuen, 1982.

Brown, Maurice J.E. *The New Grove Schubert.* New York: WW Norton, 1983.

Bostridge, Ian. *Schubert's Winter Journey: Anatomy of an Obsession*. London: Faber & Faber, 2015. (This book was given to me as a gift after I had finished writing the novel.)

• • • •

For the weather information that opens most chapters, I turned to the Area Forecast Discussion page for Western Washington State, courtesy of the National Weather Service of NOAA. I supplemented the meteorological terminology with my own experiences and impressions of weather in Victoria, British Columbia in 2008 and 2009.

Don't miss out!

Visit the website below and you can sign up to receive emails whenever Audrey Driscoll publishes a new book. There's no charge and no obligation.

https://books2read.com/r/B-A-STMDB-QHCLG

BOOKS 2 READ

Connecting independent readers to independent writers.

Also by Audrey Driscoll

About the Author

Three quarters of the way through a career as a cataloguing librarian, Audrey Driscoll discovered she is actually a writer. Since the turn of the millennium, she has written and published several novels and a short story collection. She gardens, juggles words, and communes with fictitious characters in Victoria, British Columbia.

www.ingramcontent.com/pod-product-compliance
Lightning Source LLC
Chambersburg PA
CBHW022110240626
47153CB00007B/2313

* 9 7 8 1 9 9 9 4 2 4 0 7 7 *